DEC - - 2021

Geauga County PL
Chardon
110 East Park St.
Chardon, OH 44024

"Early days and al... anything." Dani reache... her palms.

Kara rested her hands in her best friend's. She stared at the point of connection. A sigh built in her chest. Adding another lie was tempting. If she smoothed over the tense welcome, she had a chance at repairing the fractured relationship. Would one more deceit risk the temporary peace? When Dani learned the truth, would she permanently exile Kara? A moment's discomfort for a lifetime's friendship was a small price. *I'd like to be on good terms now.*

Dani squeezed. "I'm so happy you found someone. He seems really nice. We could double da—"

The kitchen door swung open and crashed into the wall.

With a start, Kara drew back her hands and lifted her gaze. She connected with Scott.

Lifting a hand, he waved.

The tiny gesture might as well be the flap of a butterfly's wings sparking a tsunami. With startling clarity, she understood. For the sake of her status in town and rebuilding her dearest friendship, she had to fake a relationship. Would he agree?

D1607428

## Praise for Rachelle Paige Campbell

Praise for LIGHTS, CAMERAS, HOLIDAYS

"It's so nice to switch off and sink into a book that you know is going to have a happy ending and just enjoy the ride."

*~Oriette S.*

~*~

"This is a delightful book to read. As Kara Kensington tries to right a wrong with her friend Dani, her fake boyfriend and Kara keep your interest going all the way to the end. I couldn't put the book down until I finished it. Another thumbs up for Rachelle Paige Campbell."

*~Cindy Z.*

~*~

Praise for HOPE FOR THE HOLIDAYS

"A sweet story about small town America where when the chips are down the town comes together for the good of all."

*~Paranormal Romance Guild*

~*~

Praise for HOLIDAYS, INC.

"Readers will surely cheer for Dani to reach her dream and catch her hero in this fresh perspective on finding love in a small town."

*~In'D Tale Magazine*

# Lights, Cameras, Holidays

by

Rachelle Paige Campbell

This is a work of fiction. Names, characters, places, and incidents are either the product of the author's imagination or are used fictitiously, and any resemblance to actual persons living or dead, business establishments, events, or locales, is entirely coincidental.

**Lights, Cameras, Holidays**

COPYRIGHT © 2021 by Rachelle Campbell Dio

All rights reserved. No part of this book may be used or reproduced in any manner whatsoever without written permission of the author or The Wild Rose Press, Inc. except in the case of brief quotations embodied in critical articles or reviews.
Contact Information: info@thewildrosepress.com

Cover Art by *Tina Lynn Stout*

The Wild Rose Press, Inc.
PO Box 708
Adams Basin, NY 14410-0708
Visit us at www.thewildrosepress.com

Publishing History
First Edition, 2021
Trade Paperback ISBN 978-1-5092-3947-4
Digital ISBN 978-1-5092-3948-1

Published in the United States of America

## Dedication

To Mom and Aunt Joanne, in loving memory of our wonderful summers on Madeline Island.

# Chapter One

Kara Kensington had never been more grateful for her unremarkable bare face. With a sigh, she nestled deeper into the first-class leather seat. Without her usual thick layer of makeup, she was anonymous in the airplane cabin. Such a strange blessing to count for an actress who prided herself on always delivering the full, movie star treatment people expected.

Heading from Los Angeles to Wisconsin via Chicago on a red-eye flight the night before Thanksgiving, however, she adapted. No one would glance twice at the bare-faced woman in leggings and an over-sized sweater. Her honey-gold hair hung in a simple braid down her back.

Reaching for her bottled water, she sipped and cleared her dry mouth. She'd need to get used to being cosmetic-free. To play the film role of her best friend, Dani Winter, Kara needed a more natural look. She snorted. Dani was blessed more than the average person with delicate high cheekbones and heavily fringed eyes. Kara needed every tool available to compete with her friend's woke-up-like-this beauty.

She recapped the bottle, tucked the beverage into the seat-back pocket, and tugged the leather tote from under the seat in front. Straightening, she opened the bag in her lap. She brushed her fingers against the three-inch sequin star safety-pinned to the lining and grabbed her cell phone. Plastering on a smile, she unlocked the device and checked her inbox. Grinning through any situation was her super-power. She'd manage her best with her latest task.

Without mascara and lipstick, she was unrecognizable but not entirely natural. Her dermatologist ensured her skin was in top shape without plastic surgery. Fillers restricted her facial movement, but she preferred cutting remarks to arched brows. Showing expressions was too basic.

For one night, she'd embrace not worrying over completing her rather elaborate makeup removal routine before bed. After the four-hour, red-eye flight landed at one in the morning, she had a two-and-a-half-hour drive to New Hope, Wisconsin. She'd collapse in the guest bedroom of Dani's house for a few hours before hustling to lead the town's parade as co-grand marshal.

Then she'd get back to work. Her feel-good, made-for-TV movie about Dani's dinner theater would be the first project of Kara's newly formed production company, Golden Age, and her first step behind the camera. She loved acting, but opportunities evaporated as she matured. If she wanted choice parts, she'd have to hire her own screenwriters and finance the projects. The holiday-themed musical was the first undertaking and a chance to reintroduce her to old fans and find a new audience.

She dialed Dani's number, pressing the phone to her ear. "Hi, girl. You ready?" She mumbled and frowned as the line rang. Dani hated the word girl. Kara had no clue when the distaste started. When Dani lived in Los Angeles, she hadn't balked at the term. Or Kara hadn't paid close attention to her friend's reaction.

The call connected.

"Dani speaking."

"Hi, doll. I'm on th—"

"Please leave your name and number, and I'll call you back."

The phone emitted a beep.

Kara dropped the cell to her lap and powered off her device. She hadn't rehearsed her check-in speech and wouldn't leave a rambling message. Leaning forward, she returned the cell to the leather tote under the seat in front of her and straightened.

The trip wasn't just about work but—hopefully—would be a resolution to the tit-for-tat game Kara started and wanted to end. After breaking the contract with Paul, Kara paid the outstanding balances for a slew of unrealized projects. She didn't tell Dani about the obligations straining Kara's finances. If Dani knew the truth, would she view signing the rights to her life story as a reasonable exchange and answer the phone? Kara wasn't sure and refused to show weakness with a detailed explanation. *Everyone has a price.* Mortgaging her home was a small cost for launching the next phase in her career.

Why hadn't the plane pulled away from the gate yet? She glanced at the smart watch on her wrist, frowning at the high blood pressure alert and willing herself to take in a deep breath and calm down. She had a detailed schedule and a strict timetable. Nothing could go wrong. She declined any hint of complication.

"Ladies and gentlemen, good evening from the flight deck." A deep voice boomed over the din of conversation in the cabin. "This is Captain Mark Sterns speaking. Along with First Officer, Tory Lang, and our entire crew, we want to thank you for flying with us. We anticipate a smooth trip to Chicago and will be pulling away from the gate shortly. We are waiting on one more passenger."

She shut her eyes and leaned against the headrest, angling toward the window. Outside, artificial light cast a hazy orange glow over the tarmac. On her previous trips to Wisconsin, she'd left almost as soon as she arrived. The only night she slept at Dani's cottage was Fourth of July. The town was illuminated with fireworks. How dark would the night sky be in winter? She shivered.

Heavy footsteps followed by shallow breathing caught her attention. She snapped open her gaze and spotted a man, looming over her. Thick brown hair fell over his forehead, almost long enough to copy the floppy haircut her 90s crush wore on her TV show. Wearing a flannel shirt completed the vintage look. He was average height, fit, and tan like he spent time at the beach. Most of her male colleagues protected their skin from the sun and its premature aging effects as ardently as the women. The corners of his brown eyes crinkled in a fine web of wrinkles she found endearing.

"Hello. I'm seated here." He pointed toward the aisle seat.

"Oh, hi." She straightened and tucked her sweater more firmly underneath, restricting her clothing to her seat. "Sorry."

"No need to apologize." He sat, nudging a leather bag under the seat in front of his feet.

"Flight attendants, please prepare the cabin for take-off," the captain said over the system.

She faced the window again, studying the gate as the modern glass and steel building disappeared. In sunny Southern California, the weather wasn't an impediment. Within minutes, the plane steered into the queue and taxied forward. When the captain landed in Illinois, would he navigate through snow?

"You okay?"

Frowning, she turned toward her companion and tilted her head.

He pointed to the seat divider. "You're gripping the armrest pretty tight."

She stared at her hands. Her white knuckles clenched the armrest with a life-or-death grip, bulging the veins to the surface. Relaxing her fingers, she dropped her hands to her lap. She wasn't scared of flying. She traveled constantly for work and couldn't even remember her first flight. A four-hour domestic trip was nothing to worry about. Except, her nerves twisted her stomach at what she might encounter when she reached her final destination. "Just been a long day. I'm rather anxious to get there."

He nodded. "I know the feeling."

The plane picked up speed and tilted, lifting the wheels off the tarmac.

Force pushed her against the cushy seat.

"And we're off." He pointed out the window.

She turned her head. The dark sky obscured the view.

"Are you visiting friends or family?"

Her instinct was to say both. But her relationship with Dani remained shaky. With any luck, a byproduct of her nearly month-long stay would be reestablishing their friendship.

"Rather complicated answer?"

Swallowing, she faced him. "It didn't used to be."

"Ah, the traveling-for-the-holidays-to-rebuild-a-relationship storyline." He stroked his chin. "I've probably seen that movie."

She flinched. His casual tone brushed close to the truth. Did he recognize her? Storyline was an industry word. She didn't want to keep her identity a secret per se. For a few hours, she relished the rare chance of honesty without judgment. A simple Internet search yielded a host of articles over the past year about her project. The opinions spanned the spectrum from hope to scorn.

Was he in the business? How far out of the loop was she if she didn't know him? After falling off the lists of stars to watch, she hadn't paid particular attention to those rising in the rankings. For years, she used to scour the listings of up-and-coming directors and producers. She created dossiers on names she didn't recognize and studied the faces until she could confidently feign an acquaintance in person. *This new movie will propel me back to the top.*

"I'm visiting family. My aunt and uncle."

She relaxed her shoulders. Her companion seemed determined to hold a conversation. What was the harm in exchanging a few standard pleasantries? She'd need the practice for making small talk with her adopted community. "Did you grow up in Chicago?"

"No, I'm from Milwaukee. But I'd rather drive the last bit of my journey than deal with connecting flights and potential delays."

*Like your arrival?*

"Like a plane being held for one passenger." He

shook his head. "I am grateful. Hope I didn't delay the flight too long and force any missed connections. If I don't show for Thanksgiving, I'd earn more than a spot on Santa's naughty list."

He wasn't the only one anticipating a coal-filled stocking. She nodded and exhaled a heavy sigh. Her apology tour barely started, and she was already wiped. "If the question isn't too personal, why the delay? You can't be running late from work at ten o'clock."

"Actually, I can." He smiled, the corners of his brown eyes wrinkling. "I'm a private chef and have the holidays off through New Year's Day. Before my vacation could start, I had to finish coordinating with the chef at the Hawaii house for the next month including the new dietary restrictions."

A chef? Her mouth watered. She lowered her arms over her stomach, absorbing an ambient grumbling noise. She hadn't eaten a real meal all year. Approaching her mid-thirties, she fought an expanding middle with the iron-clad control she exerted over every facet of her life. Carefully portioned meals approved by a nutritionist didn't make eating fun, which was the whole point. Food was fuel and nothing more. She cleared her throat.

Better to focus on something else. Her parents headed to Oahu in a few weeks and invited her along for the holidays. Would she have bumped into him on a pristine beach? She smiled. She was off the soundstage, but a perfect meet-cute was never far from her thoughts. "Why not work at the Hawaii house? Sounds like my idea of a perfect holiday."

"Not if you're working the whole time. I'm Scott, by the way." He stuck out his hand. "Sorry. Probably should have introduced myself at the start of our conversation."

She shook his hand and dropped her fingers to her lap. "I'm Kara Ke—" She shut her mouth. Offering her full name was her default. If she was one of those one-name stars, she wouldn't be almost assured of her momentary anonymity. "Just Kara."

"Hmm." He stroked his chin and smiled. "I doubt you're *just* anything."

Lifting the corner of his mouth in a lopsided grin made him almost double-take worthy. She didn't have much exposure to his brand of relaxed charisma. Most men of her acquaintance imbued every tic with meaning. His charm was effortless. *As far as I'm concerned, charisma is wasted.* She sighed. She had a plan and accepted no distractions. "Work is exactly where I'm headed. I wouldn't mind doing it in paradise."

"I'm guessing you're a California girl through and through?" He lifted an eyebrow.

"Born and raised. This will be my first Midwestern holiday season."

He dipped his chin to his chest and pointed toward the floor. "You packed stronger boots and a heavy coat?"

She adjusted the oversized sweater on her shoulders and frowned down at her Sherpa-lined, slip-on, flat soled boots. The tan suede was pristine. The boots were as comfortable as slippers. *I hope the pair is more durable than bedroom scuffs.* "I'll figure it out." She tucked her legs in the opposite direction, resting her feet closer to the wall. "What else should I know?"

"I'm sure you're aware, but in case you are not."

He stroked his chin. "Don't eat the yellow snow."

She rolled her eyes.

He chuckled.

The sound was warm as a blanket and wrapped around her like a hug.

"Your biggest hurdle will be slipping in those shoes. Do you know about black ice?"

Frowning, she bit her bottom lip.

"Sometimes a section of road or sidewalk looks wet, but, instead of a puddle, the spot is actually a patch of ice. Be aware. And always wear a hat."

Squishing a beautiful wig and smearing carefully applied foundation with a knit beanie wasn't exactly camera-ready. "I'm not sure if wearing a hat is possible."

"Tuck one in your purse. Just in case."

She opened her mouth and yawned. Raising a hand, she covered the rest of the breathy inhale with the back of her knuckles. "Sorry."

The overhead system chimed.

"Good evening again from the bridge. We've reached our cruising altitude. We're dimming the cabin lights now to accommodate sleeping passengers. Thank you."

"Get some rest." He leaned close. "I won't take it personally. You aren't the first woman I've bored with my attempt at charming conversation."

She giggled. "Thanks for understanding. Good night." Turning toward the window, she lowered the shade. Reaching into the seat-back pocket, she retrieved the neck pillow and blanket the flight attendant passed out during boarding. She positioned herself against the wall, snuggling under the fleece and shutting her eyes.

She began counting. Halfway between fifteen and sixteen, she realized she hadn't been so relaxed in a long time. On a plane, flying across the country, in the middle of the night, next to a stranger she released every tense muscle. Maybe she should do this more often and toss the sleeping pills.

****

For the better part of three hours, Scott Neil tilted away his smartphone from the beautiful blonde in the window seat and scrolled through the notes he'd recorded. Ideas for meals for his boss' family mixed with quick arguments about his plan. Heading for a small-town holiday season wasn't only about a much-needed break from work. He was a man on a mission, and he couldn't fail. His only remaining family, his aunt and uncle, needed to retire and slow down. In the ideal scenario, they moved. He hated having them so far away.

Almost two-and-a-half years ago, Aunt Shirley suffered a major heart attack. The active woman couldn't avoid the family's genetic trap. He monitored his blood pressure, exercised, and ate well. Stress remained the one contributing factor out of his and her control. He did his best to focus on the present with tunnel vision and gave up worrying too far into the future.

His aunt couldn't. Running the town's diner around the clock, she lived in a nonstop loop of triaging the present and projecting the future.

If he could convince his aunt and uncle to retire and move in with him, he would eliminate his major source of anxiety. In his career, he struck gold. His employers paid him well and enjoyed his food.

Working for a family with the means to source anything they desired was fun for a chef. He pushed the boundaries of their dietary restrictions and liked the challenge of adapting to meet the varying needs of the six-member household.

After culinary school in Chicago, he moved to Los Angeles and never thought about leaving for small-town Wisconsin. He had fond memories of visiting his aunt and uncle in their town during summer trips with his parents. The break from Milwaukee was nice, and the little town was charming. The town fell on hard times. His aunt absorbed the economic impact internally and suffered her health crisis. He'd taken a month off to help her recover and honored her promise to shield the news from the rest of the town. He agreed as long as she slowed down and considered potentially shuttering the business if the numbers didn't improve.

But then a shocking rebound happened.

Some woman moved to town and turned an old cinema into a dinner theater. The outlandish scheme worked, drawing huge crowds. Instead of taking things easy, his aunt jumped into even more work. She pitched in at the theater's kitchen, squeezing in shifts during holiday weekends in addition to running the busy diner every day.

Scott couldn't believe the pendulum could swing from economic instability to the thriving town so quickly. Often, he had a hard time reaching his family on the phone. When he did, his aunt sounded beyond exhausted, and he couldn't ignore his quadrupling worries. Until a rare opportunity appeared for time off. Conducting a quick case study of his aunt and uncle's business, he realized they could sell the business and retire. When the struggle to keep going almost stole a life, he never could have hoped for such a dramatic change. But with the opportunity, he wouldn't overanalyze the good fortune.

Shaking his head, he tucked his phone back into his pocket and scrubbed his face. All he'd managed was to deplete half the battery and not illuminate his arguments. He blinked and yawned, rolling his neck to the side. In the recirculated air, his eyes and throat felt dry. Shifting to the left, he jostled the armrest, his elbow jutting into her space. Catching his breath, he winced. He hadn't felt his arm poke her in the ribs. Judging by the thick knit of her sweater, however, the blow could have been absorbed.

She murmured and turned.

Frozen, he remained still with his arm at a perfect angle on the armrest.

Her head lolled.

At an unnatural angle, she snorted. Taking a deep breath, he leaned over and dropped his shoulder under her chin.

With a sigh, she nestled close.

He wished he could sleep on a plane. If he assisted her, he wouldn't begrudge her the rest. Depressing the button on the armrest, he reclined his chair. A light rose scent tickled his nose. An almost old-fashioned smell like an old movie star might wear filled his nose.

She snuggled and murmured.

Was she a sleep talker? He pressed together his lips, silencing his breathing. He wished she'd speak a little louder so he could listen. Something about her was oddly familiar. Would she slip up and reveal some clue about herself? Of course, in Los Angeles, he was always spotting famous faces. But typically, those people held themselves with an air of importance. Celebrities knew they were watched and reveled in the attention. She seemed normal.

"We have begun our final approach into Chicago O'Hare. Flight attendants will be through the cabin. Please move your seat back to the upright position," the captain said.

After a beep, lights illuminated the cabin.

She jerked upright and squinted. Her hair slipped from the smooth braid, and she wiped the corner of her mouth. Her blue eyes widened.

He glanced at his shoulder. A tiny spot of drool darkened his flannel sleeve.

"Well, that's embarrassing."

Shrugging, he chuckled. "Don't worry. I won't charge you for dry cleaning. Good nap?"

"Sort of." She rolled her head from one side to the other. "I still have to drive. I'm not sure if I'm more tired now than before I closed my eyes."

He nodded. "Been there." Pressing the button, he righted his seat and winced, his body aching. He'd taken a few minutes break from the upright position, but the awkward angle strained his muscles. "Do you have time before you jump into work?"

"Not much." She rubbed the corner of her eyes and tugged the tie around her braid. Unplaiting her hair, she finger-combed the strands over her shoulder.

Thick waves of gold caught the harsh overhead light and sparkled. Again, the sense he knew her somehow tickled his mind. Or maybe he just wanted a good story to tell his family. Aunt Shirley loved quizzing him about celebrities. He'd only ever actually bumped into and conversed with three. Each encounter was disappointing. He preferred the illusion of the characters they played to the very real, fallible humans. What was the point in dreaming about a better life if the possibility didn't exist?

The wheels hit the ground, and the plane lurched.

His torso jerked toward his thighs. The rough landing snapped him out of his reverie.

"Guess we're here," she said.

Maybe timing was in his favor, cutting him off from saying or asking something stupid. He enjoyed a pleasant conversation with a woman he'd never see again and shouldn't hold onto frustration for wanting more.

The plane taxied to the gate, and the captain gave the all-clear to use cell phones again.

He pulled his device from his pocket and tapped off airplane mode. From the corner of his gaze, he studied her.

She bent her head and tapped on her screen, her device dinging and pinging.

For once, he didn't have a rush of messages waiting him. He had almost six weeks to work on his plan and not a minute more. He'd focus on the task at hand.

The plane reached the gate, and the fasten seatbelt sign dimmed. The flight attendant opened the door to the jetway, and the first two rows slowly emptied.

He stood and exited the row, pausing in the aisle and letting her pass first.

"Thanks."

"My pleasure."

She nibbled her bottom lip.

Did she want to say something more? Did she feel the strange charge in the air? Not quite instant attraction but something just under the surface, like they could be honest with each other without judgment. He was pushed and stumbled an inch forward.

"Sorry, I'm taking too long." She frowned. "I'll get going. Great to meet you."

"You, too."

He held his position for a minute longer than necessary. His passive-aggressive revenge against the rude person behind him provided her time to make an exit. He didn't want to ruin a bittersweet moment with desperation. If they were meant to meet again, they would. He didn't need to race after her. When he exited the plane, carrying his leather satchel in one hand, he entered the quiet corridors of an international airport at rest. With the shops and restaurants shuttered, he strolled through the building, appreciating the soaring heights of the ceilings in some sections, large enough for the model dinosaur skeleton. He liked taking his time. Because once he reached his destination, the clock started ticking.

## Chapter Two

Deboarding the plane, Kara pulled back her shoulders and lifted her chin. She strode through the airport with determined steps past other ambling passengers. She loved a good exit and couldn't resist the opening he provided. With her oversized tote on one arm, she didn't look back, fighting the desire to engage in another conversation. Had he really not recognized her? She wasn't dressed in her typical flashy sequins and full makeup.

On only one other trip had she gone unnoticed. At the time, she'd flown to Milwaukee and hopped in a hired car to surprise her best friend in New Hope. The visit hadn't followed her perfect script. Face to face with the friend she wronged, she forgot her rehearsed lines. When her best friend dropped her off at the airport, she shielded her gaze from camera lenses and bright flashes only to be ignored. Paparazzi didn't stalk the General Mitchell Airport quite the same way they staked out LAX. She'd felt foolish.

The visit sparked her change. Watching her best friend reach for—and accomplish—her dreams of moving away from Hollywood and building a showbiz career on her own terms, Kara decided to reach for hers. With every recent casting agent dismissing her almost as soon as she walked into the room, she'd decided to create her own opportunities. She discussed the bare bones of her plan with her lawyer and used the money she'd stashed from residuals to start a production company. Her first effort, a reality show and stage act, depended on one man. When he reneged on the contract, he nearly destroyed her.

Instead, she drafted a compromise to everyone's satisfaction. She didn't head to New Hope claiming a victory. She was jumpstarting her career and fixing her friendship. Could she afford to waste time thinking about a charmed chance encounter with a cute, nice guy? Or worry her departure was too abrupt? He only carried a small duffle, the size she used for a quick trip, not a holiday sabbatical. No doubt, she'd bump into him at baggage claim, thus negating her perfect farewell. She hoped for another meeting, because she didn't know his last name.

Dropping her chin, she missed her next step. Her smooth, flat sole slid across the tiled floor. She braced her hands in front of her torso and locked her knees, jerking to a halt. Either he was right about the hazards of her boots or engaging in a daydream threatened her already over-occupied mind. Straightening, she filled her lungs with a deep breath and inhaled the faint smell of popcorn.

Scanning her surroundings, she widened her gaze. While she'd been woolgathering, she reached the row of shops, restaurants, and the full-scale Brachiosaurus model near security. Besides the handful of other passengers from her flight, she spotted no one. Stores and restaurants were shuttered. The airport never truly closed, but, with only a small skeleton crew in the early morning hours, the building was silent and a marked contrast to always bustling LAX.

She followed the handful of other passengers from her flight onto the escalator. At the lower level, the air temperature dropped ten degrees. Opposite the row of motorized belts expelling suitcases, automatic doors opened and shut. She drew her sweater tighter and continued to the correct carousel, shivering with each step. The bitter, cold wind blew past her, burning her skin. She gulped and drew her shoulders to her ears, protecting the tender, exposed skin. The windy city wasn't her final destination. Driving north promised an icier chill.

A crowd gathered at the luggage carousel.

Hurrying forward, she found a free space to the side. Cocking a hip, she pulled her cell from her bag and checked the screen. No new alert or missed messages flashed.

"Hello, again, Kara."

Lifting her chin, she smiled at Scott. "Oh, hi." She dropped the phone back in her tote and smoothed tendrils behind both ears. Glancing at the ground, she spotted a hard-sided, rolling suitcase at his feet. She liked being right.

"You all set?" He frowned.

Swiveling her gaze toward the belt, she nibbled her lip. After the seemingly never-ending procession of medium-size, upright, rolling, black bags, she spotted her pair of bright purple suitcases. "I will be."

The bags neared.

She spun on her heel and stalked over. Reaching for the first bag, she bent with her knees and heaved the overstuffed luggage off the belt. Huffing and puffing, she turned for the other bag.

He lifted the suitcase and set it next to its mate.

Despite the notoriously heavy baggage, he moved with ease. She swallowed a self-deprecating comment. Based on the temperatures inside the airport, she'd need to wear every ounce of clothing in both bags at once to stay warm. "Thanks."

"Where are you headed? Do you need a hand?"

Should she let him? She hated the whole damsel-in-distress act and watched too much true crime TV to be oblivious to the inherent risks in accepting help from a male stranger.

"I'm hopping on the bus to the rental car terminal. Can I help you outside?"

Glancing at her bags, she adjusted the large leather tote on her arm. Helping her in public with witnesses and security cameras wasn't as dangerous as a handful of other scenarios. "Yes, thank you. I'm heading to the rental cars, too. Let me get a coat first."

With a nod, he stepped to the side.

Unzipping the suitcase, she tugged the puffy jacket out of the bag's front pocket. The garment was more comforter than coat. When she slipped her arms into the sleeves, she sighed. For one night, she'd take warmth over style.

"Are you ready?" he asked.

Zipping shut the suitcase, she extended the handle on the suitcases, the metal clicking into place.

He grabbed the handle and rolled forward with one of her bags and his in each hand.

She tugged the other purple suitcase behind her, tightening her grip on the tote on her shoulder. Focusing on the signs and cameras overhead, she strode through the airport with her head held high. If the worst happened, she gave the authorities a clear picture of her departure. With any luck, law enforcement could catch the culprit quickly. She gave her head a shake. She was being dramatic. Not only had he not recognized her, he also hadn't threatened her.

At the doors leading outside, she stiffened every muscle in her body, preparing for the weather waiting on the other side. Crossing the threshold, she tucked her chin against her chest, her eyes watering from the sting of frigid air. She proceeded through a crosswalk and scanned the road.

A bus idled at the curb, smoke curling from the exhaust.

She scrunched her nose. The stale air reminded her of home. Mixed with something her mind only defined as cold, however, the smell was stronger. She approached the bus, and the doors opened. With a grunt, she heaved her bag onto the single step and rolled the piece into position on the bottom rack.

He followed and positioned the other bags on the bottom rack, setting his on its side like a barrier.

"Thank you."

With a nod, he turned and sat in the front row.

She exhaled a shaky breath and strode to the back, climbing the step to the last row. With only herself and one other passenger, she had her choice of seats. Elevated, she had a clear view of her surroundings. She appreciated his discretion at not sitting close. But she was suddenly hit with a pang of loneliness. For someone who spent much of her time on her own by choice, she struggled with her next breath, aching ribs squeezing her.

The bus lurched forward and pulled onto the street.

On the worn, upholstered seat, she turned and

scooted closer to the window. Along the side of the road, trees were wrapped with white lights on branches and trunks. Oversized ornaments dotted the median. In the glow of streetlights, she couldn't make out any snow or the black ice he mentioned. Maybe she'd luck out and have a smooth drive north.

Pulling her phone from the tote, she unlocked the screen. No message from Dani waited in her inbox. She swallowed the sour taste in her mouth and texted her friend.

*—On my way to pick up the rental car. Should be there in a few hours, doll.—*

She tapped Send and stared at the screen. Under the message bubble, she willed the notification to change from delivered to read. She didn't need a response. Earlier in the week, after the flight schedule changed by an hour, she discussed logistics of getting to New Hope. Balking at Dani's suggestion that the front door remain unlocked, Kara agreed with the plan to grab the key from under the welcome mat. Dani was probably asleep since she wasn't needed. *Isn't she curious if I arrived?*

The bus slowed and turned into a fenced lot, stopping at a smaller building.

Kara hopped to her feet and strode to the luggage rack.

"Still want a little help?" he asked.

*More than you know*. She stared into his dark brown eyes, considering her options. Her problem wasn't making friends but having other people stick around. Sometimes, she pushed away people, like Dani. She lifted her chin. "I would." She smiled. "Thanks."

He dragged both bags off the lower rack, extending

the handles. Righting his suitcase, he slipped his carry-on duffle over the handle and wheeled his suitcase and hers toward the door. Stepping off the bus, he turned and met her gaze.

*No one is nice for free.* If he didn't know who she was, why wait? She didn't like the other option that he was a reporter well aware of her identity. Was he stalling for more time together in hopes of a better selling tabloid article? Should she expect another kick-her-while-she's-down piece about her very average looks and aloof manner? She wheeled to the door and adjusted the tote slipping off her shoulder.

He grabbed her bag, lifting it off the bus and onto the curb.

She stepped off the bus. He was nice. In her life, she knew only a handful of kind people operating without a motive. She valued each one. Strolling forward, she followed him to the building entrance.

Automatic doors slid open. Warm air blew past her ear, ruffling the collar of her coat. A whiff of new car spray tickled her nose. She strolled inside and stopped behind the stanchions.

"After you." He waved a hand.

"No, please, I've taken too much of your time. You go first. I insist."

Dipping his head, he strolled past to the express check-in counter.

She reached into the tote on her shoulder, tracing the outline of the cell. With a sigh, she rolled her neck and removed her hand. The behavior was becoming a compulsion. She had to stop.

"Next," the counter agent called.

When she strolled to the desk, pulling both

suitcases, she spotted him lingering near the end of the counter. Whether or not she imagined a friendship with a wonderfully unpretentious man, she was grateful for the fleeting encounter. She pulled out her wallet, removing her driver's license and credit card. Sliding both to the agent, she retrieved the agreement paperwork and signed the bottom. If the rest of her trip continued as well as the start, she'd have no complaints.

"Have a nice visit."

With a start, she raised her head and angled away from Scott, praying her observation was unnoticed. She smiled at the tall agent behind the counter. Retrieving her cards, she slipped both into the slots in her wallet and grabbed the keys off the counter. "Thank you."

The man nodded and dashed his fingers over the keyboard.

She rolled her suitcase toward the doors, stopping at Scott's side. "I'm A6. What about you?"

"A5." He flipped up the collar on his coat and pulled fleece earmuffs from his pocket, securing them into position.

*Perfect.* She exited first. This time, she gritted her teeth and dropped her chin. The bitter cold scalded her ears, but she didn't stop strolling forward. She navigated her way through the rows of parked cars. Her jaw tightened with a brittle smile. She'd been trained to grin through almost anything and couldn't escape the expression during stress. When she spotted her vehicle, she froze.

He stopped and bumped his shoulder against hers. "Is that yours?"

She sucked in a sharp breath and coughed, the chilly night irritating her lungs. Any cool girl cred evaporated. A5 housed a sleek black hatchback. In the very next stall, she spotted a blinding white, soccer mom minivan. The vehicle was Dani's suggestion. Had Kara underestimated the level of her friend's continued ire? She frowned. "My friend said I needed all-wheel drive, or something?"

"Probably a good idea for someone not used to winter driving." He nodded. "I'll load the trunk."

With the key fob, she pressed the trunk unlock button.

He lifted the suitcases.

She walked around the vehicle, inspecting for damage. The sheer size of the thing meant she wasn't likely to return it completely unscathed. If she could claim a few dings and dents before leaving, she'd be better off. In the hazy cast of the headlights, she couldn't spot anything amiss. Her teeth chattered. She rounded the bumper, completing her circle.

He lowered the trunk door. "Okay, you're ready to hit the road." He rubbed his hands together and brought them to his mouth, blowing on his fingers.

"Thank you. I really appreciate your help." She tucked a stray tendril behind her ear. "I'm not usually so needy."

"Under normal circumstances, I don't doubt you are self-sufficient." He smiled. "Don't forget about the hat."

Covering her ears with both hands, she touched the throbbing skin. Was this embarrassment or hypothermia? She didn't want to know. "I promise. A hat will be the first thing I unpack."

"Good." He turned on his heel.

"Wait." Her voice cracked.

With a glance over his shoulder, he widened his gaze.

He looked dazed at the outburst. She was, too. "I don't know how to ask this..." Heat crept up her cheeks. She should be glad for the surge of warmth, blood pumping through her veins to her extremities. "Can we talk on the phone? As we're driving, to stay awake? I know you're headed to Milwaukee, and I'm a little farther. But hearing another voice would help me focus."

He shook his head.

Her stomach dropped. Was she really this bad at reading normal people cues?

"I grew up in Milwaukee, but my family lives about an hour or so past the city limits." He rubbed together his hands. "I wouldn't mind some company. I'll keep you talking and awake. Can I have your phone?"

Her mouth was too dry for a verbal response. She nodded and grabbed the device out of her bag. Swiping the screen, she unlocked the device and handed it over.

He tapped on the screen and extended the phone, brushing her hands.

His warmth against her icy fingers was as shocking as the initial impact of cold.

"I entered my number and sent myself a text. I'll call you on the road. You okay setting up the navigation system?"

She wasn't totally helpless. Clearing her throat, she dragged up her gaze and froze. If she initially thought his brown eyes were average, she hadn't paid attention to the details. The center ring closest to the pupil was amber and glowed from the inside out like his smile. "I will be fine. I've used the app before."

He wrinkled his brow.

"I mean. Sounds like a plan." Before she could do something stupid, she hopped in her car. She swiped her finger over the screen, scrolling to the text messages and spotting the latest. "Scott Neil," she mumbled. Darting her gaze to the side, she spotted him getting into his car. The strong name was direct and suited him like perfect casting for a role. She snorted. Couldn't she enjoy a break from business for one night?

With a sigh, she studied her phone, typing Dani's address into the navigation app and leaving the cell in a cupholder. Twisting the key in the ignition, she started the car and connected the phone to the dashboard screen. She buckled her seatbelt and checked her mirrors. In a few short hours, she'd start her redemption tour. Winning public praise was a full-time job on its own in addition to rebuilding her friendship and saving her career. She gained nothing from stalling at the airport. With a sigh, she backed out of the parking spot and drove toward the open gate. In a few minutes, he'd undoubtedly pass her on the freeway. She always loved a good exit, even if it didn't last.

****

Driving while chatting with a stranger on speaker phone at three o'clock in the morning was a definite first. Scott shook his head. For nearly two hours, he drove lead in the caravan. He hadn't laughed so much in a long time. When he tempered the chuckles, he shook his seat, the upholstery absorbing but not dampening the good humor.

He couldn't make sense of her predicament. For as pulled together as she looked, she turned to him on the airplane, as he explained the dangers of winter weather, with a wide-eyed stare. He hated to overstep or mansplain. But she hadn't stopped him from lending assistance.

At the baggage claim, he'd been glad to help with her giant suitcases. Was she moving to her destination or visiting? Whatever she headed into wasn't his concern. When he boarded the same bus, he decided to give her space. She didn't approach so she must have agreed. At the rental car building, he'd been glad to again offer assistance. As he typed a text message from her phone, she shot him a shy, earnest smile and asked again for help. He couldn't refuse.

She was such a confusing combination of self-assured and in over her head. He couldn't understand. Was the Midwest such a puzzle to an outsider? He loved the slower pace of life. Nearly two decades ago, he'd probably mirrored the bumbling desperation when he landed in Los Angeles.

The biggest question remained unanswered, and he'd probably missed the normal window of opportunity for basic information. Who was she? Kara Wilson? Kara Campbell? Did finding out her full name even matter if they wouldn't see each other again? He couldn't search on the Internet without a last name. He shook off the thought. Kara was a momentary distraction from his very real mission. He needed focus.

She gasped. "Wow, wow, wow."

Her voice shook. He squinted and glanced at the rearview mirror. "You okay?" He couldn't read the tremor in her voice. Was she worried about something? He spotted the van two car lengths behind him, driving steady. "What's wrong?"

"The interstate is covered in snow."

He pressed together his lips. Less than an inch accumulated on the shoulder. The road itself was clear and dry. Was she worried the precipitation would somehow gain sentience and jump in front of her tires? "Covered might be a stretch. Wisconsin has more snow than L.A. and a greater accumulation than the beaches of Hawaii."

She sighed. "Don't mention paradise, or I might lose my nerve and head back to the airport."

The strains of ukulele played in his memory. He spent last year's holiday working at the house on the north shore of Oahu. Long hours weren't balanced by the warm breezes and crashing waves. He preferred time off, and he wouldn't complain about the Wisconsin weather.

"Oh, what's up ahead?"

Squinting, he studied the road. He couldn't see past the illumination of his headlights. Low to the ground in the hatchback, he didn't have as clear a view as the minivan driver. She could have seen an animal or trash. Her jumpy overreactions couldn't be trusted. He shook his head. "You don't like driving. Odd for an L.A. native."

"I prefer to ride. While stuck in traffic, I get a lot of work done. Do you like driving?"

"If I can get the Pacific Coast Highway, sure I like driving. In my day to day, I consider it a necessity. I prefer wide open roads to L.A.'s traffic jam." He dragged his gaze along the forest at the sides. The interstate cut through farmland and forest. The farther north he traveled, he spotted denser trees on either side of the highway. In slightly warmer temperatures, he cracked his window and breathed deep the scent of pinesap and wood smoke. Cold had a fragrance, too. A hint of moisture in otherwise dry air, teasing the promise of snow.

"I haven't driven along the coast in years. I'm always too busy." She sighed.

"Is working over the holidays your norm?"

She didn't reply.

Scanning the signs, he checked the exit numbers. He'd pull off the highway soon. Why hadn't she turned? Had she driven too far? If his oversight increased her travel time, he'd feel awful. "Hey, do you know your exit? I'll stay alert for it. You probably turn before me."

"You make a good point. I'm Exit 267."

"Really? Me, too." At the fluttery twinge in his stomach, he frowned. The ramp wasn't a direct path to New Hope. More than likely, she would stop at the first town off the exit or continue well past his destination.

"Oh, good. Because then I'm supposed to drive for another twe—"

"Twenty miles?" His throat tightened. "By any chance, are you driving to New Hope?"

"I am. How did you know?"

"It's a small world," he muttered. "I'm heading there, too. This is our turn." He flashed his turn signal and followed the ramp to the county highway. Slowing way down, he scanned the road, pleased to see it was equally as well maintained. In years past, budget cuts impacted road repairs. New Hope and the surrounding area were too far from Milwaukee to exist as suburbs. Without a lake, the town never attracted a weekend crowd. He couldn't think of a seasonal job opening in town and definitely nothing compelling enough for a West Coaster to endure weeks of winter.

The pieces suddenly linked. "Are you?" He stopped speaking, his thick tongue sticking to the roof of his mouth. He was an idiot for even thinking the idea. If he said his suspicion aloud, he gained nothing than a guarantee she'd laugh in his face every time she saw him. Which could happen quite a lot in a small town. Throughout the evening, the coincidences stacked up one after the other. Risking ridicule was a small price for the truth. He had to know. "Are you Kara Kensington?"

"Guilty."

Why hadn't he figured out her identity the second he sat next to her on the plane? He groaned. "I should have known. My aunt and uncle told me about the movie. They are so excited."

"Who are they?"

"Shirley and Ted Olson." He tightened his grip on the steering wheel, readjusting his weight on the seat. Everything ached, including his pride. Why hadn't he figured out her identity hours ago? "My aunt and uncle own the diner."

"Ahh, so I will be seeing you again. According to my friend, the diner is the best restaurant in town."

*And your friend is Danielle Winter, the owner of the dinner theater.* For most of the past two years, Aunt Shirley rarely spoke of anything but the purchase and renovation of the old cinema. She sang the praises of Dani on every call. "Your friend owns Holidays, Inc.?"

"Yep."

*You didn't look like you.* He swallowed the reply. His shock wasn't necessarily endearing. He had a vague mental image of her in fancy dresses at red carpet events. Truthfully, he never pictured her in an everyday look. But more than appearance, she hadn't displayed starlet behavior.

She fell asleep on his arm and needed help with a minivan. As a personal chef in Los Angeles, he was used to VIPs including people who preferred smelling to eating. He catered to high-end tastes, restricted diets, and all sorts of demands only the very privileged expected. His high-maintenance radar hadn't detected her. The unnerving sense she held herself—not others—to a ridiculous standard niggled him. He cleared his throat. "You're spending the entire holiday season in New Hope?"

"I'm filming from Thanksgiving to Christmas Eve. With luck, I'll be gone on Christmas Day. The movie is based on my friend. Dani started Holidays, Inc. and fell in love with the writer she hired."

"Haven't I seen the same romantic comedy a dozen times?"

"Without the script specifics, I'd agree the plot is tired. But they had a very rocky start, making the story more drama than comedy. She bought his family's business and gutted the building. He was aghast. According to my friend, she thought she'd have to bribe him on top of his salary to take the job he desperately needed."

He scoffed. The sugar-sweet premise didn't click with the smart, sassy woman he met. Of course, he wasn't the target demographic and should drop the topic. She must be a solid actor to convince an audience of the ready-made cliché. "Facts aside, isn't the story a little unbelievable? Too good to actually happen? I understand right place and right time. What are the odds of two people in show business colliding at the exact moment they need each other? The scenario you described is a little too contrived."

"The circumstances are one-hundred percent true."

Agree to disagree, he supposed and shook his head. He gained nothing from furthering the conversation into an argument. Over the speakerphone, he heard the pitch in her increasingly short statements. "Are you filming at the theater or all over town?"

"I'll do both." She giggled. "My cast will be performing in the Christmas shows. We'll film around town in the weeks leading to the twenty-fifth. Making a holiday movie seemed the best fit for the subject matter."

He smiled. The romantic, seasonal movie business enjoyed a boom. He couldn't turn on his TV without watching an ad for a weekend premiere. "I'll look forward to bumping into you."

"Oh." She gasped. "This is me. This turn."

The right turn signal clicked, echoing over the speaker phone. In another mile, he'd make a left. He set his jaw. The odds of bumping into her again were very high. She'd be hard to miss with the crowd and cameras. Still, he hated to say goodbye. This evening was the first he enjoyed in a long time. He ground his molars together. He didn't much like the reflection of having fun on a red-eye and long drive in the early hours of the morning in the Midwest. Would he ever get a moment alone with her again?

"Thanks for keeping me company. I don't think I would have managed well on my own."

In spite of the lie, he smiled. After a short

acquaintance, he appreciated her force of nature personality. She had drive and vision. No one would stop her, and he couldn't picture her allowing any sort of delay. He'd be lucky to call her a friend. "My pleasure. Have a good night."

She chuckled. "Or morning. Bye, Scott."

"Bye, Kara."

The call dropped.

Blinking several times, he cleared his vision. His eyes itched. His body slumped. He was physically exhausted. With the emotional burdens of his visit weighing him down, he wasn't likely getting much sleep. Or maybe he would dream of unexpected connections and a dazzling smile.

## Chapter Three

Seated at the desk in Dani and Paul's guest bedroom, Kara held a vintage hand-mirror and applied mascara with the other, swiping her lashes to the very end. She stuffed the wand back in the tube, twisting shut the container. Blinking, she studied her handiwork in the reflection. Under a thick layer of concealer, she looked almost normal. She snorted. Her standard heavy-handed eyeshadow, thick lashes, and berry-pink lips hardly qualified as standard.

People wanted a movie star, and not even a few hours' sleep would stop her from delivering on the promise. She adjusted the sparkly sweater, beaded with a delicate snowflake pattern over a dark pair of tight jeans. The cinch around her waist reminded her to stand straight and suck in her tummy. When she didn't dress the part, like last night, she caught a stranger by surprise and vice versa.

Turning the mirror, she set it face down on the desk. She stuffed her mascara tube into the cosmetic bag and zipped. On the plane, her unadorned face was practicality and not an attempt at subterfuge. But she couldn't argue with the results. She liked the regular girl persona she'd adopted. For a few hours, she stopped assuming the worst of humanity and had a surprisingly nice time with a regular guy. She rolled her eyes. He might be a lot of things, most of which she couldn't even guess on such a limited acquaintance, but Scott wasn't average.

Her cell phone alarm chirped.

She grabbed the device, vibrating toward the edge of the desk. With a frown, she cancelled the alarm. She should be in bed, not applying cosmetics and styling her hair. After pulling into the driveway at three thirty in the morning, she located her essential bag in one of the suitcases, left the rest in the trunk, and trudged along the front walk. Fumbling under the doormat with icy fingers, she found the key and stuck it into the flimsy lock on the doorknob. A deadbolt would make a nice thank-you gift.

Tiptoeing through the hallway, she entered the room through the door left ajar and sank onto the bed. At first, she was too exhausted to do more than collapse fully clothed on top of the plaid comforter. She slept hard on the firm mattress but woke with a start forty minutes later. Every muscle ached. After changing into pajamas, she lay down again only to get another half hour of rest. The cycle repeated itself until six when she gave up and got out of bed. If she hadn't accepted culpability long before stepping on the plane, she'd blame him for her restlessness.

Rising from the desk, she smoothed the tunic sweater over her hips and rubbed together clammy hands. Delaying the inevitable would only strain the tense situation more. She'd never been a coward and wouldn't start now. She reached for her bag on the door handle, slipping her hand inside. She brushed the sequined star pinned to the lining. A farewell gift from her TV mom, Marilyn, nearly two decades ago, Kara carried the worn gold patch as a talisman and reminder.

Once she stopped smiling, she'd be forgotten.

With a shudder, she exited the room and strode, shoulders back, down the hall. She avoided the label of difficult her entire career and wouldn't risk everything now. She had a lifetime of experiences in separating personal feelings from professional obligations.

Step by step, she strode toward the sound, hushed voices increasing from a low rumble to a hissing buzz. At the end of the hall, past the front door, she found the doorway to the kitchen. Poking her head through the open doorway of the kitchen, she spotted her hosts.

Standing side by side, they faced the window over the sink. Dani leaned against Paul.

He wrapped an arm around her middle.

*I want that.* The realization slammed into Kara like the bitter cold air outside baggage claim. She shook her head. She couldn't lose focus on the ultimate goal. Producing a successful film secured her fledgling company and her future. She couldn't just leap into love. Besides, she was too cynical for happily ever after. Life was messy, people disappointed each other, and circumstances changed in a second. How could two people find forever when tomorrow wasn't a given? She cleared her throat.

The pair turned.

Dani stepped forward, cheeks reddening. "Hi, Kara. Did you have a good night's sleep?"

"Morning, doll. I did, thanks." Her sweater caught in the light. Kara blinked, clearing her vision. She crossed her arms low over her belly, suddenly feeling too-much in the cramped galley-style kitchen. Had she spoken too loudly? She smiled and studied her companions. "Hope I didn't wake you?"

Dani shook her head.

Paul poured a mug of coffee and extended the beverage.

Kara reached for the cup. He almost dropped the container into her outstretched hands. She grabbed the mug, coffee sloshing against the rim and lifted her gaze.

He drew back, retreating to Dani's side.

Raising the warm cup, Kara sipped, tasting nothing. She scanned his tense frown and Dani's brittle grin. Kara anticipated some amount of nerves. Over the past several months, she thought the calls were getting friendlier. Of course, by exerting her power with an iron-clad contract, she secured the movie deal. For most of the past year, she scrambled to stage a comeback after the pair nearly tanked her. With her lawyers' help, she forked out a settlement with the production company for the abruptly cancelled reality show following her act with Paul. Then came the hours of negotiations for the various venues and crew contracted for the cabaret set.

In return, she asked for Dani's story. *Everyone has a price.* She wanted to move on. Her return wasn't a plan to bulldoze the pair into her vision. She sought collaboration. Could she reach a professional middle ground with her former best friend and short-lived professional partner? She had to try. "Thanks, again for letting me crash last night. I'll pick up the key to the cottage after the parade."

"You mean after the ribbon cutting?" Paul frowned.

Kara nodded, mentally scrambling for the details about the museum and what other duties she agreed to do. In the spring, her movie plans nearly unraveled because of a vengeful article outing Kara's commitment to the town as fake. Factually, the reporter was correct. She owned the rights to Dani's story and utilized a tight, non-disclosure agreement to assume credit for her friend's hard work. At the time, she hadn't invested in New Hope, but the negative spirit of the front-page news in the Milwaukee paper threatened the fragile compromise she reached with Dani and Paul.

Kara needed claim of the feel-good story for her heartwarming comeback. Luckily, Paul's twin sister, the town's mayor Jill, approached Kara with an idea cementing her dedication to the community. Kara purchased a building to keep a longtime business owner in place. At the last minute, however, the tenant backed out. She was left with a very expensive piece of real estate she couldn't use. Jill brainstormed a museum. The idea piqued Kara's interest. Either way, she wouldn't receive rent and might as well have her name displayed prominently inside the museum slash visitor's center. "Yes, of course. First the parade, second the ribbon cutting, and third the keys."

"Oh. Wait." Dani pushed off the counter and strode to a cabinet on the other side, opening a drawer and pulling an envelope. "I already grabbed the keys."

Kara reached for the envelope and set her jaw, halting her negative response. If Dani wanted physical distance, she was probably right to take the initiative. Personal space was better for everyone involved. Inside the business-sized envelope, Kara traced the keys' outline. "Great. Thanks, doll. You're a big help." She folded the envelope in half and slid the key into her bag, brushing against the raised ridges of her faded star. "I'll get settled this afternoon." She grinned, shaking her hair behind her shoulder. "I'm looking forward to your show tonight."

The doorbell rang.

Paul pushed off the counter and strode through the house.

Kara leaned out of the way, her hair ruffling in the rush of air he stirred. With the precision of an overworked restaurant server, Dani averted her gaze from Kara's attempts to catch her eye. Draining the coffee, she swallowed. A bitter aftertaste filled her mouth. She couldn't entirely blame the drink. Setting the mug in the sink, she faced the window and lifted her gaze. Outside, a blanket of white covered the ground. She shivered. *Don't forget a hat.* She'd follow Scott's advice for the parade and ask her stylist for forgiveness later.

"Kara?" Paul asked.

Was he ready to call a truce? Or better, apologize? Spinning, she pressed her hands on either side of the counter behind her. The sharp edge dug into her palms. She frowned. He wasn't there. Why call her and run away? She wasn't a man-eater. He was safe.

"Hi, Kara." Jill stepped forward, pushing past her twin brother and extending a hand. "Ready to go?"

Kara shook the mayor's hand and nodded. "Let me grab my coat." She strolled from the room, lifting her chin. Better to look proud and snooty than to show the glisten in her watery eyes. Crying at the polite greeting of an acquaintance because it was fifty degrees warmer than the same from her best friends was ridiculous.

Back in the guest room, Kara buttoned her thick pea coat, grabbing her pristine, white beret and pulling on cranberry leather gloves. She stuffed her feet into the slipper boots and strode through the house to the kitchen.

"All set?" Jill stepped away from her brother and Dani, crossing the threshold into the hall.

*She sounds like Scott.* With a smile, Kara pulled on her hat. As far as difficult situations, her current dilemma was relatively mild. She'd endured worse. "After you."

Nodding, Jill led the way.

Without a backward glance for the pair averting their faces, Kara strode to the front door. She had a lot of work ahead to rebuild her relationships. The strained morning greeting proved her worst-case predictions were true. Focusing on her feet, she monitored her progress to the vehicles parked in front. The front path and driveway were cleared, but a water spot stained the top of her left boot. The shoes couldn't handle a few steps outdoors in this climate? *He already told me.*

"Are those your wheels?"

Kara lifted her gaze.

Wrinkling her brow, Jill tilted her head toward the minivan.

"Not quite what you'd expect, but yes." Kara shrugged.

With a chuckle, Jill unlocked the coupe parked next to the van.

Kara slid into the shotgun seat and buckled.

Jill turned the key in the ignition and backed out of the driveway, pulling onto the road. "Have you done this before? Lead a parade? I'm a little nervous."

Facing the mayor, Kara smiled and sagged her shoulders, dropping the perfect posture. "I'm a newbie, too. We'll be fine. As long as we don't fall off the back of the convertible."

"Truck, actually. My boyfriend, Rob, agreed to drive us."

Since her last visit, had the town's singles coupled up? "Wonderful, I'm sure that'll be even better."

"I wanted to thank you, too."

Kara drew back her chin.

Jill coughed. "I didn't want you to feel like you were cornered."

*Am I under attack now?* Kara pressed together her lips. Any other movement smudged her makeup. Glancing out the window, she studied the scenery. Modest houses populated either side of the street. Sidewalks formed an interconnected web through the neighborhood leading to downtown. As silence stretched, she pieced together the situation the mayor referenced. "Are you talking about the building?"

"I know you agreed to purchase the property and operate as a landlord for the hardware store. When the original plan fell through, I didn't want you to think I led a conspiracy against you." Jill's voice cracked. "But I hope you'll be pleased with the end result. We have a display about the town's revitalization and a great picture of you. We've left an area free to be filled with props from the movie, too."

What wasn't the mayor saying? Kara shrank, her posture weakening as she sank deeper against the upholstered seat. Dani, Paul, and Jill saw her as a villain. The only explanation was the simplest and hardest truth. She hadn't ever hidden her agenda or her goals. Instead of being celebrated for a take-charge attitude, however, she earned the collective enmity of the town? Jill gave her a chance to make amends, and

Kara was glad for the chance. Hadn't she shown her gratitude? "I'm sure the setup is lovely. I'm looking forward to touring the museum."

"Oh, here we are."

The car rounded a bend and neared an intersection. Jill pulled to a stop at the curb.

Unbuckling, Kara opened the door and hopped out of the car. Careful to avoid puddles, she stepped onto the sidewalk, crunching road salt under her boots. Lifting her gaze, she surveyed the whereabouts.

She stood in front of her recently purchased building, a nineteenth-century, single-story property. After starting as a mercantile, the business ended as the New Hope Hardware Store. With her purchase, she saved the local landmark. She was happy to solidify her benefactress role. But she didn't leave her mark as much as secure someone else's. In a block near the front door, a mason carved *Established 1886 by George Howell.*

A whiff of melting butter and sizzling bacon lingered in the air. Her stomach grumbled. Turning, she glanced at Scott's family diner across the street. Was he there? Could she sneak in for a quick hello? She wouldn't mind a friend and a decent cup of coffee. *Everyone has a price.*

Turning, she faced the mayor and smiled. Her costs required proving her dedication to the fans willing to give her a chance. After grinning for hours, she'd head to the cottage and collapse until the show at Holidays, Inc. and repeat the act all over again. Maybe if she smiled for long enough, she'd almost believe she was happy, and the misconceptions wouldn't pierce her heart.

****

Thanksgiving solidified Scott's desire to become a chef. He loved food. With two full-time working parents, he started cooking during his adolescence to bridge the gap between lunch and dinner. But Thanksgiving was when he stretched from reheating to creating. The summer before his senior year of high school, he worked at the diner in New Hope and solidified his career goal.

Uncle Ted wasn't much of a talker. When he did speak, he was heard. His seal of approval meant more to Scott than any pretty words of praise. Rhapsodizing on holidays of the past didn't align with his present. He should have been suspicious when Uncle Ted greeted him this morning with a—relatively speaking—effusive three sentences.

Standing in a bustling kitchen, Scott mopped his brow with a cloth and shifted his weight from foot to foot. The former restaurant turned prep station for the dinner theater next door was a return to his days as a short-order cook. Through culinary school and his first five years in Los Angeles, he worked his way up the line until catching the interest of his current boss. He'd forgotten the physicality of the labor in mass producing meals. Uncle Ted would argue he'd grown soft. Scott shook his head, cooking the cranberry sauce required constant supervision but not skill. Sugar, water, and berries created the easiest holiday side dish. Of course, Uncle Ted insisted only Scott had the ability to keep the sauce from burning. Fool he was, Scott let his ego inflate and now stirred the bubbling berries. His plan derailed rather quickly.

Last night, he had pulled the hatchback into the

driveway and collapsed behind the wheel, slumping in the seat. With a heavy sigh, he rubbed his weary eyes, grabbed the keys, and headed inside. He trudged to the guest room and fell onto the soft, feather-topped mattress fully clothed. When his alarm rang at four, he silenced the device for a ten-minute snooze. He'd greet his aunt and uncle before they left for the diner. If he planted the idea of retirement early, he could harvest before he left in six weeks. With a sigh, he turned onto his side.

Instead of hitting snooze again, he turned off the alarm. He woke at eight and padded through an empty house. After a quick shower, he wandered over to the diner. Greeting his aunt and uncle in the midst of the breakfast rush, he held his tongue and jumped in to help. Flipping pancakes all morning, he didn't have an opportunity to discuss them slowing down. The inaugural parade drew a steady stream of customers. A few years ago, the morning's crowd would have constituted one of the diner's best-ever days.

The diner closed at two. While cleaning the grill, he prepared his speech, focusing on the pertinent points. When he opened his mouth, he was cut off. His aunt and uncle had other plans. They agreed to run the kitchen for the Thanksgiving dinner show at Holidays, Inc.

Exhausted from his journey and the morning on his feet, he couldn't start a battle now. He needed time to refine his arguments, but he couldn't ignore his obligation. With a nod, he had followed them to the dinner theater's kitchen and launched into prep for the event.

Typically, he worked Thanksgiving. Since his

parents' deaths during the last decade, he was alone on the West Coast. He wasn't upset at pitching in on a holiday, but the sheer scale of the undertaking confirmed Scott's worst fears. His family stretched past their physical limits. In their mid-seventies, his aunt and uncle nevertheless maintained a pace to tire someone half their respective ages.

"Okay, let's start plating entrees," a crisp, feminine voice said.

Lifting his gaze, he spotted the kitchen manager.

Wearing a sleek black suit and chin-length hair ending in a sharp, angular edge, she was direct and no nonsense. After a curt introduction, he'd been shocked to learn she grew up in town. Her air conveyed a sophistication better suited to an East Coast city. Of course, he didn't take her clipped tones to heart. With his experiences in the male-dominated restaurant industry, he understood erecting walls and establishing authority in the kitchen hierarchy.

Servers approached in an orderly queue.

He ladled sauce onto each plate, measuring the portion with care for the hundred and twenty meals. Within twenty minutes, he scraped the bottom of the pot and served the final scoop. Rolling his neck, he eased the ache between his shoulder blades. He grabbed the empty container from the stove and joined in the dishwashing queue. After dropping off his items, he continued to the next line, getting further instructions from Nora.

Holding a clipboard, she scratched a pen against a pad. Glancing up, she widened her gaze for a second before studying the sheet.

"I'm Shirley and Ted's nephew, Scott Neil?" He

cleared his throat. "I'm not on your roster. I dropped in to help."

"Of course." She focused on the checklist. "You can prepare the decaf. Dessert service starts in twenty minutes."

Scanning the row of gleaming, cylindrical, industrial-size coffee makers on the counter, he pressed together his lips. In theory, he could handle the assignment. In practice, however, he'd never had luck with percolators. With a glance behind him, he saw his aunt slicing and plating pie. If he didn't do his part, he knew the pair would accept the job. He was supposed to be taking tasks off their list. He nodded and stepped past.

Glancing around, he pulled his phone from his back pocket and tapped the screen. In a few seconds, he found an online tutorial and got to work. When the coffee finished percolating, he poured a cup. Scanning his surroundings for any curious gazes, he sniffed the steaming mug. He breathed in a whiff of rich, roasted beans. Raising the beverage, he sipped. The decaf tasted mildly sweet with no strong after-taste. He'd made better, but this brew was fine for guests.

A single, loud clap boomed. The low hum of the kitchen quieted.

Nora raised her hands. "Let's begin dessert."

Servers filed past with empty carafes.

He filled each to the rim, emptying three percolators. Glancing around, he realized he was the very last person to finish his job.

The final server walked out of the kitchen, carrying a tray laden with a coffee service. The door swung shut.

In the center of the room, Nora applauded.

Within seconds, cheers erupted. Someone whistled.

"Thank you for your hard work." The kitchen manager tucked the clipboard under her arm and cupped both hands around her mouth. "Tonight was a great test run for the biggest shows of the year. Over the next several weeks, I hope you all enjoy your break and return rested. You are dismissed."

Rolling his shoulders, he slouched. The surge of elation at a job well-done was short-lived. He showed up and did his part. Unfortunately, he'd been the weakest link in the room.

The side door opened. A blast of chilly air swept into the room.

Bussers entered with the dinner plates, and the room filled to max capacity.

He scanned the crowd. Aunt Shirley and Uncle Ted moved toward the exit. Following the wave of people, Scott ambled forward in the slow-moving mass.

A door in the side of the building opened to an alley between the former restaurant and Holidays, Inc. The workers splintered, some walking toward the street and others continuing into the dinner theater.

He twisted his neck. Where was his family? Usually he spotted Aunt Shirley's feathered hair first but couldn't catch a glimpse in either direction. Perhaps his aunt and uncle caught the end of the show. He wouldn't mind seeing what inspired Kara to film a movie.

In a few long strides, he crossed the alley and pulled open the side door. He stepped over the threshold and entered a long, carpeted hallway. Squinting, he adjusted his gaze to the dim interior and surveyed the corridor. Brass, two-arm wall sconces illuminated the empty space. Which way did he go?

Based on his knowledge of the street, he had to imagine turning right and heading down the incline would lead him to the stage. *Was Kara here?* At the moment, he needed a friendly face. He dropped his chin to his chest. He counted a celebrity as a confidante? Nothing about the trip stuck to the plan.

Passing a door marked *Office* on his right, he stopped in his tracks. He should probably turn around. The likelihood his family lurked somewhere in the employees-only area was slim. If he retraced his steps, he could find the main entrance for customers and catch up.

But he wouldn't see her. She mentioned her friend owned the theater. What if he missed a chance for another conversation? Decision made, he kept strolling. The hall terminated with a door on the left. Twisting the knob, he pushed inside, muffling the sound with both hands.

The strains of a ballad filtered past him. Male and female voices melded together. Standing at the door, he couldn't see the singers. He didn't need a visual. The power and emotion of their connection radiated through the harmonies.

He blinked, adjusting his vision to the darkened interior. He stood backstage. From his perspective, the backdrop was a flat sheet of plywood. The ensemble cast obscured the lead actors. He tiptoed around cords and props. His aunt and uncle wouldn't be here, but maybe Kara was.

At the edge of the curtain, he spotted her, standing in profile. Her hair glinted like gold. He rubbed his eyes and narrowed his gaze. Dressed in a shimmery dress, she caught the thin beams of light from the stage. Raising a fist to his mouth, he cleared his throat.

She turned.

The moment was slow and highlighted with the sudden burst of song from the actors nearby. Wearing bright lipstick and shadowed eyes, she looked like Kara Kensington. She was beautiful and out of his league. In her relaxed, traveler persona, she might give a regular guy a chance. Seeing this version, he understood how silly he'd been.

Swiping at the corner of her eye, she met his gaze and backed away from the curtain. She brushed his elbow with a hand and tilted her head toward the stage door.

His throat tightened. The light touch pulsed through his veins. With a nod, he followed.

Pushing the stage door, she exited first.

In the hall, he closed the door behind him.

Leaning against the wall, she smiled. "Hi, Scott. Nice to see you again."

"You, too." He dragged a hand through his hair. Surrounded by scuffed walls and worn carpet, she glittered. She must have a reason for her costume and presence in the theater, and he interrupted her. "Sorry, I didn't mean to drag you away from the show."

She shrugged. "It's fine. The song is almost done. The cast has one last musical number before the finale." She held out her arms and swayed side to side. "I'll make my grand entrance."

"Were they singing?"

Her mouth turned down.

*Ask a stupid question...* He dropped his fists into his pockets. "I mean were your friends on stage just now?" His voice cracked. "The ones from the love story you're filming?"

"Oh, yeah." She cleared her throat and rubbed together her palms. "You're a good listener. Yep, Paul and Dani are performing."

She sounded off. Not quite wistful, her strained words were tired. He shook his head. He knew her for only a few hours. How would he know the rhythm of her cadence or the subtleties in her expression through the thick layer of cosmetics? *Because I've seen the real woman underneath the celebrity image.* "We just finished, too."

"We?"

"My aunt and uncle talked me into lending a hand in the kitchen. I made the cranberry sauce and decaf coffee." He scanned the corridor. Could someone appear and save him from his misery? Why couldn't he conduct a normal conversation? If he pretended she was a nobody like him, he stood a chance.

"Worthy contributions indeed." She arched an eyebrow and quirked the corner of her mouth.

He chuckled. The knot forming between his shoulders released. The flash of the woman he met yesterday surfaced. With a half-smile, she invited him to share the joke. He liked her good-natured humor. Self-deprecation was an underrated quality. "I do what I can. I was won—"

The stage door opened.

A woman in dark makeup and a sparkly gown appeared in the opening. Breathing heavily, she held a clipboard to her chest. "Kara, we're ready for you." She turned, scanning him from head to toe.

He stepped back. "See you later?"

Kara winked and spun, heading back inside and sweeping past the woman.

For a long moment, the stranger stared.

Under a steady gaze, he almost flinched. Who was this woman? Why did he have the skin-crawling sensation she assessed him? Raising his hand, he waved.

Slowly, she retreated and closed the stage door.

In the seconds before the door shut, he couldn't avoid the knowing glint in the other woman's gaze. What did he miss? He raised a hand to his neck and strolled down the hallway. His skin prickled. He'd tuned in to the final act of a movie. If he found the plot online, he stood a chance to catch up. Dropping his shoulders, he hung his heavy head. She promised distraction at the wrong time. He valued her ability to focus and complete a job with dogged determination. Convincing his aunt and uncle to move was the most important task he'd ever undertaken. He'd save female trouble for another day.

## Chapter Four

Kara parallel-parked the minivan at the end of the street and hopped out of the vehicle. Rounding the bumper, she frowned. Maybe stopped was a better descriptor for positioning the automobile roughly eighteen inches from the curb. Driving was an adjustment, but she rather liked the mom-mobile. She wouldn't admit as much. Shaking her head, she scanned the vicinity as she slipped her keys into her back pocket along with her phone and wallet.

For early afternoon, New Hope was remarkably quiet. The day after Thanksgiving was the unofficial start of the holiday season. She expected the town to burst with seasonal cheer. She spotted a few other cars parked on Main Street and a handful of shoppers perusing the downtown corridor. On her previous trips, she'd never seen the street so sparsely populated.

The relaxed atmosphere was a nice change of pace. Yesterday, she'd waved to a large crowd lining the street and grinned for photographers at the ribbon-cutting ceremony. Her few hours at the rental cottage disappeared fast. She unpacked her suitcases, dressed for the night, and found her winter hats before setting out for Holidays, Inc.

Grinning, she tugged the knit beanie over her ears. Scott was correct about the importance of headgear. When she bumped into him last night, she'd almost run to show him the hat tucked into her coat's sleeve in Dani's office. She had the strange urge of seeking his approval. She'd been all sorts of off-kilter at his unexpected appearance. From the wings, she marveled over Dani and Paul's undeniable attraction. When they sang together, they focused on each other.

As an audience member, she felt like an intruder on the acutely intimate moment. But she couldn't look away from the magnetic pair. During a short-lived tenure as showbiz partners, she forced chemistry on Paul. Staring with adoration she didn't feel, she eluded the connection she needed and pushed him too far. He ended up exactly where he should be. She was glad for each of them.

When Kara bumped into Scott, she wiped at her watery gaze. She wasn't on the verge of a sobbing breakdown but a release of the tension and stress building inside. Somehow, she had to overcome preconceptions and earn the town's good opinion. As the dastardly third wheel who threatened New Hope's favorite couple, she had quite a lot of work ahead. But then, Scott was there. Maybe she could have one friend. If he liked her, how bad could she be?

Kara scanned the ground for the dangerous, sly black ice he mentioned. Last night, after the show, she curled on her bed with the laptop and enjoyed an Internet shopping spree. Until her purchases arrived, she relied on vigilance as she navigated the pavement in the flat-soled boots he questioned.

In a few minutes, she arranged a meeting with Dani at the diner. Excitement at the potential of seeing Scott again was tempered by the tense situation with her best friend. At the end of the street, she lifted her gaze and opened the door. Pushing inside, she tripped a bell overhead. So much for an under-the-radar entrance. She caught her bottom lip.

Along the left side of the building, booths hugged large, plate glass windows. Opposite, a long counter with barstools stretched to a door, probably leading to a kitchen.

In the last booth, she spotted Dani, waving and smiling.

Kara drew back her chin and only just stopped herself from glancing over her shoulder. She must have walked in ahead of Jill or some other local. Why would Dani grin at Kara's entrance? As she approached, she scanned the room, but no one else met her gaze.

"Thanks for meeting me today," Dani said. "I'm sure you'd rather stay home and get settled."

Kara nibbled her lip. "No, it's okay. I'm glad you called." She slid across the bench seat.

Dani sat opposite and grinned.

Her blue eyes sparkled like sapphires, and her mouth tilted in the I-know-your-secret smile. Kara fumbled with the buttons on her pea coat, clammy fingers slipping. Had Dani learned of Kara's desperation? She came to town on a make-or-break mission. If her best friend grinned at her misfortune, maybe she should save time and surrender. "You wanted to talk about logistics?" Her voice cracked. She cleared her throat. "I have to call the crew and find out what was filmed during the parade. I won't have a schedule for shooting b-roll and filler landscape shots until I reach them."

"No worries." Dani waved a hand. "We can figure out everything Monday. The ensemble is ready and excited to work."

Kara nodded. Paul hadn't seemed effusive yesterday. She had yet to meet the other members of the Holidays, Inc. team but pictured a struggle to accommodate a film crew and additional cast while preparing for the biggest shows of the calendar year almost on top of each other. Christmas and New Year's were the marquee events of the entire calendar. In the reverse situation, she didn't know how happy she would be.

"So…anything you want to tell me?" Dani leaned forward and arched a brow.

"The cottage is nice?" Kara interlaced her shaky hands on the table. She'd really appreciate a script or—better yet—someone off stage whispering her lines.

An older woman with a hair-sprayed and feathered, shoulder-length, black bob and a white apron wrapped around her waist approached, carrying a tray with ice waters and dessert. She slid the beverages on the table and three slices of pie in front of Dani.

Kara widened her gaze at the desserts, calculating the caloric total.

"Thanks, Shirley." Dani grinned.

"Uh huh, I should know better than to keep supplying you with sweets, Miss Dani. I can't seem to learn." The woman turned to Kara. "Hello, Ms. Kensington. I'm Shirley. My husband, Ted, and I run the diner. Sometimes, we help out at the theater."

"More like most of the time," Dani said with a mouthful of pie.

Shirley rolled her eyes.

"Call me, Kara, please." Kara reached for her ice water, heat creeping up her cheeks. Why hadn't she thought to remove her hat and fluff her hair? Now she looked rude and overheated in front of Scott's aunt.

"Well, Kara. If you need anything when you're here, you call me or Old Ted. Promise?"

Kara sipped her water and nodded. An ice cube caught in her throat, and she coughed.

With a nod, Shirley turned and swept past the table, heading into the kitchen.

Dislodging the ice, Kara swallowed. She took another sip of water and followed the woman's progress. She welcomed the distraction, stalling for another few seconds before returning Dani's coy stare. When Kara drained the glass, she relented and lifted her gaze.

Dani propped her elbows on the table and rested her chin in a palm, pushing her pie plates to the side. "Tell me all about Shirley's nephew."

"Scott?" Kara tilted her head to the side.

"Didn't I interrupt you two talking backstage last night?"

Kara nodded with slow, deliberate motions.

"How did you meet? Oh, I'm so excited for you!" Dani dropped her hands to the table and lightly drummed the surface, rattling the utensils and the plates. "I admit. Paul and I didn't give you the warmest welcome. We were a little on edge and sort of worried…"

*I might have another, ulterior, man-stealing motive*? Kara nibbled her lip. Her plan was clear cut, but she hid her reasons from public scrutiny. Doing so exposed her need to establish herself in the long-term, and she couldn't risk any hint of weakness or vulnerability. The world-at-large preferred confidence.

Last night, Kara bumped into a familiar face when she needed a boost.

"Let's not dwell on the past. I'm sorry for expecting the worst. Tell me everything about the new guy."

"I'm not sure how much there is to tell, doll." Kara exaggerated every syllable, dragging each to twice its length. Her best friend had a history of jumping to conclusions by leap-frogging inconvenient facts.

"I get it. Early days and all that. You don't want to jinx anything." Dani reached across the table and flipped up her palms.

Kara rested her hands in her best friend's. She stared at the point of connection. A sigh built in her chest. Adding another lie was tempting. If she smoothed over the tense welcome, she had a chance at repairing the fractured relationship. Would one more deceit risk the temporary peace? When Dani learned the truth, would she permanently exile Kara? A moment's discomfort for a lifetime's friendship was a small price. *I'd like to be on good terms now.*

Dani squeezed. "I'm so happy you found someone. He seems really nice. We could double da—"

The kitchen door swung open and crashed into the wall.

With a start, Kara drew back her hands and lifted her gaze. She connected with Scott.

Lifting a hand, he waved.

The tiny gesture might as well be the flap of a butterfly's wings sparking a tsunami. With startling clarity, she understood. For the sake of her status in town and rebuilding her dearest friendship, she had to fake a relationship. Would he agree? Maybe he'd think her proposition was funny. Without paparazzi, he wouldn't be splashed across seedy gossip sites or used as late-night comic fodder. She'd have to ask him first. She turned to Dani. "We'll meet at Holidays, Inc. on Monday? Nine a.m.?"

Dani grinned. "See you then."

Sliding out of the booth, Kara turned from the bright smile. She couldn't return the expression, her cheek muscles twitching under the strain. Instead, she smoothed her shirt and approached Scott, holding his gaze with a silent *stay there* command. She slipped her hand loosely around his elbow and leaned close. "We need to talk. Outside."

He jerked back and widened his gaze. After a moment, he nodded.

She tugged him through the restaurant and out the front door. Jogging down the steps, she pulled him around the corner of the building. Dropping her grip, she crossed her arms and faced him. "Will you be my pretend boyfriend?"

****

The diner's kitchen door swung open.

"Oohh!" Aunt Shirley said. "We've got a real-life star out there."

Her sing-song tone echoed through the kitchen. Scott lifted his gaze, his pulse picking up. *She's here?* He glanced toward the entrance to the still-swinging panel. Kara's appearance shouldn't be surprising. With most of the eateries still under construction following the development boom of the previous summer, the diner was one of the few operational restaurants in town.

After the brief conversation last night, he spent

hours berating himself. She'd been upset. He wanted to ask her why, but he'd been interrupted. Should he have called or texted? He had her number but was wary of the stalker implications from an unsolicited contact.

"She's even more gorgeous up close," Aunt Shirley said. "Dainty and delicate."

At the flattop, Uncle Ted grunted and flipped a row of burgers.

Aunt Shirley strode toward him and dropped a kiss on his cheek. "You old charmer."

Scott widened his gaze at the pair. Only two people very much in love and in sync could understand each other's guttural noises. Aunt Shirley understood Uncle Ted's language with admirable fluency.

Standing at the fryer, Scott pulled the basket of fries out of the hot oil, shook off the excess grease, and dumped the crispy potatoes into the pan. He reached for the salt shaker and applied a liberal crust. Operating the machine correctly required vigilance. He found the process meditative and calming. He acted through the rituals of the lunch rush like a familiar dance, never forgetting the steps. Returning the basket, he wiped his hands on his apron. "I might step out and say hello." He lifted the sleeve of his grease-soaked shirt and sniffed. "Maybe I should change first."

Aunt Shirley gasped. "You *know* her?!"

Uncle Ted dropped his spatula, the metal clattering against the flattop.

"We met on the plane from L.A." Scott shrugged. "We were seatmates in first class and then sort of caravanned to New Hope." *I didn't recognize her.* He'd keep the little tidbit a secret. Revealing his obliviousness wasn't endearing.

"You didn't *tell* us?" Aunt Shirley covered her gaping mouth with a palm.

Scott chuckled. "When did we have time for chit chat? Between the parade crowd here and the rush at the dinner theater, I barely saw you two, let alone made small talk."

"Well.... Well... You could have told us something important," Aunt Shirley said.

*Like why I'm really here?* He swallowed the lump blocking his airway. He needed to tread lightly. While he anticipated some of the pushback, he wasn't ready for all. Until he had a counterpoint for their every argument, he feared revealing his plan too soon. He liked to be in control. With too many moving parts, he couldn't guarantee an outcome but knew his non-negotiables.

For peace of mind, he needed them nearby and safe. His life didn't work in New Hope. If uprooting was the solution, he would have done so already. Cooking the same food ad nauseum killed his creative soul. He didn't mind helping but couldn't assume control of the diner. "I'm sorry. I should have."

Aunt Shirley grunted and folded her arms over her chest.

Uncle Ted shot him a narrowed gaze stare.

With a hard look, Uncle Ted reduced Scott to a ten-year-old boy. Flinching, he turned and crossed the room to his aunt. He pulled her in for a big hug. Since the heart attack, she was smaller and no longer as soft and comforting as a favorite stuffed toy.

After the bypass, she left the hospital bonier and slightly deflated. Sticking to a restricted diet, she hadn't fully regained her old figure. To him, she'd shrunk internally as well. Her fierce, stubborn nature relaxed somewhat. The brush with death changed her. He kissed her cheek and stepped back, running a hand over his itchy nose. Aunt Shirley was his mom's sister and was his back-up parent. If he lost her…

"Go out and say hi. Charm her." Aunt Shirley wiggled her eyebrows.

Scott chuckled and dipped his chin. "As you wish."

Aunt Shirley swatted him on the shoulder.

He walked past and pushed through the swinging door. The moment his hand left the frame, he sucked in a breath, preparing for the inevitable crash. When would he remember how touchy the exit was? With an odd sense of awareness, he turned his head to the right and spotted her.

Seated in the last booth, she wore a knit hat over her hair.

*She remembered.* Warmth radiated out from his heart through his limbs.

She approached.

Her blue eyes glinted like mile-deep glacial ice. Without saying a word, he understood her command to stay put. Tucking her hand around his elbow, she scalded his skin like she wielded the metal spatula left on the cooker.

"We need to talk outside."

Her warm breath tickled his neck just below his ear. He nodded.

She pulled him through the restaurant and around the building, dropping her hold.

Cold slapped him. He stared at the spot she'd held, expecting to see a burn mark outlining her fingers on his flannel sleeve.

"Will you be my pretend boyfriend?"

He stepped back and searched her face, looking for some clue he'd heard correctly. "Excuse m—"

"Listen, please." She raised her bare palms.

Frowning, he studied her pale fingers, the nail beds almost blue from cold. He should have mentioned gloves, too.

"I know this suggestion is crazy and coming out of nowhere. But the thing is…" She rolled her neck and her shoulders. "I didn't give you the complete picture. I'm here shooting a film about my friend's dinner theater and love story." She lifted her chin and met his gaze. "What I didn't say is in real life, I almost destroyed both."

"How?" He stuffed his hands into his back jeans pockets.

"It's long and convoluted." She twisted her wrist in mid-air. "You don't have time."

"How about the condensed version?"

Her chin trembled, and she nodded. "I came to town to apologize for stealing my friend's ex. In the process, I stumbled onto the stage and started singing with her current boyfriend. I offered him a contract for several TV concepts. He was mad at Dani and accepted my deal. To garner interest in the projects I pitched, I implied we were a *thing* in meetings. The producers jumped on the idea with a reality TV show." She shuddered. "I tried my best to force a relationship."

While he was a novice at the concept of a fake relationship, he appreciated the proposal didn't involve real feelings for another person. He avoided drama and refused a role as the third in a love triangle.

"Anyway, he ran back to my friend. I threatened

legal action. We reached a compromise." She looked at the ground. "I'm filming the movie about the situation minus my involvement."

He stared straight ahead, his vision blurred. The sentences were so outlandish, and yet her delivery was achingly genuine. Scrubbing both hands over his face, he chuckled. The laughter bubbled up in his gut and escaped his dry throat. "You really can't make up this stuff, huh?"

With a sigh, she tilted her head to the side and scrunched her nose. "What do you think? Do you hate me? Am I too terrible to spend time with?"

*She believes the worst of herself.* With every conversation, he questioned his preconceived ideas about celebrity, specifically one now grown-up, child star. Her candor was raw and refreshing. He hadn't confided in another person for years. How strange to connect with someone who was paid to pretend. He glanced over his shoulder.

In the last window of the diner, two faces pressed against the glass.

He turned and waved, grinning broadly.

Aunt Shirley and the Kara lookalike met his gaze.

*The woman from backstage*. With a nod at Aunt Shirley and Kara's red-cheeked friend, he faced Kara, blocking the voyeuristic pair from view. "Is the woman in question currently next to my aunt in the window?"

"Yes, that's her," Kara muttered.

He extended his hands.

She placed her fingers in his.

Rubbing the icy digits, he raised the interlaced hands to his mouth and blew warm air. "I appreciate how hard the truth was. Thank you for trusting me."

She shrugged but didn't pull back her hands. "You're the first person in a long time who doesn't judge me."

Her soft words tugged at his heart. He knew all about loneliness and the crushing weight of other people's opinions. Maybe a fake relationship could help him, too. While he navigated a family issue, he wouldn't mind a confidante. She'd be a person to bounce off ideas and concerns before speaking to his aunt and uncle. If he kept her close, he wouldn't mentally wander into wasting his time thinking about her. She presented a neat solution. *As long as I maintain boundaries.* He had no energy or time to invest into something real. "Your idea might work. In fact, I think the plan isn't half bad."

Squeezing his fingers, she widened her gaze. "It isn't?"

He shook his head. "If I'm involved with you, a woman conveniently from Los Angeles, my aunt and uncle won't try setting me up with someone in town. I need them to move with me, not the other way around."

"You'll do it?" She lifted on tiptoe.

She held on to him for no other reason than balance. He'd be a fool to imagine she tightened her grip and shared the same skin tingling sensation from the prolonged hand-holding. "I'm not sure exactly what the proposal entails."

"Neither am I." She lowered to her heels and stared at the ground, releasing his fingers.

The candid admission loosened something inside his chest, shifting a weight. She lived a life he couldn't imagine. Her goals, needs, and demands were so foreign he'd require a translator. But he understood her motivation and respected her for trying in complicated circumstances. Although he longed for forgiveness, he placed a want in his goal. He wouldn't overthink a simple solution. "At least we're both out of our league."

"We have a deal? Should we shake?" She stuck out a hand.

"How about a hug? I'm almost certain we have an audience."

She stood on tiptoes and gazed over his shoulder. "You're right."

*I always am.* With luck, he judged her correctly. He wrapped her tight in his arms. She fit snug against his chest, her head tucked under his chin. At first, he hadn't recognized her, but now, he would never forget her.

## Chapter Five

The weekend flew past in a flurry of setting up the cottage, practicing her lines, and calling the production team. At nine o'clock on Monday morning, Kara knocked on the glass front door at Holidays, Inc. and crossed her arms. She would not scan the street for a glimpse of Scott. Instead, she'd wait patiently at the door. She sighed.

Besides a few text messages back and forth during her grocery run, asking for tips on easy meals for one, she hadn't connected with Scott. She was glad for the cover of a fake boyfriend and pleased the arrangement was mutually beneficial. She didn't relish owing favors. But she had a few questions. Should she ask him on a pretend date? Or would he? How often should she be spotted around town on his arm?

In the past, her transactional relationships required a few red-carpet events and several photo opportunities. The situation with Scott was different. With separate agendas for coming to New Hope, she didn't want to overstep and impose on his time. At home, she often spent time alone. In the foreign surroundings, however, she fought an ache in her chest. If she wasn't determined to ignore unhelpful feelings, she might describe her pangs as loneliness.

Her cell rang.

Unbuttoning her coat, she reached for the device

inside her pocket and smiled at the familiar number. The director finally returned her calls. Swiping the screen, she wedged the phone under the knit hat against her ear. “Hello?”

“Good morning, Ms. Kensington,” Lydia Williams greeted. “I received your messages. Sorry for the delay over the holiday weekend.”

Kara gritted her molars at the edging-on-snide tone. If the woman objected to working on typical days off, she’d accepted the wrong job. *Holiday weekend* was the whole point of the project. “Of course. I haven’t had any luck contacting the camera crew. I’m ready to review the footage from the Thanksgiving festivities.”

“They didn’t record anything. They are still here.”

*I needed that footage.* Kara squeezed shut her eyes. During the parade, the weather was ideal. Happy faces crowded both sides of Main Street. Excited cheers bounced off the buildings. The real atmosphere couldn’t be faked.

Hadn’t she spotted several photographers? From the back of the pickup, she smiled at the woman operating a video camera. With a walkie-talking clipped to her belt and an assistant carrying a boom, she couldn’t be an amateur testing her skills with expensive equipment. Could she? “The agreement was to begin filming with yesterday’s events. When was the plan changed?”

“When I had a discussion with the location scout at the beginning of the week. I was assured the same shots can be captured during rehearsals for the stage show. We didn’t want to waste money on redundancies.”

*Why wasn’t I told?* Drawing in a deep breath, Kara

counted to four. With her first project, she couldn't be labeled as difficult, or she'd struggle with any future collaborations. Her heavy exhale didn't ease her tight chest.

Firsthand, she witnessed how quickly a label snuffed out a star. On her sitcom, she remembered the creative tug of war between Marilyn, the actress playing her mom, and production. During hiatus, the studio changed the course of the show. Marilyn returned for a final episode and was written off. *Don't show the toil.*

"Ms. Kensington? Do you have any other questions?"

"I wasn't aware of the change."

"My apologies, I thought you'd received the latest schedule. My assistant will send it again. Thanksgiving wasn't included in the script. We made a decision to hold back the crew to cut down on the budget and extra pay."

Kara couldn't argue about financials. With the project, she assumed far more control than a typical producer. Both to ensure she stuck to the tight timeline and firm budgets, she handled many responsibilities normally delegated to assistants. The filming hitch proved she still wasn't entirely in charge of the direction of her career. "I'll look forward to reviewing the timetable."

"Everything is set for the start of rehearsals on Wednesday?"

*Unless you changed the script since the table read.* She shook her head. "I'm at the theater now, finalizing the details and meeting with the mayor. I confirmed the hotel is ready for the cast and crew."

A loud cough echoed nearby.

She spun on her heels, scanning the block and spotting a familiar face. "Please keep me updated on any changes on your end, and I'll do the same."

"I'll look forward to Wednesday morning."

Ending the call, she dropped the phone into her pocket and fisted her icy hands in the coat's warmth. She rocked back on her heels and slowed her breathing. In the small town, she was never free from an audience. Life in a fishbowl was nothing new.

Jill Howell and another woman strode toward her.

"Good morning, madam mayor." Kara smiled.

"Call me Jill, please." Dressed in a dark coat over a pantsuit, the mayor smoothed a rogue hair back into her neat, low ponytail. "Kara, let me introduce my assistant, Ms. Graves." Jill turned to the woman at her side.

Holding a clipboard to her chest, Ms. Graves lifted her chin.

Kara grinned and extended a hand. Graves suited the dour older lady with the silver pixie haircut and flat features. "A pleasure to meet you."

Ms. Graves shook her hand, pumping the arm once before releasing. Readjusting her grip on the clipboard, she scratched a pen against a legal pad.

"Why are you standing outside?" Jill tilted her head.

"I knocked, but no one answered." Kara shrugged.

"If you're waiting for someone to welcome you inside, you'll be here all morning." Jill crossed to one of the glass doors and pushed the bar. With her back, she propped open the entrance. "When Dani arrives, she leaves the front unlocked. Her office is too far back to hear knocking, and my brother is no help either. He's usually playing with loud abandon on the stage in total oblivion of the world around him."

Kara arched an eyebrow and clasped her hands behind her back, entering the lobby. She should know such tidbits about Dani. But the town changed her oldest friend. In the tight-knit community, she blossomed, finding family like she always wanted. *I used to be her sister.* Kara caused the rift and accepted full blame. With luck, she could redeem more than her image on the movie. She drew back her shoulders and lifted her chin. No one would see her flinch.

In the tiled lobby, strains of piano music filtered under the doors leading into the theater.

Jill shut the front door behind Ms. Graves. "See what I mean?"

"I'll remember next time. Are you heading to the meeting?" Kara scanned both women.

Ms. Graves continued writing.

Jill nodded. "We are. Since we intercepted you…"

Ms. Graves unclipped the board and pulled several sheets from under the legal pad. Extending the documents, she lifted her gaze and shook the papers at Kara.

Kara reached for the bundle and scanned.

"We are delivering your permits. You'll find every request has been approved," Jill said.

Kara browsed the first lines of the sheets. "Including the trailers?"

"Last one in the stack." Jill grinned. "These are date and time specific to accommodate you during the town's special events. If you go over time or are delayed and—"

"We won't." Kara shook her head. *I can't afford it.*

"But if you do…" Jill said. "We need time for another meeting with the town council for approval."

Kara nodded. As sole financer of the project, she was stretched beyond thin. She'd poked several holes through the flimsy covering hiding her desperation. If she couldn't deliver her film on time and budget, she'd be moving back into her childhood home. Her parents were lovely, but for a fiercely independent person such a need would bring her lower than the ground.

"We are eager to work with you and are very excited." Jill rubbed together both hands. "Wayne previewed his footage from the parade. It'll make a great advertisement for the town."

"Footage?" Kara frowned.

"Yes, our go-to town photographer. He made a special trip for Thanksgiving. His wife operates the video camera, and an assistant helps with sound. Don't worry. He's heading back to warmer weather now. He won't get in the way of your cameras."

Relief flooded through her. Kara shook out her trembling limbs and rolled her neck. "I'm not worried. Could I get his phone number? He might solve a minor scheduling snafu. My crew wasn't here for the parade. I'd appreciate seeing what he and his wife captured. If I use any of the footage in the movie, I will pay and give them screen credits."

Jill widened her gaze and grinned. "He'd love to help. I'm sure the added incentive will spur a rush processing and delivery."

The cheek-to-cheek expression brightened the mayor's whole face and transformed the somewhat average-looking woman into a beauty. *With a little makeup and a haircut…* Kara wouldn't force a makeover on someone. “Thanks, I really appreciate it. You have no idea.”

“Hey, you’re practically a local now. We look out for our own.” Jill winked.

Ms. Graves ripped a sheet of paper and extended it.

“Thanks.” Kara nodded. Accepting the scrap with the name and number, she stuffed the note in her purse next to the permits. “Should we go inside?”

Jill sauntered forward and opened the doors to the auditorium.

Crossing into the theater, Kara clutched the purse on her shoulder and spotted the group near the front. Being the boss required diplomacy and strength, she learned. She pulled back her shoulders and lifted her quivering chin. *No one expects more out of this project than me.* The thought wasn’t the mantra she needed. Navigating through the rows, she reached the round table and smiled, infusing the expression with every ounce of brightness she possessed. “Good morning. Thank you for meeting with me today.”

Dani approached and stopped at her side. “We’re looking forward to the movie. Let me introduce the team. You know our musical director, Paul Howell.” She smiled and winked at the tall man, tipping his head. “I believe you know Rob Carroll. He used to own the hardware store but runs construction and storage for the theater.”

“Hello, Rob. Nice to see you again.” Kara relaxed her shoulders, appreciating every familiar face.

In his late thirties, a brawny, bald man with startlingly jade green eyes nodded. “You as well, Ms. Kensington.”

“I don’t think you’ve met our stage manager, Andy

Jacobs?" Dani asked.

A man with sandy blond hair extended a hand.

Kara stepped forward and shook. "Hello. I'm Kara Kensington. I'm very pleased to meet you, Mr. Jacobs."

"Call me, Andy." He looked at the ground, and his cheeks reddened.

She liked the sheepish expression and held his grip for a second longer than necessary. How many fans did she still have? She couldn't overlook a single one.

A throat cleared.

Releasing the grip, she turned toward the sound.

A woman with a smooth, brunette bob and dark brown eyes crossed her arms and arched a brow.

"Last, but not least, our kitchen manager, Nora Thomas." Dani waved a hand toward the woman. "With years of experience, we are lucky to have her."

*And she seems to agree.* Kara inclined her head, slightly, and clasped her hands behind her back. She refused to otherwise greet the impertinent woman. "Should we start?" She sank into the chair. With her purse on her lap, she grabbed a notebook and pen. Setting both on the table, she uncapped the pen and hovered the tip over the first page of the spiral bound paper.

Chairs scraped the floor, and the table tipped under the unbalanced weight of someone's arms.

"Who would like to go first?" Dani asked.

"I've already spoken with the mayor. Thank you, Jill and Ms. Graves," Kara said.

"I'll go." Rob held up a hand. "I have a listing of the set pieces in storage next door." He pulled several paper clipped sheets of paper from a back pocket and slid them across the round table. "Let me know what, when, and where you need something. I'll gather the supplies."

"This is great. Thank you." Kara grabbed the pages and scanned the first, dragging her finger down the table row by row. The detailed account would be helpful. She lifted her chin and turned toward Paul. Seated on the other side of Dani, Kara leaned forward to study him. "How is the next show? Will my cast be included? I know you have your fan favorites."

"I'm writing the musical to include your actors." Paul looked at the table. "Of course, Sherman and Margaret are involved. I can't imagine leaving them out."

Kara nodded. With his head lowered, he couldn't see her response. But he was probably sure of her agreement. The octogenarian couple earned a well-deserved reputation for dynamic, scene-stealing performances at Holidays, Inc. TV audiences would love the pair.

"I've finished viewing the casting auditions. I have parts in mind for the cast," Paul said.

"Wonderful." Kara smiled. Was she making progress in thawing his icy disdain to cool professionalism? "I appreciate you taking the time to review the tapes." The Christmas musical at the dinner theater formed a central plot point in the movie. She and the TV leading man would fall out over the rehearsals and a misunderstanding. During the finale song of the Christmas Eve performance, Kara and her co-star would reconcile and kiss.

The show within a show element complicated everything. Kara and cast would perform for Dani's audience and simultaneously film the movie. In addition to scenes around town, the cast would rehearse Paul's musical and separately film the script showing the staged rehearsals. The dinner theater was the crux of the movie but also proved the most complicated aspect of the project. She'd follow up with Paul and Dani about the musical's score and script later.

"This morning, I received a call from your food service vendor." Nora rested her arms on the table, interlacing her hands.

At the cool-as-ice tone, all warm feelings evaporated. Kara tilted her head and returned to studying the sheets in her hand. She wouldn't meet the woman's gaze. "Hmm?"

"Your food service cancelled."

"What?" Kara gasped and stared at Nora across the table, widening her gaze.

Nora curled her upper lip. "The kitchen staff is on holiday until the week of Christmas."

Across the table, the manager lifted a shoulder in a small shrug. "When did you find out?" Dani knitted together her brow. "I haven't heard anything."

"Only moments before we came into the meeting. Otherwise, I would have made other calls myself on behalf of the film."

Kara gritted her molars, creating a dam against the unfriendly response. She hated the sugar-sweet expression the kitchen manager shot Dani. Sure, Nora just found out. From the corner of her gaze, Kara spotted Jill rolling her eyes and smiled. She counted one ally against Nora. Kara wouldn't be outmaneuvered by an amateur with poor acting skills. An idea popped into her mind. She pushed back from her chair and rose. "I might have a solution."

"Keep us posted." Dani grinned.

Kara liked the smile in her friend's gaze. The warmth swept her from head to toes. Maybe she could have redemption both professionally and personally. The only requirement was embellishing a lie.

****

Sinking his wrists into warm, soapy water, Scott scrubbed the plates. In the short-term, he didn't mind washing dishes. He didn't hesitate to jump in and help wherever he could. Pitching in gave him firsthand understanding of the tasks on his aunt's and uncle's plate, he needed every shred of information before starting the talk.

After his initial plans failed, he counted luck in his favor. Aunt Shirley was skilled at debate. Once he began the conversation, he'd have only one chance to argue his side. He could imagine her counterpoint. If he wanted family nearby, why didn't he move? With the back of his hand, he lifted the tap, rinsed the dish, and set it on the rack to the side. New Hope held nothing for his future.

Engaging in the diner's monotony was fine in the short-term. If the job was his everyday routine, he would have run screaming. For a few weeks, he could engage in repetitive tasks without complaint.

Of course, he wasn't sure what constituted normal in New Hope. The Monday after a holiday weekend was deceptively calm. The regulars arrived at opening for the usual orders of coffee and the weekday pancake special. A few other customers trickled in for a steady breakfast service. Unlike Thanksgiving, the kitchen was never overwhelmed.

Turning on the faucet, he rinsed the last dish and

set it in the rack on the side of the sink. He tugged the stopper and angled the running water, clearing residue from the stainless-steel basin as suds swirled into the drain. Was he circling an abyss, too? He wanted a chance to catch up with Kara and pinned his hopes she'd stop in for a bite.

Over the weekend with back-and-forth text messages, he guided her through the aisles at Frank's grocery store on Main Street. He offered tips on easy-to-prepare meals and almost invited himself over to help with meal prep. The problem was him. He wanted to see her but wasn't sure how to act under the guise of a fake relationship. He vowed to wait for her next move. If he agreed to her plan, he had to follow her direction. With the back of his hand, he shut off the faucet and dried his hands on a towel slung over his shoulder.

The door between the restaurant and the diner swung open and crashed against the wall.

He turned and blinked.

Panting, Kara scanned the room from one side to the other.

Scott followed her line of sight across the galley kitchen.

Uncle Ted flipped a row of pancakes at the flattop and didn't stop his work.

Dragging his gaze back to hers, he reached for the knot on the apron at his waist and quirked an eyebrow. "To what do we owe the pleasure?"

"Is your aunt here? I didn't see her outside." Kara tipped her head to the side.

He approached. With each step, he focused on her face, her expression coming into clearer view. She looked anxious, darting her gaze and bobbing her head. Her chest rose and fell with rapid, shallow breaths. Aunt Shirley was at a doctor's appointment. His aunt delayed her well-visit for several weeks. Intercepting the call from the nurse over the weekend, Scott assisted his aunt with booking the visit and dropped her off himself. Glancing at his watch, he still had half an hour before he needed to leave and pick her up. "She'll be here later. Is this an emergency?"

"Okay, okay." Kara nibbled her lip and studied the ground.

A few feet away, he felt the heat rolling off her like a wave. Inside the tight kitchen, she was liable to pass out from the high temperatures of the grill and oven. "Follow me. You need some air."

She nodded.

With a hand to her elbow, he applied gentle pressure and steered her through the kitchen to the back door. In his grip, her joint seemed impossibly tiny and fragile. Kara was petite, being both slim and short in stature. Her big personality erased the differences in their physical dimensions. Today, however, she seemed small. He hated seeing her vulnerable.

Continuing around the dumpsters, he led her deeper into the eight-foot-wide alley between the diner and the building next door. The tight space couldn't accommodate the city's equipment to asphalt the road and retained its original brick paving. He dropped his grip and leaned back against one wall.

She twisted together her hands. "I need help."

"What is it?"

"More than a faux beau can handle." She smiled.

He liked the little, lopsided grin lifting the corner

of her mouth. He preferred her being cheeky to overwhelmed. "Clearly, you've been disappointed in your previous fake relationships."

She shook her head. "Those have all been transactional situations."

He crossed his arms and arched an eyebrow. A sour taste filled his mouth, contrasting the sweet smell of perfume tickling his nose. "I thought you hadn't been in a situation like ours before?"

"Well, not exactly like..." She pointed between them. "Our aim is convincing people who know us. But you live in L.A. You've seen it. There a certain number of mutually beneficial relationships exist, offering paparazzi a hint of something romantic with someone unexpected to boost a mention in the news cycle."

She was right. But he hated to think of her being involved in something similar with someone else. He scrubbed a hand over his face, wiping the scowl from his features. Dropping his hands to the wall, he flattened both palms against the rough brick. "Let's try this again. What's the problem? Why do you need my aunt?"

With a heavy sigh, she dropped her shoulders. "I lost my food service contract. I don't know what happened, but I need someone serving my cast and crew. I was hoping maybe your aunt could help. Your aunt and uncle have come through for the dinner theater time and time again."

*They can't keep riding to the rescue.* Digesting her words, he nodded. If he hadn't intercepted her, he knew his aunt and uncle would have agreed without hesitation. They did any and everything in their power to help the community. "What about the Holidays, Inc.

kitchen staff? Won't they be eager for more work?"

"Maybe the staff would." She rubbed her brow with both hands. "But the kitchen manager isn't amenable."

He chuckled. He hadn't sought an ally against Nora but was glad to have one.

"What's funny?" She dropped her hands and tipped her chin.

"Nothing." He shook his head. He'd never been on the same page with someone else and was almost in lockstep with Kara. Should he consider the phenomenon a byproduct of being a pair of outsiders in a tight-knit, small town? "What did the manager say?"

"Until the week before Christmas, her staff is on holiday and unavailable. My previous vendor was entitled to full access to the kitchen. Getting the manager's agreement in the first place wasn't easy. But the caterer backed out." She flipped up her palms. "I don't know what happened. The entire cast and crew arrive on Wednesday. I'm out of time."

He should mention the gloves. Her hands were almost blue from cold. He wanted to warm her fingers. To do so, he'd step away from the wall and stop very close. He hated to erase her flustered and frustrated expression. She was adorably frazzled. "I'll do it."

"You will?" She arched an eyebrow.

He covered his heart with a hand. "You wound me, madam. Of course I can help. I'm a chef."

"I know you are, but I'm asking for more than a few meals for a handful of people. I need large amounts of food prepared and served every day of production."

*I'm a much better option than my aunt and uncle.* Familial obligation demanded stony silence. If telling the community the truth about his aunt's slowly recovering health would help, he'd have done so already. The job promised a lot of work and plenty of distraction from his purpose.

Exhaling a heavy sigh, he dropped both arms to his sides. He had no choice. In truth, the diner was well-staffed and didn't need him. But he could provide valuable aid to her project. "I have a varied history in food. I've been a short-order cook, a *sous* chef, and—for one very tense weekend—a caterer."

"Can you get up and running quickly? Like in a couple days?"

"*Like* meaning as soon as possible, but I could take a few days if needed?"

She shook her head.

"You really need help in forty-eight hours?" He ran a hand through his hair. She didn't strike him as a woman accepting any answer besides yes. If he stripped away his other concerns, he reached the same kernel of truth. He wanted to be dependable.

"I wouldn't push if I wasn't desperate."

"If I'm your boyfriend, I'd help. Catering is a good excuse for hanging around the set."

Widening her gaze, she snapped both forefingers and thumbs. She pointed at his chest and smiled. "I didn't consider the angle. You're exactly right. The production is supposed to last three weeks. You're here until after New Year's, right?"

Lifting the corner of his mouth, he almost levitated off the ground. *She remembered.* He nodded. "On my honor, as a fake love interest, I promise I won't let you down."

"Oh, thank you." She lunged forward and wrapped

her arms around his neck.

The hug was more relief than romance. He didn't return her embrace. If he held her, he might tighten his grip and test how she felt snuggled against his chest. She wasn't the person he thought she was. What else was he wrong about?

She stepped back, her blue eyes sparkling. "Can I forward you the contract I had with the other vendor? So you can see what the agreement entailed?"

"Yes, please." He stuffed his fists into his pockets. If he didn't, he might reach for her again.

"Great. I'll get you the details. Thanks, Scott." She spun on her heel and stalked to the street between the two buildings.

Monitoring her progress, he held his breath.

She disappeared around the corner.

Then he exhaled a sigh and sagged his shoulders. He'd either dodged a bullet or taken one to the chest. Unfortunately, he'd have to bleed to know which hit he took.

# Chapter Six

The next day, Kara strolled the long hallway at Holidays, Inc., wall-to-wall carpet muffling her high-heeled steps. With the kitchen catering crisis in good hands, she focused on the show within a show aka the source of her throbbing temples. Without a script, she couldn't schedule rehearsals, block time for the crew, or instruct the cameras where to shoot. In normal circumstances, she'd avoid the middleman and head straight to the problem.

Ambushing Paul, however, was out of the question. She wanted no hint of impropriety or working around Dani. She knew how words and situations could be twisted. For years, she'd been a master of spin, engaging every trick for optimum positive publicity. She shook her head. How strange she never stopped to consider the calculation in her actions. With a fist, she rapped once on Dani's office door.

"Come in," Dani said.

Opening the door a crack, Kara peeked inside. "Hi. Do you have a minute?"

"Sure, come on in." Dani nodded, keeping both hands on the keyboard.

Kara stepped over the threshold and shut the door behind her. Turning slowly, she took in every detail in the room. The pale blue walls reflected a warm glow from a desk lamp near the monitor and a floor light in the corner. The airy room almost fooled Kara into thinking a transom window hid in some upper part of the tiny space. She'd only stepped inside Dani's sanctuary once before. On the previous occasion, Kara focused on her goal and failed to notice the surroundings. Dani transformed the office from claustrophobic to breezy. Take less-than-ideal circumstances and brighten the whole scenario with *trompe loie* and a smile was Dani's hallmark.

"How can I help you?" Dani interlaced both hands behind the computer and tilted her head to the side.

Kara pursed her lips. If she blurted the reason, she cut her chances for success in half. "Do you want to read the script?"

"Excuse me?"

Kara swept the thin strands of hair peeking under her beret over her shoulders. Her hair required regular maintenance to tame. She didn't have thick locks like Dani. She didn't have a lot of what her friend naturally possessed and took for granted. Their differences kept Kara on edge, searching for any excuse to pull ahead. Competition didn't happen without two parties, and Dani never participated. Instead, Kara dragged her along. For years, the arrangement suited both. When Kara used her sense of noblesse oblige to justify hurting Dani, however, Kara destroyed everything. If given a chance, she'd take back every action of the last two years. "I can drop off a script for your review."

"Was my approval part of the agreement? I didn't think any input was necessary." Dani yawned.

*No, but I'd like to find a truce.* The tone of nonchalance rattled Kara. While she didn't want a fight, she preferred some feeling to the indifferent void. She planned, scheduled, and coordinated everything within her power. From hotels and permits, to screenplays and trailers, she tackled the massive project to save her career one task at a time. In all her preparation, she failed to anticipate feelings. Initially, she viewed the situation with professional detachment. She hated emotions and preferred facts. After a few days in town, she needed a new approach for getting back her friend.

Dani shook her head. “It is what it is, I suppose. I won’t fight about whatever words you put in my mouth. I’d prefer not to read the script.”

The dismissive comment slapped Kara’s cheek. She raised her left shoulder half an inch and pressed a hand to her collarbone, shooting her friend an unbothered stare and froze. Why was she posing? Affectations weren’t the key to her former body double’s good graces.

She slid the purse off her shoulder. “If you’re sure…” Unbuttoning her pea coat, she hung the garment on a hook near the door and pulled off the beret. Reverting to her old, over-the-top ways felt off. She wanted Dani’s approval and blessing. For better or worse, the movie would be forever associated with both of them and the town.

“Let’s cut to the chase.” Dani propped her elbows on the desk. “What do you need? Any luck with a new caterer?”

Kara scrunched her nose. Bending, she grabbed her purse and stuffed the hat inside. “Scott can step up.”

“Wonderful.” Dani jumped to her feet. The rolling chair hit the wall behind the desk. She wrinkled her brow. “I suppose the next piece of business is the Holidays, Inc. musical. Should we talk to Paul?”

*If that will help...* Paul was a complication. Kara trusted Dani to handle the talent. Nodding, Kara smiled.

Dani exited the room, leaving the door ajar.

Kara spun on her heel and followed.

With heavy steps, Dani strode through the corridor to the lobby. She didn't glance over her shoulder.

*She knows I'm still learning to follow.* In the course of their friendship, Kara never assumed the submissive role. She led, finding opportunities for both and hearing no complaints. For her second chance, she had to flip the script. Studying her steps, she gripped the purse with one hand. She was on Dani's turf and couldn't forget it. Light spilled onto the floor, illuminating a sliver of faded, red carpet. She lifted her gaze.

With her back, Dani held the door to the lobby. "Paul gets easily startled. If he's working, I don't walk across the stage." She chuckled. "I enter through the auditorium."

Kara pressed together her lips. Paul's quirk wasn't universally charming. With a few months' cohabitation, she remembered his particular ways. Crossing the tile, she craned her neck and glanced through the lobby's glass walls overlooking Main Street.

She didn't catch a glimpse of Scott. He had plenty of prep work before he catered for a hundred tomorrow. Vowing not to micromanage, she wouldn't seek him out. An accidental run-in was okay. She liked who she was around him. She forgot all the studied movements and witty lines, embracing a personality she hid from the public.

A door scraped the floor.

Turning, she spotted Dani entering the auditorium. Quick on her heels, Kara followed. From the back of the room, she had an unobstructed view of the stage. The former cinema maintained the slight slope of the floor, maximizing every guest's experience. Kara could imagine quite a few things, but she would never have had the vision for the renovation. The old theater was two separate screening rooms, which Dani combined both into one grand space.

A jaunty piano tune flitted through the room.

On stage, Paul dashed both hands across the keys. He reached for jingle bells on the bench. Playing piano one-handed, he shook the bells with the other.

Dani stopped in the middle of the room.

Kara stood at her side.

The music paused.

Dani clapped and grinned. With a sideways glance, she raised both brows.

Belatedly, Kara joined her, her cheeks stretching with a tight smile.

Paul drew back his hands and turned, squinting at the audience. "Hello?"

Dani cupped hands around her mouth. "Sounds great!" She resumed her approach, navigating around the tables toward the stairs at the side of the stage.

A few steps behind, Kara studied the ground. She'd never seen Dani overact. If love meant fluffing a man's tender ego, she wanted no part. With a hand on the rail, she climbed the stairs. Focused on the boards, she tiptoed her way through the tangled mess of cords and cables.

Her order of Scott-approved, snow boots hadn't arrived yet. She unpacked a pair of leather, heeled booties. Better than nothing became her slightly more optimistic New Hope mantra, supplanting her cynical statement of everyone has a price. If Scott spotted her, he'd frown. She'd explain her reasoning and ease his tight expression into a warm smile. She enjoyed every opportunity for banter.

"Kara? Don't you agree?" Dani asked.

Lifting her gaze, Kara found Dani leaning against the upright piano.

Paul turned and studied her.

*Flattery smoothes every awkward moment.* Another nugget of Marilyn's wisdom popped into Kara's brain. She smiled. "Yes, absolutely. You're the composer, Paul. With so much success this year, I trust your vision." She rubbed together both palms. "When can I hear the whole show?"

Paul blanched.

Dani widened her gaze.

Kara gritted her molars, smiling her movie-star grin and considering her best response. The show within a show benefited both the movie and the dinner theater. For the biggest shows of the year, Dani had a trained cast of screen credited actors. A *Sold Out* sign was stuck to every poster throughout town. In return, Kara expected professionalism at Holidays, Inc. "Do you have a timetable for blocking? We're planning on starting filming tomorrow. After we work through our script, we'll have plenty of time to rehearse yours."

With one finger, Paul tugged the collar of his crewneck shirt. "How many days do you think you'll be shooting?"

Kara darted her gaze from Paul's twitching cheek to Dani's stiff smile. Would the wrong response shove the man into a nervous breakdown? Why hadn't Dani explained the modus operandi to her boyfriend and prepared him? She'd been in Hollywood nearly as long as Kara. Clearing her throat, she focused on Paul. "If we stick to the plan, we film for twelve days including our scripted shots at the theater. Do you have a book we can start learning?"

Paul shook his head, looking at the floor. "I usually work out a lot of details in blocking."

*Like, all of them?* Stifling a gasp, Kara plastered a smile on her face. When in doubt, grin it out.

"The musical won't be a problem." Dani stepped forward, leaning against the top of the upright piano. "Paul always delivers a great show. Things get really messy right before they are cleaned up."

"Would repeating last year's musical be an option?" Kara crossed her arms, tucking both hands against her ribcage and holding tight. The small action was better than kicking herself. With her friend's assurances Paul would be ready, Kara hadn't micromanaged Holidays, Inc.'s contribution to the movie. "To alleviate some pressure? Do you still have the music and pages floating around somewhere? Should I ask Sherman and Margaret for their copies?"

Dani shot her a wide-eyed look, pursing her lips.

Paul frowned. "I didn't have a chance to work on the show."

*Because you were in my house*. Ice clogged Kara's veins. Any reminder chilled her in a second. She waved a hand. "Never mind. Let's just keep each other informed of where we are."

"You start shooting tomorrow?" Dani looked at Paul.

Nibbling the inside of her cheek, Kara ignored the flutter in her stomach. Why didn't Dani meet her gaze?

Was Kara about to fall into a trap? Honesty was her only option. "The cast arrives tonight. We'll meet for coffee and pastries in the morning and begin production." *Do you want to watch on set? I can save a chair.* She hated to put Dani on the spot more than she already had. "I'm heading next door to give Rob a list of props. We're filming a Valentine's scene." *Please ask me more.* If she was bolder, she'd stop the internal monologue during every conversational pause and speak direct.

"Great. Do you need anything else from us?" Dani pushed off the piano bench.

*Not that you're willing to give.* Kara bit the inside of her cheek. She still had much more work to prove herself worthy of friendship. For years, she considered Dani her real sister and assumed the relationship could withstand any test.

When Marilyn left the TV show, she warned Kara never show herself as anything less than a perfect star. She maintained the persona with ease until work opportunities evaporated. With dwindling roles, she betrayed her best friend and secured a couple jobs. After years of lying to herself, she thought nothing of doing the same to her nearest and dearest. She lost her most important relationship because of a guy.

As much as she hated it, she brought the troubles on herself and accepted responsibility. Under the strain of her fake grin, she struggled and twitched. Whatever she needed to do, she would. "No, doll. I've got everything I need. I'll see you both tomorrow."

She jogged off the stage, racing through the auditorium. She pushed out the front door. Icy wind slashed her cheeks. Reaching for her collar, she grabbed air. Her coat hung on a hook in Dani's office. She'd have to fight the scalding breeze and keep going. Returning to the building and fetching her outerwear would put her at a disadvantage, displaying a lack of foresight. With so much to prove, she understood how much little time remained.

****

Tuesday morning, Scott sat in the back booth of the diner. With an elbow propped on the table, he pressed a cell to his ear and drummed his fingers.

The line rang and rang.

Since agreeing to help Kara, he'd leaned into the little patience he possessed. He must have been a fool to agree. *Or desperate.* He reviewed the very thorough contract she'd signed with the original food service company. On shooting days—detailed calendar and timetable enclosed—she needed three meals and two snacks for no less than a hundred. With filming scheduled around the clock, he only marked a few days free between December fourth and Boxing Day.

If he backed out, he risked disappointing her and adding hours to his overworked aunt and uncle. His plan to encourage them to slow down and let others lend much-needed assistance would implode.

He still hadn't approached the pair about retirement. Finding both at home at the same moment was rare. One was always at the diner and the other heading over. Should he take a chance and discuss the idea separately? Was his best bet divide and conquer or stare down the united front? The delay wasn't his typical procedure, but rushing into the unknown wasn't a character trait either. With a month in town, he'd take his time handling the delicate situation.

The line connected.

"Hello? Brixton Catering. Kay Brixton speaking. How may I help you?"

"Ms. Brixton? Hi. This is Scott Neil calling. I'm not sure if you remember me. I'm Shirley and Ted Olson's nephew."

"Shirley's sister's boy? The chef out in California?"

Heat crept up his cheeks. He tugged the collar of his crew neck shirt. How did she know so much? Was Aunt Shirley bragging? "Yes, ma'am."

"Well, goodness. What a surprise," Kay said.

If possible, Scott heard a smile in the woman's voice. Decades prior, Kay lost her husband in a tragic accident, and she was a neighbor in need. Aunt Shirley and Uncle Ted helped her. By providing staff, space, and support in the diner's kitchen, his aunt and uncle lifted the fledgling business from obscurity to success. During his summers in New Hope, Scott pitched in at fancy events. Almost fifteen years ago, she moved to a bigger town with more opportunities. He hated to exploit the connection, but Ms. Brixton was exactly the person he needed. "I'm calling with a big favor, Ms. Brixton."

"You are? How can I be of any assistance to you all the way in California?"

"No, ma'am. I'm in New Hope." He lifted his gaze, surveying the half-full restaurant. At the counter, a handful of regular customers sat on the barstools. A few tables were occupied. No one was close enough to listen. "At the moment, I'm sitting in the diner."

"Oh, okay." She chuckled. "I can't imagine why you'd need my help. But I'll always lend a hand."

"I have a big ask, and I don't want to put you on the spot." He reached for the pen and notebook next to his cup of cold coffee. "I'm sure you're busy with the holiday party season."

"I am, but tell me what you need. Whatever it is, I can try to figure out something. I'd do anything for Ted and Shirley."

*Hoping you'd say that.* "Not sure if you heard, but a movie is being filmed in town starring Kara Kensington."

"Wasn't she on a TV show about twins?" Kay squealed. "Ooh, my kids loved her."

*Everyone did.* Kara starred in a long-running sitcom as a pair of identical twins getting into mischief. As a kid, he eagerly waited for the new show on Friday nights. In middle school, he lost interest. The cancellation wasn't surprising. Almost immediately, the show went into syndication, cementing the star as America's sweetheart.

The woman he'd met definitely earned the moniker. If he could maintain his supposed involvement without giving away the truth, he was excited for a behind-the-scenes glimpse from the sidelines. He coughed.

"Are you feeling all right?"

"Sorry, Ms. Brixton. Something stuck in my throat." He reached for his cold coffee and sipped. "Anyway, I'm in town for the holiday. The food service for the film's production fell through. My aunt and uncle are slammed at the diner. I figured I'd try to help out."

"Did she ask you? What's she like?"

*Surprisingly unsure*. He bit the end of his tongue.

Offering a candid impression of the kind person he met was too personal. He tapped the pen against the notepad. "Yes, ma'am. Kara Kensington is here and did ask. The requirements are pretty lengthy, but the budget is adequate. I have access to the kitchen at the dinner theater in town."

"What do you need from me?"

Studying his notes, he gripped the pen until the veins bulged on the back of his hand. He drew in a breath, uncurling his fingers. "I need a crew for cooking, contacts for ordering, and supplies for service. Really, I need anything you can spare for seven days a week, starting in the morning."

"Hmm."

He wasn't sure if conducting the ask over the phone was a way to ease the awkward situation or added to the brittle pain of the moment. At least she couldn't see the tight pull of his mouth or his lips moving with his thoughts. As the seconds ticked past, he squeezed shut his eyes. He didn't have a big network in the Midwest and specifically not in the nearby vicinity. What was his next plan if she told him no?

"You're aware I moved out of town? I'm about a forty-minute drive from New Hope."

Scrunching his face, he shut his eyes. She had every right to refuse. He was glad he didn't have to see the regret in her expression. "Yes, ma'am."

"My staff is located here."

Rubbing a hand on his tight jaw, he nodded. "I know."

"I think we can work out something."

She said the words with slow deliberation. He fisted the free hand and pumped the air. "Ms. Brixton, thank you. I really owe you."

"Oh, never mind. I could never repay your family. Besides, I'm sure my staff will love meeting movie stars. I will, too. When do we start?"

He sucked in a sharp breath. "Tomorrow afternoon."

She whistled. "Not a moment to waste? Please send me the details. I do have two non-negotiable conditions. I don't want my staff working past seven, and the servers can't work weekends. We are booked solid."

*Better than nothing.* "Yes, ma'am. Thank you. I'll email the specifics."

"Please do. I'll see you tomorrow. Goodbye."

"Bye." He tapped the screen, ending the call. With a few swipes, he pulled up his inbox and forwarded the scanned contract to Kay. Dropping his phone to the table, he leaned back and studied the ceiling. He had seventy-five percent of a solution but would face the next problem, no weekend servers, in three days. Somehow, he'd find the answer.

"Scott?"

With a jolt, Scott straightened. He blinked and cleared his vision.

A tall, slim man approached.

Scott tipped his head to the side. The guy looked to be about Scott's age and was vaguely familiar but not remarkable.

The man stuck out his hand. "I'm Andy. The stage manager at Holidays, Inc. Sorry to invite myself to your table. I was discussing the kitchen staff with Dani. She mentioned you were helping out with the film?"

"Yes, I am." Scott waved toward the opposite bench. "Please sit. Shouldn't the kitchen manager help?"

"Normally, yes." Andy scooted to the center of the booth. "She's taking a vacation and won't be back for a week or so."

Exhaling a heavy sigh, Scott rolled his shoulders. "Thank goodness for small miracles," he muttered.

"Sorry?"

Scott lifted his gaze. Andy frowned with almost comedic exaggeration. Scrubbing a hand over his chin, Scott loosened his jaw and considered. If he was working alongside the crew for a few weeks, wasn't honesty within reason his best policy? "I helped at the Thanksgiving show. I didn't have a favorable impression. My breathing disturbed her."

"She can be formidable on show days. Understandable under the circumstances." Andy raised a hand mid-chest. "High pressure." He lifted the hand over his head. "Even higher stakes."

*If you say so*. Andy looked utterly unconcerned by Nora's fiery demeanor. Scott nodded and smiled. Contradiction would earn him nothing, and he needed every asset he could collect.

"Thank you for helping. This isn't your job, or what you came to do here. We appreciate it. I have a full list of Nora's contacts including our serving staff. If you want, I'm happy to pitch in and make phone calls."

*Oh, thank goodness*. Exhaling a heavy sigh, Scott dropped his shoulders. "I should be the one offering gratitude. You have no idea how grateful I am."

"Don't you dare. Pulling up each other is just what we do here."

*For everyone?* Scott held his breath. If his aunt and uncle shared the news about the doctor's retirement recommendation, would they have support? Or were they too fundamental to the town? If they couldn't help, could anyone? He wanted to unload the secret but instead found himself drawn more tightly to the core. Add in his newly acquired fake relationship, and he appreciated the simplicity of honesty. As soon as possible, he wanted a return to the truth.

# Chapter Seven

Leaning against the cloth, director-style chair in front of City Hall, Kara watched the replay on the monitor setup. Under a moonlit sky, she shivered. The air stung her exposed skin. Without smearing her makeup or mussing her hairpiece, she bundled into the long puffy coat as much as she dared. Wasting valuable time in touch-ups before the next scene was the sort of trouble she avoided. Similarly, while watching playback, she refrained from emitting any noise.

She wasn't a fool. Lydia saved her a seat in consideration for Kara's financial role on the project. Barring any major errors, Kara vowed to keep her mouth shut and her opinions to herself. She wanted a reputation as an easy-to-work-for producer slash star. With the first day nearly complete, she fared better on set than in real life.

Yesterday, after the awkward departure at Holidays, Inc., she'd taken several steps backward with Dani and Paul. Physically, she hadn't gone far. While reviewing the list next door with Rob, she was reunited with her pea coat courtesy of Andy. She offered the stage manager profuse thanks, slipping on the garment and rubbing a finger against the sequin star secured to the silky lining with a safety pin. With a chuckle, she blew off her error as dizziness and not the truth. She'd escaped. She wasn't searching for sympathy but a chance to prove she changed.

The first day of production had started with morning coffee at Holidays, Inc. overseen by Scott, Rob, and Andy. She didn't have a spare moment for chatting. Poised for action, she thrummed with nerves.

In front of the cast and crew, she opened her mouth, and her mind blanked. Her welcome speech disappeared en route to her tongue. Standing before a crowd, she understood the stakes like never before. She invested everything into the project and encouraged others to follow. She accepted responsibility for providing employment for a crew and couldn't disappoint them.

*This pressure is what Dani felt, too.* She turned her head and met her friend's gaze in the wings of the stage.

Dani flashed a thumbs-up.

With a nod, Kara faced the group. She cleared her throat and spoke. After introductions with the Holidays, Inc. team, the cast and crew departed for the blocked-off portion of Main Street in front of City Hall, the library, and the war memorial. The day was a series of block, rehearse, film, and repeat. They'd knocked off three daytime scenes between Kara and the actors playing Paul and Jill, renamed Josh and Jennifer.

Rob and Andy had used props to dress the area for Valentine's Day for the night's final shots.

After the first few takes, the crew prepared to shoot the same scene from Josh's perspective. Tweaks of body language from one character's perception to the other added hints of the internal thoughts to the visual picture.

Kara reviewed the script in her lap, tempering her

excitement. The cast and crew stuck to the timetable within minutes. If the rest of the shoot continued at the same pace, the production would wrap on schedule. The film started and ended in one calendar year, emphasizing the winter months with key conflict to best utilize the shooting location in December. During the daytime shoot, Kara as Charlotte was at odds with Josh while filing for her business license. Tonight's scene showed the pair reluctantly agreeing to a truce and accidentally sharing dinner on Valentine's Day, eating takeout on the steps by the war memorial.

As the script's conflict eased from lethal to playful, the actors dialed up the flirtation. In the next scene, Charlotte and Josh nearly kissed. Kara glanced over her shoulder, hoping to spot Dani and not Paul.

"Do you think you could lean in more?" Lydia asked.

Kara straightened and swiveled toward the director, her stomach clenching. Had she been caught wool-gathering?

Lydia pointed toward the screen, flashing with a still of the leads sitting close on the steps.

With her focus on her work, she hadn't noticed Kara's distraction. She slowly exhaled and nodded. "Of course."

"We're ready." Lydia donned her headphones.

Kara hopped from the seat and reluctantly unzipped the puffy overcoat. Underneath, she wore a white dress coat over a red, V-neck, silk shirt and skirt. For the most flattering proportions, the outerwear was unlined. She draped the heavy, duvet-like overcoat on the chair and strode toward the steps.

Patrick, the male lead, waited on the top step.

Kara took her seat at his side and grabbed the empty takeout container and spork. Angling her knees toward her co-star, she scooted into position. "Ready to wrap up?"

"More than you can know." Patrick sighed. "I have a video call in an hour. My little girl's dance recital is tonight."

*I'm sorry you're missing it.* Kara stared at the props in her lap. She didn't want to be an apologist. He took the job knowing the requirements. But she had a heart. "How will you celebrate Christmas?"

"My wife and daughter are flying in. They're excited about snow." He chuckled. "The reality might be a little different."

Lifting her gaze, she grinned.

The three-person hair and makeup team approached, retouching the pair's on-camera looks.

Dutifully, Kara widened her gaze and parted her lips as Cassandra reapplied cosmetics and Leo combed her hair. She was glad for the break from conversation. For several years, she wanted to partner with Patrick. He had a good professional reputation and a cult following in the holiday, feel-good, made-for-TV love story market. The specific niche exploded in recent years, attracting an avid viewership. In hopes of building her brand in the field, she needed a dynamic rapport. If she wasn't careful, she'd act her desperation.

"Ready?" Lydia called over a megaphone.

The artists stepped away.

Kara silently counted to ten and filled her lungs with a deep breath, assuming the character like slipping on a hat. She nodded.

"Action," Lydia called.

Glancing at the takeout container, Kara twirled her spork in an imaginary dinner and lifted the corner of her mouth. "Thanks for dinner."

"The least I could do." Josh shrugged and poked the spork into his prop container.

From under her lashes, she glanced up and leaned toward him. "No, you could've pretended not to see me."

He jerked back. "Leave a beautiful woman to her own devices?"

She dropped her jaw, her pulse pounding at the base of her throat. "You think I'm…beautiful?" she murmured in her lowest tones, avoiding the edge of huskiness sometimes shading her vocal range.

He reached forward and brushed a strand of hair over her shoulder. "When you're not badgering me? I guess you're all right." He gently clipped her on the chin.

Pursing her lips, she flared her nostrils. "And here I thought you'd gotten sappy because it's Valentine's Day."

"I'd almost forgotten." He lifted a shoulder, his blue eyes sparkling. "Charlotte, promise you won't read anything into an accidental date?"

"I won't." She straightened and tightened her jaw, turning her knees in the opposite direction while scooting her bottom closer toward him. "If you won't."

"Cut," Lydia called. "Great work. Tomorrow, we're at the theater. Call time is ten am."

"See you tomorrow," Kara said to Patrick. Rising off the icy step, she strode toward her heavy coat and abandoned chair.

Dani was in her seat, using the garment as a

blanket.

Kara gaped. *She came?* Biting the inside of her cheek, Kara refrained from grinning. Clearing her throat, she plastered on a smile. “Dani. Hi, doll.”

Dani hopped to her feet and held out the puffy outerwear. “You were great. I forgot how natural you are on camera. You make acting look easy.”

“Thanks.” Kara grabbed the coat. With a sigh, she slid her arms into the sleeves, crossing both over her chest. “You know I return the compliment. Seeing you onstage during the Thanksgiving show gave me goose-bumps.” *You had it all.* She pressed together her lips. Each woman was entitled to guide her own life. Some days, she couldn’t fight the worry her friend figured out something important that still eluded Kara. “I appreciate you coming to watch and support the crew. What brings you by? Do you need something?”

“I read the script and wanted to see it in action.”

Kara fussed with the zipper. “Oh?” With her chin on her chest, she muffled the exclamation. Dropping off the script was her idea, and Dani rejected it. As time passed, Kara reasoned maybe not being in the know was for the best. If Dani was unhappy about any lines or details, she’d be frustrated. Rewrites were too costly in both time and money. How did she get a copy?

“Lydia insisted.” Dani picked lint from her shoulder. “She wanted to see if I had any requests for the shoot at the theater tomorrow.”

*Do you?* Kara tugged up the zipper halfway, focusing on her fingers and not her friend. “What did you think?”

“Surprisingly…”

Cringing, Kara lifted her gaze.

"I like it," Dani murmured.

"Really?" Kara scrunched her nose and closed an eye.

"You improved the original scenario. I like your version much better than the truth."

*Me, too.* Kara shrugged. Inside she cheered. She had no desire for the fight over Paul to be dramatized for the world. The moment wasn't good for either woman's reputation. Still, she'd been nervous to have her friend see the changes. Kara wanted the story to have a broader appeal. The heart, Dani's big dream inspiring a whole town, remained the same. With her friend's official seal of approval, Kara relaxed. Perhaps the movie could heal the rift. She had another idea to prove herself to Dani, too. But it involved trusting other people and wasn't necessarily shaping up quite as easily. She needed every ounce of New Hope Christmas magic. "I'm glad you approve. The movie will be forever associated with Holidays, Inc. I want to be your ally and not your nemesis."

Dani shook her head. "I don't want to be enemies. But I need more time before I can trust."

"I know," Kara murmured.

Dani turned away.

"Thanks for stopping by. I'll see you tomorrow?"

"Yep. Can I have Rob and Andy break down the props now?"

Kara nodded, scrunching her nose. Turning, she headed toward the small trailer parked nearby. She made progress, but she still had much more to go to prove herself. If only controlling all the variables was as easy as rewriting history.

****

Standing in front of the microbrewery, across the street from City Hall, Scott blew on his hands. Fingerless gloves were the best option for serving coffee, tea, and cocoa in zero-degree wind chill. Instead of a reasonable solution, however, he was forced into not quite getting what he needed. He should have brought his lined, leather gloves and removed them when required. He stomped his feet, recirculating blood in his frozen legs, and drew in a deep breath. In L.A., he didn't miss the cold but did long for the pitch-black sky dotted with bright stars. He dropped his gaze from the heavens to the action.

From his position, behind a table, he spotted Kara and her on-screen love interest on the steps above the war memorial. As an onlooker, he found the process boring. A flurry of activity proceeded a few minutes of filming. Then came another round of waiting. The director called announcements, and the cast and crew scurried. If he was an actor, he'd lose his mind with the repetition.

"How are you? Can I get you anything else?" Andy approached with hands tucked in his jacket and collar raised.

"I'm almost out of everything. The hot chocolate went first." He held an empty container, waving it in the air.

"One more take, I heard."

Scott nodded and set the jug on the table. "Thanks for helping me set up tonight and staffing food service for the weekend."

"I'm glad it worked out." Andy shrugged and pointed to one of the giant coffee carafes on the table. "Mind if I have a cup?"

"Please, help yourself." Scott grabbed a paper to-go cup and handed it to the man. A warm beverage was the least thanks he could offer.

True to her word, Kay Brixton had arrived at Holidays, Inc. with a full staff.

The team's entrance was like watching the cavalry ride in to save the battle. With help, he set up a light buffet for breakfast and returned to the kitchen, preparing lunch and dinner.

After dinner, Kay and the catering crew departed.

The Holidays, Inc. staff agreed to start on the weekend.

Scott was left on his own for the final snack service of the day. He could have asked for help from his aunt and uncle. With frustration bubbling, he hadn't trusted himself to address the pair.

Yesterday, Aunt Shirley's doctor again advised retirement.

If Scott hadn't driven her to the appointment and spoken to the physician himself, he wouldn't have learned the news. The car ride home was silent. He hoped she processed the gravity of an expert's judgment. Almost as soon as she opened her mouth, however, she dashed his hopes.

While she shared the doctor's opinion with Uncle Ted, she explained the words were a suggestion and not a directive.

In a contest of which of the pair was more irksome, Scott wasn't sure the winner. Was he frustrated with the woman who always got her way or mad at the man who never questioned her? Scott couldn't force either to acknowledge the truth. Pretending she was fine wasn't helping her.

The community would rally and help them. But they ignored the truth.

He'd have a fight moving the pair to California. In the past ten years, he lost both parents and wouldn't give up his only remaining family. As he sat alone and frustrated in the guest room, he fought the urge to call Kara. She was the only person who knew the reason for his visit. He liked confiding in her. But she was too busy for a moment to chat. He dove into work and pushed aside his family concerns. His first day had proved channeling his energy into the job was easy with constant demands.

"Do you want to get closer and watch the filming?" Andy asked. "You can't see anything from here."

Scott frowned. Had he been craning for a glimpse of her? He raised a hand to the back of his aching neck. He wasn't sure he wanted images of Kara and her co-star recorded in his brain for posterity.

"I don't mind holding down the fort here."

"I've got to start washing up." Scott reached for the insulated jugs and crossed to the rolling cart, loading both onto the bottom rack.

Andy rounded the table from the other side. "Go. It's only a couple minutes. I'll tear down the table."

Straightening, Scott dusted his hands on his jeans. "You sure?"

Andy nodded.

"Thanks. I'll be back in a second."

"Take your time." Andy grabbed one of the large carafes and carried it to the top row of the rolling cart.

Scott stuffed his icy hands into his pockets and tucked his chin into the collar of his coat. Main Street curved around the war memorial, creating a cul-de-sac for the library and City Hall. With the road blocked off on either side of the turn, he didn't have to watch for traffic. Instead, he focused on cables and cords taped to the ground. Tripping and falling wasn't very incognito. He wanted to observe from the back. A few yards away, he spotted her sitting near the director.

Unzipping her coat, she shimmied out of the heavy garment. Her body shook from the chill. Lifting her chin, she pulled back her shoulders and walked up the steps.

He reached a hand forward and paused, hanging the limb in mid-air. He was too far away for a warming hug. Embracing her in front of a crowd? His instinct was probably wrong. Dragging back his arm, he stuffed the hand into his pocket and clenched the fingers into a fist. At the first row of additional lighting, near a group of assistants, he stopped. He had a clear view of the top step.

Makeup and hair artists hustled over to the pair.

"Ready?" The director's voice echoed over the speakers.

The touch-up team backed away. The camera crew moved in, focusing over her co-star's shoulder on her reactions.

Kara faced her co-star.

Scott saw her profile.

"Action," the director called.

Kara leaned close to the man, her knees almost touching his. "Thanks for dinner." A microphone carried her voice through the still night.

The sultry, deep voice wasn't the one he recognized. He frowned.

"The least I could do." The co-star stared with

unwavering intensity and inched toward her.

Scott pressed together his lips. The scene was oddly intimate. He was intruding on something and felt awkward. *In the alley, did I look at her with adoration?* He rolled his neck.

"No, you could've pretended not to see me."

Her voice almost shook. She sounded hesitant like when she asked for his number at the rental car lot.

"Leave a beautiful woman to her own devices?" The co-star nudged her with a shoulder.

*Impossible. I'd always see you.* Scott gulped. Good thing he wasn't writing the scene, or he'd share too much.

"You think I'm…beautiful?" Her voice cracked, and she widened her gaze.

The icy air burned Scott's lungs. Standing still, he fought the urge to approach and reassure her. She was so achingly vulnerable. But she wasn't alone with him. She acted opposite another man.

The co-star reached forward and grazed her shoulder. "When you're not badgering me? I guess you're all right."

"And here I thought you'd gotten sappy because it's Valentine's Day." She arched a brow.

Her tone edged between sarcasm and hurt.

"I'd almost forgotten." He lifted one shoulder in a shrug, and his blue eyes glimmered. "Charlotte, promise you won't read anything into an accidental date?"

She twisted, simultaneously moving away her face and her lower body toward her co-star. "I won't, if you won't."

With an unobstructed view, Scott studied her. In

the moment, she exaggerated annoyance with her pursed lips. Executing every gesture with care and emphasis, she wasn't herself. At the start of her speech, she was so fragile. He reacted like she spoke to him alone.

"Cut," the director called. "Great work. Tomorrow, we're at the theater. Call time is ten am."

Exhaling, Scott dropped his chin and rubbed a hand over the back of his neck, smoothing down the raised hairs. Perhaps he needed to avoid her performances. He knew she was an actress. Growing up, he'd watched her show. After spending time with her, however, seeing her performance shocked him.

She became a different person, but hints of the woman from the plane, her tone and her expressions, shone through the act. Had she acted with him, too? How could someone fake candor with such conviction?

He shook his head. When he first spotted her on the top step so close to the co-star, he'd been struck deep in the chest with a pang. Was it jealousy? *I'm not really dating her, so I have no reason to be upset.*

A hint of familiar perfume danced past his nose. He lifted his gaze.

Steps away, she stared at the ground as she descended.

He wanted to call out for her attention. What would he say?

She strode to a chair.

Spinning on his heels, he retraced his steps to the table. He had plenty of work left and another long day ahead. Another time, when he had rehearsed, he could greet her.

## Chapter Eight

By Monday afternoon, Kara was simultaneously hitting a groove and more overwhelmed than ever. Assuming a dual role as star and financer raised her stress to new heights. Her jaw ached from forcing a smile around the clock. If she kept up her current obligations on other films, she'd schedule recovery time after capping her teeth between projects. She was ready to move behind the camera. With any luck, the production would earn rave reviews, proving the company's qualifications and securing the future.

Sitting behind the monitors in the auditorium at Holidays, Inc., Kara studied the playback of the day's shoot. Paul had yet to finish his musical. The movie team took advantage of the empty theater to film interior shots. With only a little over two weeks until Christmas Eve, she aimed to wrap as many scenes as possible before the influx of tourists into town and rehearsals took over use of Holidays, Inc.

"You look like you ate a lemon," Patrick said.

Frowning, Kara swiveled in the cloth seat.

Patrick stared at the screen.

She hadn't been in the shot. The lens focused on him at the piano as "Jennifer," played by soap opera mainstay Ali, approached for a heart-to-heart conversation. Kara unclenched her jaw, massaging the pressure point under her ear.

"Mine is only a fleeting expression," Ali said. On the other side of Patrick, she shrugged and tossed her hair over her shoulder. "Could be worse. I could be stuck with a face like yours."

At her side, her co-stars chuckled. Patrick and Ali elbowed each other, continuing the pattern of the day. The pair bickered like siblings, bantering off camera much the same as on.

Kara sighed. Platonic chemistry was just as important—and difficult to quantify—as a romantic spark. Casting landed the perfect twins. Her heavy breath wasn't solely due to exhaustion from her responsibility. She hated being left out.

With the hotel devoted to housing the film's cast and crew, the group formed a summer-camp-style bond during shared meals and carpool trips. Instead of joining in the fun, however, Kara was the camp director, forced apart by age and duty. She should have stayed on location with the others. In planning the schedule, she opted for personal space, eliminating any worry completely her cues and tics were misinterpreted.

But she missed the networking opportunity. She hadn't thought she would. On location for other projects, she kept to herself as much as possible. In her new role, she monitored her cast's and crew's happiness and frustration. She figured she'd really need time off the clock. Instead of seeking escape, however, she wanted to linger and dive deeper into conversations. What had she missed over the years with her narrowed-gaze focus? In her past, she blocked distractions with her guard raised. With the highest stakes of her career, she couldn't get side-tracked and sentimental.

"Well," Lydia said from the other side of Ali.

Kara snapped to attention, straightening.

"I'm pleased. Let's wrap here. We'll pick up tomorrow." Lydia stood and removed the headphones from her ears.

"Wait." Kara's voice was a too-sharp bark. Three heads swiveled her direction. Smoothing her hairpiece behind her ear, she ignored the pounding pulse point in her throat and counted to ten. Taking time was a power move and a chance to control her response. "Shouldn't we stay on top of the schedule?" She glanced at the timestamp in the corner of the monitor. "It's only four o'clock. We could keep going."

"We're already ahead on filming," Lydia said. "Besides, the hotel is hosting a karaoke competition tonight. Teams have been practicing all week." She stared at Patrick and Ali. Turning in the seat, she tipped her chin. "You should come."

*Pity invite?* Kara held the director's gaze and kept her expression blank. The significant look the director shot the *twins* before addressing her could not be mistaken. Kara was an afterthought. When forming teams, she wasn't included. She refused to embarrass herself by sitting on the sidelines and cheering for the others at a group activity. "Thanks for the invitation, but I should double check permits and supplies for next week's shooting schedule."

"Production is wrapped for the day. Tomorrow, be here at eight am sharp." Lydia turned and strolled to the exit.

Her personal assistant followed.

The announcement was met with whoops and hollers. Crew began disassembling lights and booms, pulling up cables.

Kara hopped off the chair and ambled toward the exit.

Dani and Jill hung near the doors, viewing the scene.

Kara rubbed together her hands and approached the pair.

“Everything okay?” Dani wrinkled her brow.

Her friend’s mouth downturned in a perfect frown. Relaxing her jaw, Kara stopped grinding her molars. Had Dani heard? If she thought Kara was on the outs with her co-stars, what happened to the ceasefire? Kara lifted a shoulder and grinned, forcing a beaming smile. “Great, doll. We’re making good progress.” She studied Jill. “What did you think of today’s scenes?”

Jill fidgeted with her glasses and smoothed her hair. “The experience is surreal. I never imagined I’d watch someone pretending to be me.”

*I wouldn’t know.* Instead of admitting the truth, Kara nodded. Would she ever be enough of a star to warrant a movie about her life? She wasn’t sure a dramatic re-telling would be flattering. Meeting Jill’s gaze, Kara winked. “No one can compare to the original.”

Jill turned bright red.

“Wrapping up already?” Dani tipped her head to the side.

Kara lifted one shoulder a quarter of an inch. “Not a bad spot to end.”

“Convenient for me.” Dani grinned. “Double date tonight.” She nudged Jill.

*Did everyone have plans?* Kara tightened her face into a smile.

Jill coughed and turned toward Dani.

Staring at the back of the mayor's head, Kara didn't miss the nods exchanged in silence. *Dani and I used to talk without words, too*. Kara twitched her nose, clearing her tight throat.

"You and Scott are welcome to join us." Dani clasped her hands in front and smiled.

Her voice pitched with a too-bright tone. Kara cringed. Her second sympathy olive branch in less than ten minutes. Under the strain of being forgotten, her ego buckled. She wouldn't exacerbate the situation by accepting. *But maybe I should call Scott*. He was her supposed love interest. They hadn't spent more than a few moments in each other's company since shooting started. "I already have plans. See you both in the morning."

With a wave, she breezed past and through the doors, heading toward the hair and makeup trailer parked outside the main entrance. She pushed the front door and stopped, her eyes adjusting to the light. Night fell quicker every day, and four o'clock in the afternoon might as well have been midnight. She filled her lungs with cold air, a hint of pine hanging in the night. Spinning on her heel, she scanned her surroundings and spotted the newly hung boughs, framing the Holidays, Inc. entrance.

"Hey. Can I get an autograph?"

Kara grinned, her first real smile of the day. Slowly, she lowered her chin and glanced over her shoulder, spotting Scott. "Depends." She turned.

With hands tucked into his jeans and a scarf wrapped around his neck, Scott ambled forward.

He moved with a deliberate slowness, like he had all the time in the world. *If only*.

Stopping a few feet away, he shrugged. "What's the price?" He arched an eyebrow.

"Dinner and a movie?"

Turning, he scanned the façade of Holidays, Inc. "Dinner I can manage. Movie might be hard. The only theater in town is out of business."

"My place?" Her voice cracked. She cleared her dry throat. Until she asked, she didn't realize how much she wanted time off the clock and out of the limelight. Being with Scott was lovely. She liked the person she was when around him. Spending more moments only complicated the future without him. Neither she nor he suggested a no-strings-attached association. But the terms of their agreement hadn't been spelled out. "I mean. No pressure. You don't have to come over last minute."

"You'll send me the address?"

Meeting his gaze, she nodded.

Wind howled, blowing past with force. She stumbled a few steps backward and hit an iron bench with the back of her legs. "Ouch."

He rushed forward. "Are you okay?" Stopping nearby, he extended both hands.

If she leaned close, would he embrace her? She raised her chin, breathing fast.

"What's this?" He bent toward the ground.

She sighed and pulled back her shoulders. He was a fake boyfriend. She had no need to twist the practical situation into anything else. Stepping to the side, she leaned against the back of the bench. In her costume dress, without a coat, she felt the chill of the iron slats on her legs through the skirt. The cold couldn't pierce through the warmth radiating off him.

Straightening, he dropped his head and looked at something in his hand.

Without standing on tiptoe and leaning close, she couldn't see the item in his palms. If she got any nearer, she might do something crazy. For her mental equilibrium, she needed distance. She patted the coat near her ribs for the talisman but couldn't feel it. A flash of sparkle caught in the corner of her eye, and she stood motionless, her pounding heartbeat drowning all other sound.

He lifted the three-inch patch to the light.

"Mine." Her voice cracked.

Widening his gaze, he stared.

She flipped up a palm and wiggled her fingers. "Please. I need the star."

"Of course." He dropped the star into her open hand.

The sequins remained intact and undamaged. After nearly two decades, the patch was delicate. She slowed her breathing to normal.

"Why do you carry it?"

Smoothing the sequins in the same direction, she flattened the star in her palm and tipped her head to the side. "I don't know. A talisman? A relic?" She stood still. With any movement, she'd dislodge the tangled web of emotions, buried deep inside. She met his gaze.

He softened his expression, crinkling the corner of his mahogany eyes.

*He listens.* When was the last time she'd been heard? She cleared her throat. "It's part of my past and a warning to my future. Marilyn, my TV mom, was everything I wanted to be as an actress. Dani didn't care for celebrity. I did. I soaked up every moment with a bona fide star. Marilyn won several Tony awards before heading to Hollywood. She was on the EGOT track. She knew everything and everyone. When she left the show, she gave me the star."

"How does a little sequin thing protect you from evil?"

"It's a reminder. Keep up my head and smile no matter what." With a shudder, Kara curled her fingers over the star, tightening her grip. "She couldn't follow her advice. Within a couple years, she wasn't getting hired and disappeared from the scene. She passed a few years ago, and none of the media outlets reported her death. She was forgotten."

"You won't be." He ran a hand through his hair. "I watched filming last night."

His tone was stilted. She tilted her head to the side and assumed a placid expression. "Oh?" She managed the question with nonchalance. Her heart pounded.

"I wasn't... When I saw..." He shrugged and sighed, meeting her gaze. "A couple times, I saw the you I've gotten to know sneaking through. I guess, I'm wondering if you act around me."

Shaking her head, she sagged her shoulders. Hadn't he seen the difference? Around him, she was brighter and lighter. She moved without choreography and spoke from the heart. With more time, would he see the difference? "I've never been less of an actor around you."

He smiled. "The movie is sure to be a hit.

She dropped her free hand to the back of the cold bench. If she wasn't careful, she'd share too much. Having a friend was nice. "You're sweet for saying that, and I hope so. My career is a constant struggle to stay relevant and vulnerable while toughening against outside attacks. My greatest strength is not showing emotions or voicing opinions." *Except with you.*

"If I heard lies about myself, I'd react. I can't imagine how you deal."

Could he try? If she pursued a real relationship, she subjected him to press and paparazzi. Would she be worth the trouble?

"Okay. Well…"

"I'll text you the cottage's address?"

He grinned. "See you soon."

His smile warmed her from the inside out. Before her cheeks achieved full flush, she climbed the steps to the costume and cosmetics department trailer. For the first time in a long time, she was nervous and excited. And her inner turmoil had nothing to do with work.

****

With Uncle Ted's grilling apron tied around his waist, Scott stood behind the kitchen stove at his aunt and uncle's home. He ladled the final cup of marinara from the sauce pan, covering the lasagna in the white baking dish. He should have asked Kara if she had preferences for dinner. After agreeing to the date suggestion, he hadn't asked questions for fear of losing the invite.

Erring on the side of caution, he omitted meat and loaded the layers with veggies. Once settled in town, he hadn't expected to feel drawn to her. After a few friendly exchanges, he imagined she'd fade into the background. He came to visit family and celebrate the holidays. Meeting her was a random opportunity. While he appreciated having a confidante, he had other purposes in town. She was busy, too. The tug toward being together—in any capacity—deepened every day.

She was kind and funny. Tonight's date wasn't real, and yet he cared about serving a delicious meal. He wanted her praise and smiles. Maybe he was ridiculous for exerting himself and imagining glimpses of the woman behind the role. But each moment spent with her felt more honest than his typical day-to-day in L.A. He wanted to know her better.

Grabbing the last cup of shredded cheese, he topped the noodles with mozzarella and parmesan.

"Something smells good," Aunt Shirley said.

He glanced over his shoulder and smiled.

Entering through the arched doorway, she shuffled into the room.

Narrowing his gaze at the wall clock near the entryway, he frowned. "You're home early. Everything okay?" Dusting his hands on the apron, he leaned against the counter. The sharp edge dug into his lower back.

"I was tired and wanted to rest for a little bit." She patted her hair and popped a hip. "Looks like I came home in time to see you messing with my kitchen."

"I'll clean."

"Hmm, 'n so?" She folded her arms over her chest and squinted.

In a second, he was a little kid. He shifted his weight foot to foot. "Really. I'm finishing up." He cleared his throat. "But you should sit." He crossed to the peninsula and grabbed one of the high-backed stools. He carried the seat to her and rested a hand on her shoulder.

With a sigh, she sat.

Only a few inches away, he studied the dark,

undereye circles visible through the thick layer of peach-colored cosmetics. He'd never known Aunt Shirley to come home during dinner service. Every morning, she left for the diner with Uncle Ted at four forty-five and returned home at eight. The long hours were brutal on someone half her age, but she never complained.

Hovering behind her, he couldn't stop from analyzing her slumped posture. She looked frail. He'd never associated the word with his force-of-nature aunt, but he couldn't think of another description to encapsulate her dampened spirit. He strode to the refrigerator and grabbed a bottled water, returning with the beverage.

She accepted the drink and sipped. "Thanks. Don't look all worried. Didn't you want me to take it easy? I'm following your directions."

He nodded, pressing together his lips into a flat line. If he overtly displayed his level of concern, he missed a moment to discuss something of vital importance. She'd shut down. "Aunt Shirley, do you have a plan?"

She scrunched her nose and drew back her chin. "A plan?"

"Somewhere to go, in case…" His throat closed. Dragging in a deep breath, he gripped his biceps. Inside his chest, his heart skipped a beat. "Maybe we need to think about the next step."

"Do you mean like one of those TV places?"

"Huh?" He widened his gaze.

Adjusting on the stool, she leaned forward on the peninsula counter. "You know the sorts advertised during daytime soap operas. Commercials showing communities of lonely, old people."

"When are you watching soap operas?"

"We leave the TV on behind the counter for patrons." She drained the rest of the water. "I'm not moving into a senior living facility."

"Of course not." He crossed to the pantry and grabbed the aluminum foil. He needed action. With busy hands, he pushed aside his swirling thoughts. Ripping off a large rectangle, he returned to his lasagna and covered the noodles. With his back to Aunt Shirley, he opened the pre-heated oven and slipped inside the baking dish. He set the timer and considered his next move. "If you lived close, I wouldn't worry."

"Honey." She released a long sigh. "Uncle Ted and I are fine. Don't get yourself worked up. We have help and support. We're not alone here…"

*Like I am?* Turning toward his aunt, he met her gaze. Did he want his family to uproot their lives for their sakes or his? He missed them. Until coming for the visit, he hadn't considered his loneliness. He rubbed a hand against his aching ribs. His simple mission twisted into a complicated problem. A few hours away would do him good and clear his head. He needed a break, too.

"What time is supper ready?"

"I'm cooking for a…date."

Her eyebrows stretched into her hairline. "Really?"

"Just dinner and a movie." Straightening, he narrowed his gaze and scanned her wrinkled face. "Do you need me here? Would you like me to reschedule? If you don't feel good, I can stay."

"Please, go." She held up a hand and stood. "I'll help. Let me whip up my famous garlic bread. You can start the dishes."

With a chuckle, he stepped forward and pulled his aunt into his arms. Her head barely cleared his shoulder. He breathed in her smell of hairspray and kitchen grease, twitching his nose. Nothing was more important than family. He didn't need a health scare to remind him, but he had to finalize his plan. The emotionally-charged visit heightened every worry and concern to anxiety-inducing levels. He'd take a night and formulate a better approach.

## Chapter Nine

Yawning, Scott buried his face into the plush pillow. Velour rubbed his cheek, catching on the slight abrasion. On the guest bed at his aunt and uncle's, he slept on smooth, flannel sheets that invited snuggles. He snapped open his gaze and stared at an unfamiliar ceiling. Pushing off the couch cushion, he scanned his surroundings.

He'd fallen asleep on a sectional. Every muscle in his upper back cramped from forcing his body into an awkward contortion. He spotted her. Curled in the corner, she formed a ball. Massaging the back of his neck, he replayed the night. He had brought lasagna, salad, and garlic bread for dinner. After insisting she couldn't eat the carbs, she caved and ate generous portions of the entire meal.

At the coffee table, he dished up the plates.

She played a black-and-white movie on the TV.

He never watched old films. His cinematic tastes tilted toward thrillers. Settling on the couch, he found himself entertained by the vintage story. While the plot veered toward silly, the entire production was good-humored. The movie didn't take itself too seriously like Kara.

With more time together, he appreciated the difficult path she navigated. Besides his aunt and uncle, he observed locals treat her with wary deference.

Instead of erecting a snobbish demeanor to shield herself, however, she persisted with politeness. He admired her patience. What did she think of him?

He helped clean up the meal, including a quick scrub of her kitchen. When he wiped the fridge, he brushed off her protests at his unnecessary thoroughness. He didn't want to leave. The evening was his first break in a while. While her film added considerably to his workload, he couldn't lay blame squarely at her tiny feet. He underestimated the emotional toil of his holiday plan.

She queued another movie and snuggled under a blanket.

With permission, he joined her. The cadence of East Coast accents from the forties combined with a stomach full of pasta lulled him into a profound state of relaxation. He had fallen into a deep sleep.

Careful not to disturb her, he rose. The snug, one-bedroom, one-bathroom cottage was maybe a thousand square feet total. The front door opened directly into the living room. To the left, he faced an eat-in kitchen. To the right, he spotted a small hall leading to the bathroom and bedroom. He couldn't peer through the shut curtains in the living room without disturbing her. He'd sneak out and get home before the morning.

Strolling toward the kitchen, he stopped. Faint streaks of light poured through the blinds on the backdoor and under the curtain of the window above the sink. In the awkward position, he couldn't have slept more than a few hours. At the sink, he pulled back the curtain and gasped.

Snow covered the screen like sand drifting on the wind across the desert.

Shielding his gaze with a hand, he squinted. At least two feet of fresh powder accumulated overnight. Snow continued to fall. Twisting his neck, he glanced at the oven clock. The display flashed seven forty-five. He turned toward the couch.

With a massive yawn, she stretched her arms overhead and rolled off the couch. She landed with a thud on the ground. "Oof."

In a couple long strides, he reached her and knelt at her side.

She rubbed a hand over her eyes and squinted. "What time is it?"

"Morning. Are you okay?"

"What?" Scrambling to her knees, she pushed to standing. "How early in the morning?"

"Seven forty-five."

Dropping her jaw, she widened her gaze. "Oh no, no, no. I have to be on set in fifteen minutes."

He shrugged. "Actually, I don't thi—"

With her shoulders back, she strode to the bathroom and shut the door. Running water echoed through the cottage.

He returned to the kitchen, opening the blinds on the back door. Outside, everything looked white. He couldn't distinguish the ground from the overcast sky. The wind increased, creating fast-moving drifts of dancing sparkles. The last blizzard he experienced was during childhood. He remembered a day spent indoors wearing pajamas and building pillow forts.

Patting down his jeans, he found his phone in his back pocket. He typed a quick text to his aunt and uncle. Last night, he told them where he was headed but expected to wake under their roof. A man in his thirties didn't need to worry about curfew, but he didn't want his family sending out a search party either.

His phone beeped, and he tapped the screen, pulling up a text from Aunt Shirley.

*—Stay there until the plow reaches you. Might be a day.—*

*—Got it—*

Leaving the phone on the counter, he surveyed the space. With his day on hold, he might as well be useful. The coffee pot occupied the corner of the countertop nearest the window. He filled the reservoir with water and spotted the filters in an upper cabinet. Searching through the fridge and freezer, he found an unopened tin of ground coffee. He set up the coffee and hit Start. The machine whirred and percolated. He smiled. This was a coffee maker he could manage.

Curving his lips, he whistled and bustled about the space. Sliding drawers and opening doors, he acquainted himself with the food supply. He grabbed what he needed and started whipping up chocolate chip pancake batter in a glass bowl. On a snow day, he embraced the sudden halt of normal activity. He could think of no better way to unwind than enjoy a sweet treat. Butter sizzled in a pan. He dropped the batter, forming three silver-dollar sized pancakes.

"What are you doing? We don't have time." She reappeared, wearing a sweater and leggings. Around her head, she wrapped a towel.

"Time is all we have." He grabbed a spatula out of a drawer and flipped the pancakes.

"What do you mean?" She widened her gaze and her stance.

She could fight him but not Mother Nature. He

shrugged and studied the pan. "Check your phone. I'm pretty sure we're snowed in."

"Did someone call and tell you? Did you get an emergency alert?"

With a hand, he waved to the back door. "One glance out the window told me everything I needed to know." Grabbing a plate, he deposited the first batch of pancakes. He poured batter into the pan and started the next round.

"Yes, hi. I'm just checking in. How's it going over the… Oh?"

Her voice pitched high, almost a squeak. He pressed together his lips. While he wouldn't mind a day off, he wasn't the one with a huge, financial stake. His goal wouldn't be impacted by a twenty-four-hour delay.

"Well, sure. No, no. Of course, I get it."

She sounded far away.

The coffee maker beeped.

With the spatula, he flipped the pancakes and glanced over his shoulder.

Standing near the table in the opposite corner, she angled her body toward the wall.

From the corner of his gaze, he spotted her sink into the chair like she was made of molasses. A burnt smell tickled his nose. He pulled the pancakes off the pan and inspected the hint of dark brown edging the discs. The chocolate should cover the well-done taste, but he wouldn't risk offending her. He grabbed another plate and dished those for himself. Moving the pan to the back, he turned off the burner and angled the handle toward the center of the stove.

"Yes, please keep me posted."

Carrying two plates, he slid both onto the table.

Backtracking, he filled a mug with coffee and found utensils. “Everything okay?” He handed over a fork and knife, setting the mug next to her breakfast.

“You’re right. We’re stuck for the day.” She stuck her fork into the stack of pancakes and reached for the mug, blowing across the steaming surface.

He retraced his steps and poured himself a cup of coffee. Leaning his back against the counter, he sipped. “I promise not to take your tone as a comment on my abilities as a fake boyfriend.”

“What?” She raised her chin and frowned, setting her mug on the table. “Sorry. I didn’t mean it like that.” With the knife, she sliced through the pancakes, speared a bite, and stuffed it in her mouth then moaned.

“Much better.” He grinned. Grabbing another set of utensils, he crossed to the table and sat opposite. “I am sorry. I’m sure a delay isn’t ideal. When’s the last time you had a day off?”

She reached for her mug and sipped again. “I don’t know. My birth?”

“Really?”

Stuffing another bite in her mouth, she widened her gaze and chewed. She covered her mouth with a hand. “I’m not a workaholic.”

He drew together his brows. How did she add two and two and reach seventeen?

Swallowing her bite, she dropped her hand. “I’m a planner working in a freelance world. I probably shouldn’t be in such a volatile work environment. I like security.” She shrugged. “Show business is what I know and love.”

“How is behind the scenes going?”

“Not great.” She stuffed the last bite of pancake in

her mouth.

He pointed at her empty plate. “More?”

She nodded, gazing at the table.

Standing, he crossed the room and turned on a burner. He poured perfect rounds in the pan. “I love snow days. For one day, the whole world rests. When I was a kid, I’d stay in pjs. My mom always let me sleep in and whipped up chocolate chip pancakes.” With the spatula, he lifted the edge of a bubbling pancake and flipped. “The smell woke me up. I miss my parents.”

“How long have they been gone?”

Clenching his jaw, he ground his molars. He hadn’t intended to share so much, seeking only a conversational shift. As often happened in her company, he dropped his guard. In L.A., he didn’t have any close friends. He didn’t speak freely or open up with his employers or his acquaintances.

With her, he was himself. Discussing his beloved parents, he prepared for the dull ache that usually accompanied missing them. Instead, he relaxed, pressure releasing like steam escaping a vented lid. “Several years ago. My aunt and uncle are my only remaining family.”

“Did you often visit New Hope? Any special childhood memories?”

“I spent a few summers here during high school. Those days are a lifetime ago.” He flipped the pancakes. “Mostly, my aunt and uncle visited us. They loved Milwaukee.” Lifting the pan off the stove, he crossed toward her and tipped the pancakes onto her plate. “I have a confession. I don’t think I’d be cut out for living here full-time.”

She lifted her chin. “I’m not a small-town fan

either. It's charming in small doses. I like the excitement of the city, and I prefer being anonymous." She popped another bite in her mouth.

He crossed to the sink and dropped the pan in. "I don't think I've ever been the subject of gossip. I'm not interesting. After today, my status might change." Glancing over his shoulder, he spotted her pink cheeks. He wasn't a fool. His presence would be remarkable to the tight-knit community and solidified the supposed relationship. Still, he felt bad she'd have to deal with the aftermath. "Is it easier to have gossip articles printed about you? Or for the locals here to comment?"

"Good question." With her knife and fork, she cut the remaining piece of pancake in half. "I assume facing people who think they know a secret is difficult. In L.A., I brush off rumors and remember the reporters don't really know me. But occasionally a headline hits close to the truth. Then it hurts. In a small town, you have people who know you, but kind-hearted folks jump to their own conclusions and judgments." She speared the last two pieces onto her fork.

He returned to his seat. "Like they'll say about us today?"

She shrugged. "I don't mind."

"Do you have any chores planned? Any wintertime activities you want to check off the list of Midwestern experiences?"

Chewing, she lifted a hand and held up a finger. "Eat? Watch movies?" She tipped her head to the side. "Can we do anything else?"

*Good point*. He leaned back and studied the room. The cottage was neat and clean. With demands on set, she spent limited time in the four walls. The property had no hint of her or the holidays. “We could decorate. Make the cottage a little more festive. You leave on Christmas Day?”

“If I stick to the plan…” She sighed. “I’ll be home in time for a festive swim in my pool.”

As the snow piled up outside, he couldn’t imagine outdoor swimming. Of course, she probably had a difficult time appreciating the accumulating snow. “Will your parents miss you?”

“Probably, but they aren’t home either. We haven’t really celebrated both days since my childhood. If I suggested spending the holiday under their roof, I can almost hear their gasps.”

“You’re not sentimental?” He stuffed the last bite of pancake in his mouth.

“I don’t know why I’m being so honest.” She shook her head. “You’re the first person I’ve ever met who doesn’t find the real me boring. I never really understood what people meant about being themselves. On a whim, my mom signed me up as a baby model. She started fielding offers before I could walk. If I’m not acting, I don’t know who I am.”

He swallowed the last bite. Chocolate chips melted on his tongue. “I do.”

She gulped. “You do?”

“The Kara I’ve met is kind and caring.”

“I don’t think many people would agree.”

“Their loss.”

She stood, her chair scraping the linoleum tile. Grabbing both plates, she crossed to the sink and turned on the water. “You want to see if the cottage has any holiday movies or decorations in hiding?”

He nodded and finished his coffee. In a second, she

brushed off his words. He wouldn't rescind the sentiment. Lately, he hadn't enjoyed much normalcy. How strange to have found the sensation with a celebrity.

****

Kara stood in the center of the tiny attic. She could only remain upright within a three-foot wide by eight-foot-long space marked with plywood over the insulation. When she climbed the pull-down steps outside the bedroom, she bent almost in half until slowly reaching this spot. Considering she was barely five foot two inches, the storage space wasn't practical for any long-term residents at the cottage. Her chances of success in the search for Christmas decorations dwindled.

"Any luck?" Scott shouted.

She tilted her phone, flashlight activated, toward the dark corners. She spotted something. *Please don't be a mouse*. "Maybe," she called. "Hold on." On tiptoe, she crossed the thin board and shined the light above what was the bedroom at the front of the house. With each step forward, she tightened her body, shrinking from imagined spiders and probable rodents. At the end of the plank, she sighed, staring down at a four-inch, fake pine tree branch. "False alarm. I'm coming back."

Strolling slowly along the center of the board, like a balance beam, she didn't see anything moving. She hoped. The little cottage on the edge of town was her first experience alone. In her Malibu beach house, she had a constant influx of visitors and an armed surveillance system. If she hadn't invited Scott for dinner and an accidental sleepover, she would be stranded.

He peered through the opening in the attic floor. "Nothing? I'm surprised."

Stopping a few feet away, she nibbled her lip. Finding anything would have shocked her. Was he an optimist? She hated to kill his bright-side approach. But she had trouble seeing any unexpected situation as inherently good. On set, she grew up quickly and lost her blind acceptance and trust before she could spell. She cleared her throat. "May I come down now?" She folded her arms over her torso, rubbing her shoulders.

With a nod, he descended.

She sat on the floor and shimmied to the edge, gripping the phone in one hand. Lowering her legs inch by inch, she swung one foot and then the other to the risers. She shut her eyes tight and dropped her weight to her feet on the thin treads. She descended, shaking the pull-down steps.

She wasn't the do-your-own-stunts kind of actress. Although, to her way of thinking, she should have been entitled to a body double for locking lips with a handful of her former co-stars. She shuddered. At the last step, she hopped to the floor and tucked her phone into her waist band. Dusting both hands on her leggings, she folded the stairs along the first hinge. The steps snapped shut along the next hinge, dangling in mid-air. With a yelp, she jumped.

Moving between her and the spring-hinged ladder, Scott blocked her with his body. He grabbed the edges of the plywood backing and pushed the stairs flush with the ceiling. "Are you okay?" He glanced over his shoulder.

Her chest rose and fell with shallow breaths. She stepped back. Without hesitation, he leaped into action, like he anticipated the need. Did he?

"We could make decorations."

She met his gaze.

He leaned against the door leading to the bedroom.

*Like he belongs here.* She crossed her arms. What would she do without him? The question unnerved her. She was always fully in control, but she couldn't command the weather to her whims.

After breakfast, he had retrieved a shovel from the trunk of his car and cleared the paths leading to the front and back doors. He continued to dig around the perimeter of the cabin, explaining the dangers of snow drifts causing carbon monoxide build-up from blocked vents, and showed her the important spots to check outside. She had listened carefully and ordered a shovel to be delivered in a few days.

"From what? Do you have construction paper in your hatchback?" She arched a brow. "If the attic was a bust, I can't imagine we'll find a trove of arts and crafts in a cabinet."

Lifting one shoulder, he smiled. "Popcorn?"

She rolled her eyes. "Always food related."

"Occupational hazard. Don't tell me you don't have popcorn."

"Of course, I do." She curled her upper lip. "Occupational hazard. I'd rather make a bowl and watch another movie then stab myself with a needle threading a garland."

He stroked his chin. "You make a strong case. I agree on one condition."

*Like a kiss?* If she could, she would have kicked herself. Why were her thoughts constantly straying? She'd never felt a hint of attraction around a fake love interest. With Paul, she forced herself to relax instead of recoil at his never-ending scowls. With other men, she flashed a smile for the nearby cameras but essentially forgot her date's presence. Scott was completely different and dangerously distracting. She gulped.

"With cocoa?"

"You're on." In her back pocket, her phone vibrated. "Hold on." She pulled the cell and frowned at the screen. Why was Dani calling now? The time flashed one o'clock. Was another problem on the horizon?

"Everything okay?" Scott asked.

Lifting her gaze, she smiled. "I'm sure it is. But I better answer."

He nodded and stepped away from the door. "I'll get started on the snacks."

Her stomach grumbled loudly. Heat burned her cheeks.

With a chuckle, he strolled to the kitchen.

She slipped into her bedroom and closed the door, pressing her back against the solid panel. They almost shared a moment. She wanted to drift toward him and see what could happen.

Recognizing a lot of her same traits, she'd never experienced a real, non-judgmental connection with another human. Her career set her up in competition to someone but not Scott. He understood her drive and compelled an honest vulnerability she'd never tapped into. She almost closed the distance between them and then her treacherous body ruined it. Under her breath, she groaned and crossed to the bed.

Sinking into the covers, she sat cross-legged and

swiped a thumb on the phone screen. The timing wasn't favorable for pursuing a relationship. She focused on her last-ditch effort to rebuild her career. A real romance promised distraction and threatened her next step.

At the moment, fake dating was all she could handle. She pulled up her missed calls and tapped Redial. Holding the phone to an ear, she slowed her breathing to normal.

"Kara?" Dani asked. "Hi. Sorry I'm so late checking in. We had a bit of a situation at the theater."

"What happened?" She scrunched her nose. Maybe no news wasn't always good news.

"Nothing too serious, and no one is injured. The snow's weight on the roof caused a partial collapse over the staff hallway."

"Oh no." *Would filming be impacted?* Kara hated to ask. "I'm glad everyone is okay."

"Yeah, I am, too. I didn't know until Jill called. I can't get out of my driveway. Our street is one giant snow bank." Dani sighed. "Luckily, Jill lives in town and saw something strange. She went over and investigated. Rob has a snowmobile and met her there."

Pinching the bridge of her nose, Kara fought against the pressure building in her forehead. "Did Jill say how bad the damage is?"

"Nothing on the main stage. They climbed onto the flat roof, shoveled the snow, and threw a tarp over the hole. Your production won't be impacted."

Dani's voice was strained and tired. Kara's moment of relief was tempered by her friend's circumstances. She shifted on the bed, tucking the blanket around her legs. "Can I do anything?"

"For the time being, I'm praying the snow stops," Dani said. "Any good vibes you want to send up to the universe are much appreciated. I'm not sure I can do much more than hope."

Could Kara offer better? Could she rework the schedule and alleviate crowding of the theater? She bit the inside of her cheek.

"I'm sorry I took all day to call. How are you? Do you need anything? Is Scott there?"

With one hand, Kara covered her burning earlobe. If Dani assumed he spent the night, mission accomplished. The whole purpose was to convince her Kara moved on to someone new. But she didn't want people thinking poorly of him for his association. "Yes, he's here. We fell asleep watching old movies."

"Sounds lovely. I'm glad you're not stranded alone."

*I'd be lost without him.* "Me, too. He's been a big help."

"I'm sure."

Kara frowned. Was Dani's singsong tone innuendo or exhaustion? "I don't know what I would have done."

"Probably gotten stuck in a snow bank on the side of the road heading to town." Dani chuckled." I like him. He's nice."

"He is." At the universal truth, Kara smiled.

"How's your impromptu, romantic rendezvous going?"

*Not like that.* Kara bit the inside of her cheek. As the conversation continued, she risked compounding the lie. She hated duping Dani. After the messy love triangles with both Dani's ex and current boyfriends, Kara forged ahead for the sake of the uneasy reconciliation. Ceasefire was probably the better term.

"Okay, keep it to yourself. I'm happy. You have a reason to visit in the future."

Had Dani warmed to the idea of welcoming Kara into her life? She tilted her head, straining for the rest of the sentence. "What's the incentive?"

"Scott."

"He lives in L.A."

"If you get serious, you'll spend the holidays here with family."

Dani's bright tone hinted at wistful nostalgia. At one point, Dani and Kara were family. Did she have a chance again? Could she hope for a Christmas miracle? First, she needed to focus on work. "Will you need to close the theater?"

"Not officially. Until the roads are plowed, every business is shut down." Dani sighed. "It'll probably be another day before I reach the insurance agent and find a crew to fix the roof. I don't have to totally close the building. The stage is fine. If we didn't have to worry about noise, we could finish repairs so much faster."

Pinching the bridge of her nose, Kara breathed through the pain building in her forehead. She wanted to restore their friendship, but did she have to drain her bank account in the process? *Everyone has a price.* She nodded. "If I extended the filming schedule…"

"Could you?"

Dani's voice cracked. Was Kara such an unfeeling, task master her friend sounded desperately relieved? If she couldn't film, she could at least shoot some promotional stills in costume. "I'll do my best to rework the schedule and discuss the potential changes with the crew. No promises."

"I understand. I appreciate you even considering adjusting the production to accommodate me."

"I'll see you soon. Tomorrow, hopefully."

"If you need anything, please call. I think you're in good hands though."

Kara was grateful Dani couldn't see her bright red cheeks. "Bye, Dani." She ended the call and dropped the phone onto the bed.

Extending her trip hadn't been in the plans but would give her more time with Scott. The relationship started as an opportune cover. Under the facade, she discovered real feelings. With time, she wasn't sure what might develop. *At what cost?*

She didn't want to rush the days they spent together, but could she relax as her bank account drained? How much of a delay could the remaining budget handle? Could she hit pause, focus on work, and plan a reunion in L.A.? Would he care about her once her life resumed its normal, hectic pace?

****

Crossing to the kitchen, Scott opened the lower corner cabinet, grabbing a small saucepan. He pulled the chocolate bar and milk out of the fridge and started his task. In his opinion, hot cocoa packets couldn't compare with the real, from-scratch deal. He'd convert her. *Not that she probably drinks the stuff and has a baseline for comparison.*

Normal life was an unwelcome intrusion into the happy, cozy day off. She was totally out of his league, and he needed no reminders. For the time being, she existed on his turf, and he'd take the lead. What was a snow day without excess sugar consumption? If a little extra work impressed her, he wouldn't object to the resulting praise. He grabbed a spoon and stirred the contents of the saucepan, slowly heating through.

In his back pocket, his cell phone chirped. With one hand, he removed the device and smiled at the screen. *Finally*. After breakfast, he tried calling the house number but got a busy signal. Either Aunt Shirley was on the line, or Uncle Ted left a receiver off the hook.

Instead of calling back, he sent a text but should have known better. His aunt and uncle barely used their cells. Swiping the screen, he pressed the phone to his ear and kept stirring. "Hello?"

"Hi, Scott. Are you still at Kara's?" Aunt Shirley asked.

"I'm still here and not likely to leave anytime soon. The snow is several feet deep. How about you and Uncle Ted? Everything okay in town?" Kara's rental cottage sat on a dead-end road on the very outskirts of town. His family lived in a neighborhood of single-family homes with generous yards. The buildings insulated each other somewhat better than Kara's cottage. Within a mile to town, his aunt and uncle could walk to Main Street if necessary. *Oh, no.* A lump lodged in his throat. "You didn't go to the diner, did you?"

"We didn't even try. Everything is quiet here. No one has driven down our road."

"Did Uncle Ted shovel?" Until Scott asked, he forgot about the physical tasks at home, too. With his concerns about stress from overworking focused on the diner, he neglected the chores of living in a stand-alone home on a quarter acre of land. Yard work was a lot of maintenance, and winter multiplied the physical demands. *They can't stay here*.

"Our neighbor's high school son, Robert, came over and cleared the driveway. He's a sweet boy." Aunt Shirley sighed. "Don't worry. We are holed up inside. How's it going?"

"Good. Nice." He sighed and rolled his neck. "I'm glad I was here."

"Us, too. She seems a little lost."

*Yeah, she does.* He swirled the melting chocolate until it completely dissolved in the warm milk. Was he disloyal if he agreed with the frank assessment? He frowned and pulled the saucepan off the stove. What were the terms of being a fake boyfriend? *Especially if I'd like a chance at something real?* "Glad to hear you're okay. I'll come home after the roads are plowed."

"Probably won't be until tomorrow at the earliest. Might be a couple days."

"I know. Call if you need me."

Aunt Shirley snorted. "You're not much help stuck on the outskirts of town. We'll call Rob. He has the snowmobile."

A retort tangled on the tip of his tongue. He pressed together his lips and focused on his task. Grabbing two mugs off the dish rack, he set a spoon in each.

"Oh, wait. Do you hear that?" Aunt Shirley asked.

A distant *beep-beep-beep* echoed over the line.

"Maybe we'll be cleared soon. You might still have a few hours of captivity. I don't know how many trucks the mayor employed. Have fun with the movie star. You're living one of her films."

"I am?" With a shoulder, he held the phone to his

ear. Carefully, he tipped the chocolate from the saucepan into each cup, aiming the stream for the spoon's bowl to minimize splash.

"Well…you should be. I don't suppose you'd have to share a b—"

He frowned. Aunt Shirley wasn't one to cut herself off from sharing an opinion. "A what?"

"Never mind," she mumbled. "Thinking about my favorite romance novels."

*Romance?* He set the saucepan in the sink and turned on the faucet, filling it with water. He couldn't contradict his aunt without giving away the deception. While she hadn't made any overtures about matchmaking—like he initially feared—she was known for meddling. If she knew he was single, she might involve herself in pushing him toward someone else. He didn't want to waste a second that could be spent with Kara. "I'll see you soon. Take care of yourselves. I love you."

"Love you, too. Bye." Aunt Shirley ended the call.

He set the phone on the counter and opened the corner cabinet, spotting a box of microwave popcorn. Not everything could—or should—be gourmet. He opened the pack, ripped open the plastic covering, and set the package in the microwave, tapping the popcorn button.

The turntable rotated, and a dim light powered on inside. After thirty seconds, kernels popped, beginning slowly and reaching a fervent crescendo just before the microwave beeped.

"Smells like heaven," she called.

He stepped back, peeking around the fridge.

She stood in the living room near the doorway

leading to the bathroom, holding a pillow and sheets.

"I made a snack." His voice cracked. "You need help?"

"You don't trust my bedmaking skills?" She wiggled both eyebrows.

Crossing his arms, he stroked his chin and studied her. "Well…."

She scrunched her nose. "Rude." She strode toward the couch.

He chuckled and retraced his steps. Grabbing the warm mugs, he strolled toward her.

She dropped her bundle in the center of the couch and sat to one side of the fluffy pile.

Extending a mug, he set his on the coffee table and retreated to the kitchen. He needed to grab the popcorn while it was still hot. If he stood around, analyzing the warmth of her smile, he'd serve a subpar snack. He grabbed the bowl. Returning to the living room, he left the popcorn on the coffee table and sat on the floor, resting his side against the sofa and draping an arm over the cushion.

With her eyes shut, she sat cross-legged, sipped the cocoa, and moaned. "This is so good."

He grinned. "Better than the mix?"

She shrugged. "I wouldn't know."

His throat squeezed, cutting off his airway. What else was he right about? Did she sense the real connection between them, too?

"It's official." She took a long sip and met his gaze. "You can't stay here any longer than necessary, or my costumes will have to be altered."

He reached for his cocoa and sipped, savoring the bittersweet bite of the semisweet chocolate. A few extra pounds were a miniscule price for taking pleasure in his food. But he couldn't make her choices. Building a career out of creatively working around dietary restrictions, he could find an alternative for her requirements. If he pursued her, he could adapt his favorite recipes for dinner dates. Could she be flexible about including him in her life? "Is everything okay?"

Leaning forward, she returned the half-empty mug to the table and rested her forearms on her thighs. "What do you mean?"

"Your phone call?"

She frowned.

Maybe he shouldn't be asking something personal. "I'm just wondering… If your friends are…" He cleared his throat. "I called my family."

"Oh, goodness." She pressed a hand to her cheek, widening her gaze. "How are they?"

"They're fine. They live close to town and have plenty of neighbors. They want me to stay put until the roads are plowed. Are you okay if I stick around a little longer?"

"Of course." She tilted her head. "Thus the sheets. My call went fine. I might extend my stay in town, too."

*Will we get more time together?* "How long?"

"Holidays, Inc. experienced a partial roof-collapse. No one is hurt. Thankfully." She shuddered. "Dani says it won't impact filming, but I can't ignore her plight. Combined with the delay, I might be here until New Year's Eve."

Warmth spread through him faster than the first sip of cocoa. He wanted as many opportunities to be with her as he could get. "Just like me. Guess you'll get to ring in the New Year with a fake kiss."

"You should be so lucky."

He threw back his head and laughed. The deep belly rumble shook loose something inside him. If he ever had an ounce of good fortune, he'd utilize every drop at present. "Movie time?"

"I thought we could wa—"

*Beep-Beep-Beep.* A blaring horn cut into the cozy conversation. Orange lights flashed in the thin crack of the curtains at the window near the door. He scrambled to his feet and crossed to the window.

She reached the spot first and pulled aside the floral pattern drapes.

A snowplow barreled down the road toward the dead end, clearing several feet. At the cul de sac, the truck lumbered into a slow turn and pushed the accumulation on the other side. After the truck passed, the sun came into view, hovering low on the horizon.

"Sounds like our rescue." She sighed. "Guess the mini vacation is over. Thanks for being here."

Was she kicking him out of her home? He froze. Today, he enjoyed himself. Stranded with her, he hadn't experienced a moment of awkwardness. Instead, he was more aware of how well their personalities meshed. "I'm surprised at the prompt response. I wouldn't have thought the town had any plows big enough for the accumulation."

"Really?" She tipped her head to the side. "I'm not. The mayor has worked hard on the town's civic rejuvenation. Improved utilities and public works were the handiwork of the Jill Howell I've gotten to know."

He nodded, bobbing his head like a car dashboard toy. Perhaps the snowplow arrived at the right time to save him from an epic mistake. He could have ruined everything by overstaying his welcome and asking her on a real date. His coat hung in the closet near the door. His escape was moments away. He turned and extended a hand. "Good night. Guess I'll see you tomorrow?"

She shook his hand and stepped back. "I'll be there."

The corner of her mouth twitched like she had more to say. On wooden legs, he hobbled toward the closet, grabbed his coat, and stuffed himself into it. She could stop him. But she didn't.

He crossed toward the door and twisted the knob. With a final glance over his shoulder, he smiled and waved. Then he stepped outside into a snowy, silent wonderland and trudged to his car. He vowed not to think about what he almost said and accepted the day for what it was, a fun anecdote he could share at dinner parties. His audience might not believe him. Regardless, he'd cherish the recollection. How could he want more?

## Chapter Ten

Standing in the carpeted hallway at Holidays, Inc. the next day, Kara rolled the sticky lint brush over her dark green, velvet pants. With filming cancelled for the day, as work proceeded on the roof, she assembled the main cast for promotional stills in the auditorium. Until called to the set, she could do little more than fight a losing battle with the shedding white angora sweater grazing her hips.

She liked the costume. It looked beautiful and aspirational, wearing a light color over tight, unforgiving leggings highlighting every bump and bulge. But the outfit wasn't practical for the real work of running a dinner theater and couldn't last the test of even pretending to do so. If she sat, she'd wrinkle the smooth pants and shed more light-colored fuzz onto her thighs.

After a few weeks of living in town, she understood how out of place she'd always been. Her clothes only made identifying the out-of-towner easier. *Look at the sequin-gowned onlooker*! Replaying her initial visit, she shuddered. Until her relocation, she hadn't appreciated the tone she set during her first few trips to New Hope. She made no attempt to blend with the community. Standing out wasn't—in itself—a bad thing. But she used her clothes as a barrier, separating herself both physically and emotionally from people she'd like to get to know better.

Like Scott.

When she spotted the snowplow yesterday afternoon, she panicked. Her initial disbelief morphed into devastation. She expected another snowbound night. He was planning the dinner menu. She found the perfect, follow-up, classic film for the second movie night.

As she tracked the orange lights flashing against the living room walls, she felt her hopes fracture in the strobe-like effect. Turning, she studied him. His flat expression hinted at nothing. Her heart nearly snapped, and she made a decision. She couldn't let him know how desperately she wanted him to stay.

The accidental sleepover was nice. Spending time together was lovely. Waking up on the couch, eating breakfast, searching for decorations, and shoveling the front walk hinted at domesticity. She relaxed, not once lowering her voice or leaning too close. She'd dropped every act.

Had she been herself? Without costuming, she was discovering herself. She liked her personality around him. If he left, he took the best part of her. She wanted him to stay.

Her offer for another film viewing wouldn't be an invitation for more than what they had already shared during the day. When she heard the snowplow, the illusion shattered, she decided against the question. They both had early morning starts and couldn't afford distraction. He didn't need another bad night's sleep on her couch. So she gave him the chance to leave.

She couldn't blame him for taking the opportunity.

A door crashed against the wall. An icy breeze

filled the hall.

Kara jumped.

In a tartan-plaid shirt and puffy vest, Dani strode inside through the side door.

A group of four men dressed in worn jeans and heavy-duty coats carried tool boxes and wiped their feet outside the door before entering. The last man shut the door.

"Thanks, Tim." Dani smiled at the man and waved an arm down the hall, indicating the blue tarp-taped ceiling to the floor near the office. "We removed the snow and ran fans all night to dry the carpet. Please focus on operational over aesthetics. I don't know what insurance will cover, but I don't have much choice. I can't have a draft freezing the movie crew or my staff."

Tim nodded. "We'll get to work. If I have any questions, I'll find you."

Dani stepped to the side.

Tim and the other three men strode past. At the end of the hall, they parted the blue divider, plastic crinkling.

A second, cold blast of air swept through the hall.

"Brr." Kara shivered, her teeth chattering.

Dani swiveled and widened her gaze.

*I wasn't supposed to intrude*. Kara held her friend's gaze steady and rolled the lint brush down her thighs in exaggerated measure. "Sorry, doll. Don't mind me. I'm staying close but out of the way."

With a hand, Dani batted the air and ambled forward. "No worries. I didn't see you."

*That's a first.* Kara scrunched her tickling nose, fighting a snort.

"Everything okay?" Dani stopped a few feet away.

Kara shrugged. "Just waiting until I'm needed. You know how it is."

"I saw Jill for breakfast and mentioned the filming delay. She is already submitting new permits on your behalf."

Pressing her tongue against the roof of her mouth, Kara gripped the lint brush with both hands. As always, the mayor proved herself kind and indispensable. She was a good friend. What chance did Kara have if stacked against Jill? Did Dani have room for two best friends?

Loud footsteps echoed overhead.

Lifting her gaze to the ceiling, Kara studied the drop tiles.

"Rob is shoveling the roof," Dani said. "He's checking for any other weak spots for reinforcement."

"Oh, of course, probably a good idea." Kara smiled and returned to her lint rolling.

"How is the cottage?" Dani rubbed together her palms. "Did you stock up at the store? Do you need anything? Sorry I couldn't help."

Kara waved the roller in the air. "I'm fine. I ordered a few shovels to store in the minivan. Just in case."

Dani chuckled. "Bet you never thought you'd say that sentence."

Kara tipped the corner of her mouth, relaxing in the contagious good humor. Joking without agonizing over her words, Kara almost returned to the old pattern of their friendship. All she had to do was take out another line of credit to finance the additional production delay. *Everyone has a price.*

A call to her accountant reassured her she wasn't in

dire straits, yet. But she had to manage the remaining time effectively. When she called Lydia, she got the director's agreement to the additional changes. In the background, she heard the lively scene at the hotel. She wasn't jealous for the crowd but felt a pang of envy at the new connections being forged.

If she redeemed her friendship with Dani, her costs would be worthwhile. *As long as the film is a hit, and I get another production started.* "Can't say I did. I'm not too far off my usual mark here." She held out her arms and spun in a circle.

"Beautiful." Dani nodded and wiped her hands on her jeans, underneath her flannel shirt. "Thanks again for staying longer. I know it's not ideal to rearrange the schedule or add days. But I'm grateful."

Besides her never-ending penance, Kara didn't entirely mind the circumstances. She was glad for a chance to spend more time with Scott. Last night, she hadn't slept well. Blaming work stress would be a lie. She never sugarcoated anything for her fragile ego, preferring clear-cut absolutes.

Tossing and turning tied back into the strained goodbye and words better left unsaid. He couldn't possibly be interested in the woman under the glamour. If she wanted any chance, she had to tap back into the persona that built her career. Could she? The familiar contortions of her facial features felt too studied. She didn't want to lean close and gaze through heavy-lidded eyes anymore. She wanted something different.

But maybe he didn't. If he expected the star, he'd escape the woman. The love trap was almost a Hollywood legend. Clearing her throat, she snapped back to the present. "Of course. Let's hope for smooth sailing from here on out. No more hiccups."

"Well, speaking of..."

Kara kept her face still as possible. A reaction threatened her on-screen makeup. If she opened her eyes too wide, she'd smudge mascara against her upper lid near her eyebrow. If she pressed together her lips too much, she'd lick off her lipstick. She had one option, holding herself frozen.

"Since you are officially staying until New Year's Eve, Paul and I wanted to invite you over for Christmas morning."

*You're inviting me?* Kara held still, unsure of the appropriate response. Fighting the urge to utter her initial response, she swallowed the lump in her throat. "Oh?" She could have kicked herself for the single word. Did she sound annoyed?

Dani nodded. "We don't do anything big. We can't because we're working the night before and twice on Christmas day. In the midst of a busy week, the little break is calm and cozy. We have cinnamon rolls and coffee. We listen to carols and open presents."

Growing up, Kara endured Kensington Christmas parties as work events. Christmas Eve was a fancy, dress-up party catered toward adults. She had been so glad the first year Dani joined her. They snuck into the kitchen. The catering company fed them dessert before dinner and then—after being paraded around as the TV twins—they retreated to Kara's room and watched movies. The scenario Dani mentioned reminded her of the holiday specials on TV. "Sounds nice." Kara smiled. "Thanks for inviting me."

"Bring Scott, too."

*Of course.* Kara nodded. Here was the catch.

Without her fake boyfriend, she threatened her best friend with a solo appearance. She did this to herself, wrangling Paul into an exclusive contract and forcing a romance where none existed. In truth, she never wanted him but capitalized on every opportunity for press coverage she could. If she explained, she risked offending both.

The employee-only entrance to the auditorium opened. A headset-wearing assistant peeked out into the hall.

"Guess they need me." Kara stepped past.

Dani reached out a hand.

With a start, Kara turned toward her friend.

"I really am grateful. I was skeptical about the movie." Dani shook her head. "I don't know why I would ever be so foolish as to doubt you." She grinned. "This production will be a big hit."

"From your lips to destiny's ears, doll," Kara murmured. She pulled back her shoulders and held her head high, scrunching her stinging nose and blinking her watery eyes. She was a professional. Feelings served no purpose.

****

Only a handful of cast and crew members were on set at Holidays, Inc. for the morning photo shoot. Scott could go home soon. Submerging his hands in the soapy water, he grabbed a sponge and scrubbed the baking trays. Earlier in the morning, he called Kay Brixton and updated her on the schedule change.

Holidays, Inc. needed several days to repair the roof. The film crew adapted from indoor primary filming to promotional and outdoor shoots for the rest of the week, accommodating Holidays, Inc. and staying clear of the roofers. He was glad to give the caterer a few days off. With the help of Rob and Andy, Scott served from-scratch maple scones and fresh coffee for the slimmed-down cast and crew.

He wanted to chat with Kara alone. Shaking his head, he tightened his grip on the sponge, applying pressure to a stubborn stain on the rectangular, aluminum sheet. He hadn't figured out what he'd say. Admitting the truth, he had wanted to stay at the cottage for a while longer, was pathetic and might give the wrong impression.

He didn't expect anything more than what they already shared, listening to her movie analysis and abundant compliments about his food. Alone at the cottage, he sensed a shift. She wasn't concerned about prying eyes. Back on set, however, he was more mindful of others than ever.

Exhaling a heavy sigh, he rinsed the sudsy pan, set it on the dish rack, and grabbed the next tray. The repetitive work gave his mind an almost meditative break. But hyper-focusing on one situation didn't help find peace. Instead, he circled the problem, rubbing his nerves raw. When he left last night, had he saved himself an embarrassing moment or missed an opportunity?

Across the long, banquet table this morning, he handed her a scone and pressed his tongue to the roof of his mouth, stilling the questions. Did she need anything? Had the plows covered her driveway in snow? Had the shovel arrived? Dressed in a fluffy white sweater with heavy makeup, she looked unattainable. He preferred the woman who devoured chocolate chip pancakes.

Based on the saturated red color on her mouth, she probably couldn't taste anything without marring her lips. If he had insisted on staying and making dinner, would casual Kara have agreed or would professional Kara have asked him to leave? Both incarnations smelled of rose perfume lingering long after she left. Behind the table, the woman avoided his gaze, giving no clue to her thoughts. He read her avoidance and posture as all-business.

Turning on the faucet, he rinsed the last tray and set it on the dish rack, pulling the stopper from the full sink. The dirty suds swirled, forming a whirlpool until disappearing completely. Everything happened for a reason. The snowplow rescued him before he asked for a real date. If he had said the words yesterday, he wouldn't suffer a burning stomach nonstop for the past sixteen hours. He never lived with regrets. Why start now?

In the end, he arrived at his aunt and uncle's house to find Aunt Shirley on a ladder in the unheated garage, reaching for Christmas ornaments stored on the highest shelf. After helping her down, he took her place and nearly fell from the weight of the enormous, plastic bins. He repeated the action three more times. How did she equate lifting heavy items with following her doctor's orders to *take it easy*?

At least he discovered the plan to get a tree before his aunt wielded an ax. He focused on the next problem. Had he projected transparency when he issued Kara an invitation? Would she come? He had to figure out a way past the awkward handshake good-night and back to normal ground. A fake couple would spend time together engaged in seasonal activities. He appreciated the excuse and could ignore the change in his feelings for a night.

"What is going on?"

A sharp, feminine voice carried over the rushing water. With the back of a hand, Scott shut off the faucet and turned, drying both palms on a nearby cloth.

The kitchen manager barreled through the room, clicking her heels against the tile floor.

He frowned. The sound echoed in a room used to rubber-soled clogs.

She twisted her neck side to side and widened her gaze. Proceeding through the row of stainless-steel workstations, she tutted and shook her head.

Unsure where everything went, he established a system with Andy's help. He cleaned the items he used and stacked them in neat towers of similar things. Later, Andy returned and organized the goods, putting away objects into their places. So far, the system worked. Scott didn't like adding hours to Andy's day but heard no complaints.

Until the boss returned.

Twisting the cloth in his hands, he wrung the fabric in a tight spiral. He wasn't a naughty child and wouldn't quake during a stern lecture. He threw the towel over his shoulder and strolled forward. "Good morning, Nora. Didn't expect you back so soon."

"I cut my trip short." She smoothed hair behind both ears. "Good thing I did. What is going on here? Why is everything out?"

She avoided his gaze, and he frowned. "Well, it's sort of an agr—"

"My idea." Andy jogged through the kitchen, letting the door swing shut behind him. At Nora's shoulder, he stopped and touched her elbow. “Sorry, I was double-checking something for Paul. I didn’t want you upset at the disorganization. I told Scott and the catering team to leave out everything, and I put it away.”

With hands on her hips, she faced Andy.

Did her glower soften at the corners of her mouth? Scott shook his head. Townsfolks’ love lives weren’t his business. The pairing—if real—was interesting. If Andy and Nora had feelings for each other, they argued strongly in favor of opposites attracting. Scott appreciated Nora’s determination. In a demanding and male-centric field, she probably had to assert herself at every moment. At least, the women he’d met in his rise up the ranks had. But Andy wasn’t hard or unflinching. With a kind smile and easy-going spirit, he radiated gratitude. The pair made sense. *More than me and a star.*

“I suppose if it works, it’s fine.” Nora crossed her arms and lifted one shoulder. “But, Andy, you can’t take on everyone else’s job. You have enough of your own to do.”

“I don’t mind.” Andy shrugged and inched closer. “Only another week and a half left.”

“Andy, still,” Nora said.

Scott winced. Her voice pleaded with familiarity. Was he intruding on a personal moment? She didn’t know the new schedule. He couldn’t let Andy take on all the difficult tasks, especially if the man pursued a relationship with the woman. Scott coughed. “Actually. There’s been a delay.”

Nora tilted her head and wrinkled her brow. “What do you mean?”

"Not sure if you've been inside the theater yet, but a minor roof collapse at Holidays, Inc. has pushed everything back."

"How far back?" Nora asked.

"The cast and crew will be filming until New Year's Eve," Scott said.

Nora flared her nostrils.

*Why won't you help?* Scott held himself in check. Instead of immediately defending Kara, he studied Nora's frown and analyzed the scene from another viewpoint. The domino effect of the roof collapse had far-reaching consequences. Kara fell back to help Dani, but no one spoke with Nora about the adjusted schedule. She was collateral damage. If she hadn't stopped in, she wouldn't have known.

As a dinner theater, food service comprised half the business and should be equally important. Was she valued? Or was she expected to flow with last-minute changes and demands on a regular basis? Was she the bad guy because she was never allowed a win?

Running a kitchen wasn't easy, and constantly changing demands contributed to the difficulty. He needed her as an ally and not an enemy. "I understand your frustration. Losing control of a kitchen is hard. I work as a personal chef specifically to cut out the middleman between me and my client. Your situation isn't ideal, but you don't need to add more complications."

She tipped back her chin and stared.

"I'm sure you're still getting the domain under your command, and everything keeps changing," he continued. "But it has to happen. The filming is extended to accommodate Holidays, Inc. Your boss is grateful for the adjustment. You can't fight back. If we reach an agreement, we can find terms we like. Otherwise, your boss will be dragged into finding a resolution."

Narrowing her gaze, she curled her upper lip.

*If looks could kill...* He'd rambled for too long and knew he should stop. But he couldn't quit if his words could help a friend. Holding up both hands, Scott stepped back. "I'm not threatening you. I'm just explaining the situation."

"I can't have my staff constantly cleaning up for the catering crew. Starting the week of Christmas, I'd rather have my team in here."

*Would have been easier if you helped from the start...* Scott swallowed the cheeky remark. The blame game was never helpful. He nodded and forced his lips to lift in a pleasant smile. "Let me discuss the changes with Kara and Ms. Brixton. I'm sure your staff will be fine. Ms. Brixton has a full calendar of holiday parties. She'll probably be glad for the break. She helped me as a personal favor."

"I'll need all the specifics. Andy, come talk and walk with me." She spun on her heel, stalking toward the door.

Andy flashed a thumbs-up and jogged after her.

The door opened and shut, the lock softly clicking into place.

Scott released a pent-up breath from inside his chest. His involvement on the fringe illuminated how much was at stake for everyone involved in the movie, dinner theater, and town. The community was tightly interwoven.

He'd suffocate here. Without question, he had to

extricate his family. If he didn't move them close, who would look out for their best interests? While many neighbors were giving, others took without returning the favor. Slowly, he watched the emotional, physical, and financial resources draining to zero. He couldn't let his aunt and uncle be victims of their own goodwill.

# Chapter Eleven

Friday morning, Kara trudged from the makeup trailer toward Holidays, Inc. for the day's outdoor shoot. Strolling along the pavement, she scanned the block in front of the theater. On either side, snow stacked in giant mounds in front of the Holidays, Inc. kitchen and Rob Carroll's handyman store respectively.

In the median in front of the theater, a pair of street lamps flanked a bench. Instead of slushy ground, bright-green fake grass rolled over top of the mud. Hanging baskets overflowed with artificial red and yellow tulips, flashing like emergency lights against an otherwise white and gray landscape.

Lifting her gaze, she studied the lighting and heaters brought in to aid the actors in pretending warm weather and sunshine days. She pursed her lips. Movie magic was something else. While the set looked fake up close, she knew every prop would photograph perfectly.

The day's shoot focused on her burgeoning relationship with the on-screen love interest. Too bad she couldn't skip ahead to the break-up scene. Two days after the strained goodbye with Scott at the cottage, she still agonized the moment until her stomach twisted. She fisted her hands inside her coat, clutching the pocket warmers she ordered online.

First to the food service area, she couldn't find a second to speak alone with Scott. What was the point of full hair and makeup if she couldn't deliver the star treatment while flirting?

Following the return of the kitchen manager, Scott finally had help and a staff.

She uttered a few, brief hellos and stopped, unsure how to act. She never had trouble performing in front of an audience. When she didn't have a script, however, she found her tongue too thick to speak. She missed him. Surrounded by the crew and plenty of onlookers, she never felt so lonely in her life. Was this the downside of a real connection? She got close only to have the comfort snatched away?

With her gaze unfocused, she strolled ahead. Her tea-length sundress swirled at mid-calf, catching in the light breeze. Under the cotton, she snuck a thin pair of capri leggings. But she couldn't add more layers without creating bulk. The camera crew banned pantyhose for the glare. In truth, she didn't feel so cold today. Could she possibly be getting used to the climate? While she moved forward, she caught one of her three-inch heels in a sidewalk crack and turned.

Her eyes widened. Her jaw slackened. A strong arm grabbed her waist and steadied her against a solid wall of muscle.

"You okay?" Scott asked, breathing heavily.

For a moment, she stayed still. He gripped her middle and held her wrist, tucking her against his side. If she stretched on tiptoe and turned her head, she could kiss him. Would he want a smooch from the woman driving a minivan or the movie star? *Men always want the star*. In this instance, she searched her memory for her old lines with an appropriate meaning. Slowing her breathing, she batted her lashes. "Much better now."

Her voice was low, almost gravelly scraping against her throat. Licking her bottom lip, she leaned in.

He dropped his grip. Stepping back, he reached for her chin and tilted her head side to side.

Narrowing his gaze, he scanned her face. "No, really, I'm serious. Are you okay? Is something in your eyes?"

So much for her usual tricks. Annoyance bubbled up, flaring her nostrils. Before she could correct him, however, she studied him. Up close, she noticed how his rich, dark brown eyes obscured his pupils. If she wasn't careful, she'd lose herself in staring deep enough to see his soul. She smoothed her skirt. "You must be right. Some fuzz or something floated into my eye." She blinked several times, exaggerating the gesture. "Thanks."

"No problem." He stuffed his fists into his jeans pockets, rocking back and forth on his heels.

Did he have something to say? She switched her stance, angling her body and popping her front knee. The pose photographed well. Utilizing the posture in high-stress scenarios, she highlighted her best angles and assumed command. Growing up in show business, she never did anything she didn't want to do. When she flirted, she played her own game and remained in control. *Except around him.*

"Seriously, is something wrong?" He frowned.

*Only you are not responding.* She swallowed the sigh building in her throat. "I'm great. Heading to set. How about you?"

"I'm on my way back to the kitchen." Stepping forward, he extended a hand.

He brushed the back of her hand, her skin prickling

with awareness. Lifting her gaze, she sucked in a breath and internally groaned. He stared with the unwavering intensity and concern of a caregiver. Why was she so affected by him, and he interpreted her actions as feverish? Why did she feel like a brand-new actress flubbing her lines? The more she replayed his abrupt departure, she increased her frustrations. She wanted another dinner but couldn't afford another break in the production schedule.

If she could, she'd hit pause for another day in the little cottage on the outskirts of town. But that choice was impossible. The longer she stood on the sidewalk, the colder and more ridiculous she felt. New Hope didn't have time for stars, especially not her. "I better not keep you." She forced a smile and stepped forward.

"No, wait. Please." He reached out again. "I was hoping to get a chance to see you. I've been a little busy."

Drawing back from his touch, she crossed her arms over her chest, nibbled her lip, and nodded slowly. Had the tables returned to her command? His skin wasn't heightened in color from flush, but his brown eyes flashed. As the silence stretched, she coughed.

"What I wanted to ask was…" He tipped his head to the side. "Are you free tonight?"

At the lopsided grin, she felt her insides slip and slide. She rose on tiptoe, feeling lighter. "I'd love to."

He wrinkled his brow. "You don't even know the plan. Are you really sure? Don't you want me to finish my question?"

A dare? She hadn't been challenged in years. Shrugging, she glanced at the ground. "I'm not one to back down."

He chuckled. "I didn't think you were. Well, if you're game?"

Lifting her chin, she pursed her lips and nodded.

"Christmas tree shopping."

She rolled her eyes. "Oh, for goodness sakes. You think I can't manage picking out a tree down the street?"

"We'd be joining my aunt and uncle."

Was the clarification his easy way out of spending time alone? When she offered him an exit at the cottage, she hadn't realized he'd leap at the chance. If he didn't want her to come, why invite her? *Or maybe he doesn't want me to think he's asking me on a real date.*

He stuffed his fists into his pockets. "I can promise pie and coffee at their house while trimming the tree."

She arched an eyebrow. "You are suggesting a very challenging evening."

Grinning, he stepped forward. "I'll make the effort worth your time."

With a hand, he brushed her shoulder. She swayed toward him and grabbed his hands. She was growing uneasy with all the back and forth. Did he like her? Would they reconnect in Los Angeles? Or was this only supposed to be a brief interlude in a small town so far from her normal life? Why did she have to know the answer? *Because I've got to be in control.*

For one night, she'd give herself a break. He wasn't setting up a seduction. He invited her to a family-friendly, seasonal event. Maybe the activity would even help elevate her holiday spirit in time for the next phase of the production—performing the actual musical. "Sure, I'll come."

He squeezed her hands. “Great. Dress warm and wear good boots, not the flat-soled pair from the plane.”

She scrunched her nose to the side and narrowed her gaze. “Just so happens the shovels weren’t my only online purchase. I’ll be fine.”

“I’m sure you will.” He lifted her hands and dropped a kiss on the back of her knuckles.

The light press of his lips to her bare skin reverberated through her nervous system. What would happen with a real kiss? She eased back her hands, shaking her hair over her shoulder. “I better go.”

“One more thing.”

His low words rumbled through her. She widened her stance and locked her quaking knees. Her palms itched. She needed her little star safely stowed inside the coat in her trailer. At least she could blame her physical reactions on improper costuming for the chilly weather. She tipped her head. “Hmm?”

With fingertips, he caressed her cheek. Stepping forward, he narrowed the distance from feet to inches. He lowered his face. “I’ve been meaning to do something.”

His warm breath tickled her face. She twitched her nose. “What?” Her question was breathless.

Moving closer, he pressed his lips against hers.

She sighed. Her legs went boneless, and she swayed into his hard chest.

He wrapped an arm around her waist, steadying her as he deepened the kiss.

*A gentle promise*. The thought flitted through her mind. He hadn’t grabbed her in a fit of possession or held her firm to satisfy his demands. The strong bicep around her back offered support. If she broke away, she knew to her bones he wouldn't fight her. With him, she could share anything without fear of the consequences or the judgment. *Leave him wanting more*. Breaking the kiss, she tipped back her chin.

Heavy lids covered his gaze, and his breathing was shallow.

Warmth spread through her. She grinned. Maybe she could push aside feelings in the name of professional integrity but find honesty with one person. "See you tonight." Stepping back, she strode past him. She didn't know what he wanted or how to act around him, but she could always deliver an excellent exit. As she executed a superb example, she could have sworn she heard him mutter, "I can't wait." Her knees almost buckled. She had to get herself back to normal as a cool operator. Without self-control, what did she have?

****

With hands cupped over his mouth, Scott blew hot air on his icy fingers and lifted his gaze to the cloudless night sky. At the outermost edge of the downtown tree lot, he had plenty of light for scanning his surroundings. Overhead lights strung across the street in a web of interconnectivity, adding a touch of holiday magic. The full moon shone bright as a flashlight.

Near City Hall, he had a clear view along Main toward the theater. After filming, the crew restored the landscape in front of Holidays, Inc., dumping snow over the mud. The smiling, bustling passersby gave no indication to noticing anything out of place. With less than ten days until Christmas, tourists flocked into town, lured by the small-town celebration and added intrigue of watching a movie production.

Scrubbing his face, he wiped away the deepening

frown and curled his fists inside his pockets. Waiting on a star to arrive could take all night, and he blamed himself. *I didn't tell her a time.* He should have driven to the cottage. The front cab of the pick-up truck wouldn't accommodate another person. He could have gone separately. In the midst of escaping the friend zone, he gave nothing else—like logistics—any attention. She'd probably been kissed a thousand times. Did he warrant a memory?

He sighed and rubbed the back of his neck. Fearing a full interrogation, he hadn't told his family about his guest. *If I left in my own car, I wouldn't have been questioned.* He swallowed the groan scraping his throat like a windshield brush. Riding with his family presented an opportunity for a discussion on retirement, but he hesitated and missed the chance. After his crash-and-burn conversation with Aunt Shirley, he didn't want to ruin another night. He needed this moment to be special so she wouldn't forget him.

"You gonna help look or what?" Aunt Shirley asked from a few feet away near a balsam pine.

For tonight's outing, she stuffed a hat on top of her sprayed helmet hair. He wouldn't have thought it possible for knit to stretch so far without ripping. He knew better than to share his opinion about fashion. But he couldn't hold back his argument any longer. He had to plant the seed about their retirement and hopefully harvest it by New Year's Eve. "Actually, I wanted to talk to you about something."

She tipped her head to the side and rubbed together her hands. "So serious. What's wrong, honey?"

"Nothing with me," he murmured.

"Huh. 'N so?" She folded her arms and arched an

eyebrow. "You want to clarify your statement?"

Pulling back his shoulders, he stood tall. Aunt Shirley held his gaze. His cheek twitched. Instantly, he was a little kid crying because he hurt himself disobeying a direct order. But he couldn't back down. The stakes were too high and too emotional. He hated the uncertainty and worry of living so far away. New Hope was the perfect getaway for a few weeks at most. He'd never establish a permanent residence. He couldn't leave them here.

"Before you get started." She held up a hand. "I can see you puffing out your chest and preparing for one of your speeches. I want to say I'm so happy you're here. Spending this much time with you has been a real gift." She sniffed and rubbed a mittened hand on her nose.

The tiny gesture cracked his determination. He sighed. "I'm glad, too."

"Look how well everything worked out." She wiggled her eyebrows. "Dating Kara Kensington. Who would have thought it?" She chuckled. "Only in New Hope."

"Well, no, not really." He wished the ruse meant something more but had to face facts. In helping her, he'd helped himself. His aunt hadn't suggested any potential mate. "She's from Hollywood. I'm in Los Angeles, too. We could have met a hundred times and not known it."

"But it takes a small town to spark a connection. You'll both have a nostalgic tie. Maybe you'll spend more time here. Together." Aunt Shirley grinned, her smile stretching across her face.

He dropped open his mouth, but no reply bounced

off his tongue.

"Speaking of…" Aunt Shirley straightened. "Good evening, Miss Kensington. What brings you here?"

Whirling around, he faced the newcomer, and his next breath seized in his lungs. Dressed in her puffy coat, she beamed with a cheek-to-cheek grin. Under the string lights and street lamps, her hair glowed like gold, and her blue eyes sparkled. She'd probably heard her eyes compared to every jewel from sapphires to aquamarines. When he stared deep into her eyes, he glimpsed her shine from the inside out. Without the layers of heavy makeup she'd worn earlier in the day, she looked brighter. He didn't have a preference. He liked everything about her in any incarnation she chose.

"Good evening." Kara dipped her head. "I was invited." She turned toward him. "I was told there would be pie?"

Raising a fist to his mouth, he coughed. The playful gleam in her gaze teased him. "As it so happens, I was getting ready to te—"

"Doesn't matter, doesn't matter." Aunt Shirley waved her hands. "Of course I'm serving pie. We always have dessert at the house and especially during the holidays. You are coming to help us decorate?"

Kara arched an eyebrow and held his gaze. "If I'm still invited…"

"Absolutely, you are welcome to our home any time." Aunt Shirley pulled back her shoulders and lifted her chin. "Oh, let me get Ted. He's probably already found a tree." She bustled past, pinching Scott's upper arm as she hurried away.

"Ouch." Scott rubbed the spot on his bicep. He'd have a bruise. "Sorry. I really was getting ready to tell them. You can see how she reacted. With my silence, I avoided a full interrogation on the drive here."

Kara chuckled.

The light sound was as joyful as tinkling jingle bells, promising something good on the way.

"I don't mind. I'm just giving you a hard time." She clasped her hands in front. Nibbling her bottom lip, she stretched on tiptoe and leaned close. "But I did sort of want to ask you something."

*Can I kiss you?* The air heated to boiling. If he kissed her here, would she object or lean into him to maintain the façade of mutual interest? After accosting her in front of the movie crew, he wouldn't again put her on the spot. The next time he kissed her would be without an audience. She would have a choice. He stepped back and studied the ground. "You are wearing good snow boots."

She rocked back to her heels and lifted her right leg behind her, knee bent.

*Just like old movie stars kissing for the camera.* He had to wipe making out from the brain.

"Told you I was doing some online shopping." She dropped the boot back to the ground and pointed her toes in front.

The quilted boots laced to her knee. She could probably wear the pair in the arctic tundra. He frowned at the overkill. She didn't do half-measures, did she? Was she acting interested, or did she feel the same spark? Extending a hand, he held his breath.

She reached forward.

He interlaced her gloved hands in his and squeezed.

Her blue eyes shimmered, and the corner of her

mouth lifted.

If he wasted every moment with second-guessing, he'd regret every lost second. Whether or not the faux relationship materialized into a full-blown romance, he wouldn't deny the peculiar circumstance enhancing his time in New Hope. While he continued to fail at his ultimate goal for the visit, he valued the unexpected distraction. "I've been mean—"

"Good news," Aunt Shirley called.

*Interrupted again.* He'd be lucky to finish a thought let alone a sentence tonight. Dropping an arm to his side, he readjusted his grip on Kara's hand and turned toward his aunt.

Aunt Shirley strode forward, and at her side, Uncle Ted carried a five-foot pine tree bound with twine.

"He found the tree. We can get started decorating." Aunt Shirley grinned.

"Wonderful news," Kara said. "Since you're here, I had a question. Or, more accurately, a favor to ask."

"Shoot," Aunt Shirley said.

Kara darted her gaze from his uncle to his aunt and ending with a smile for him.

She looked so earnest and unsure. Scott was touched she turned to him for encouragement. He didn't know what she'd ask, but he nodded anyway.

"We can't film at Holidays, Inc. for a few days. The theater needs a thorough cleaning before guests arrive for the Christmas shows. Stage rehearsals are on hold."

Aunt Shirley mumbled her acknowledgment.

"I had an idea to shoot some additional scenes on Monday. We might not use anything. I can't make any promises but..." Kara drew in a deep breath. "Could we film at the diner tomorrow? I'd love to have you in the movie. If you're willing?"

Aunt Shirley gasped.

She sucked nearly all the air from the downtown block. Scott breathed deep from what oxygen remained. Should he worry that she stood as still as a statue? With mouth agape, she widened her gaze resembling a fish more than a person.

Uncle Ted rubbed his wife's upper back. "We'd be honored, Miss Kensington."

Scott twisted his neck and stared at his uncle. The man wasn't known for responding, ever, and especially not to strangers. His uncle's stoicism protected his shy nature, and his gravelly voice sounded harsh from disuse.

"Thank you so much. These shots will be marvelous. I'm thrilled to add a real slice of town to the movie." Kara leaned against Scott's arm, clasping her free hand on his bicep.

The light touch was familiar and exciting. He grinned. Kara was lovely. She stirred feelings he'd ignored for the better part of the last decade. As an actor, she instilled a sense of instant connection with complete strangers all the time. He wasn't special, but she was. By giving his two favorite people something to cherish, he found his admiration deepening. Asking for more would be overstepping. Stolen kisses aside, he'd do better to focus on the purpose of his visit and not get swept up in what could never happen.

## Chapter Twelve

Sitting in the last booth at the diner on Monday morning, Kara dragged a finger along the script she was supposed to be reading. She knew the words by heart. After the impromptu idea to film at the diner, she called the screenwriter. For an exorbitant fee, the writer would draft a new scene. Kara hoped the lines and setting added another layer to the plot of the film, including a beloved local institution fans could visit in real life. Instead of paying someone else, she wrote the new dialogue.

If she had to discuss the adaptation—and screen credit—later, she would. But she didn't fret over potential contract snafus now. In the present, she enjoyed the act of creation and eagerly anticipated filming her words. The editor would decide what to include in the movie's final cut.

She'd be happy to hand control to someone she could trust and wasn't so sure she included herself in that category. When Scott invited her to find a Christmas tree, he surprised her and misunderstood her best simpering and flirting as something stuck in her eye. At the tree lot, she thought he wanted another kiss. He leaned forward. She stretched up on tiptoe, and nothing happened.

She couldn't quite figure out how to act around him. He constantly threw her curveballs and left her questioning everything she assumed she knew. She stepped back and had the spontaneous thought to include his family the same way they welcomed her. After picking a tree, Scott had driven her minivan to his family's house. She ignored any thoughts of romance and relaxed, enjoying the evening.

His aunt turned on a TV holiday special and brewed a fresh pot of coffee.

Without comment, his uncle positioned the tree in the stand and methodically wrapped lights around the tree.

In fascination, she studied him as he strung each branch with multi-colored bulbs from trunk to the very tip of each branch. She could only imagine removing the lights would require an advanced degree and exceptional patience.

When he finished, he plugged in the string of lights.

Everyone oohed and aahed. Then came the next step.

Shirley and Scott opened the first plastic bin and started the process of hanging ornaments.

Kara appreciated the pair's time-honored methodology to decorating.

As they unboxed each item, they shared stories, detailing the history of each bauble. From elementary school crafts to vacation purchases, they related a sentimental attachment to nearly every item on the tree.

Nodding and smiling as applicable, she listened to the charming anecdotes but couldn't relate. Truthfully, she was shocked how many memories could be stored in a few plastic bins. Her parents hired decorators to set up the house per each year's theme. She didn't remember any misshapen, lumpy, childhood relics. Instead, her mother picked glass balls based on the year's color scheme and returned the decorations in January.

Her family rented Christmas. She'd always liked the practical solution. In more recent years, her parents often booked a tropical vacation in lieu of the holiday. Instead of devoting storage space for boxes of knick-knacks never displayed, they maximized their attic for the luggage and sporting equipment in constant rotation.

But she wouldn't mind starting a small collection of ornaments and decorating a little tree in her beach house. She could start with something to remind her of New Hope. She'd have to pay more attention to the shops in town and find a suitable souvenir.

Once finished trimming the tree, Shirley served dessert, cutting large slices of pie.

A thick graham cracker crust set off the slightly bitter chocolate and sweet fresh whipped cream top. As she ate and sipped coffee, savoring each, Kara listened. Shirley talked about everything from the movie to the changes in town to their excitement for the future.

Kara caught her breath. When she first stopped in the dinner theater a year and a half ago, she hadn't understood Dani revitalized an entire town, jumpstarting the economy. Kara nearly wrecked everything by contracting Paul for a scheme on the West Coast. She shook her head at the memory. Dani changed a whole community.

Kara felt rather stupid with her attempts to change only her life. She wasn't as big a thinker as her friend. Her rationalization for doing her part was self-serving and fell flat.

Dani didn't have a clue about the far-reaching implications of her dream. She came to make her own way. Maybe Kara wasn't so far off the mark. Perhaps, her movie could still do some good, too. After thanking everyone for a lovely evening and avoiding another awkward handshake with Scott, she climbed into her car and had driven home.

"Kara? You ready?"

Kara snapped to attention, lifting her gaze to Lydia. "Absolutely." She shut her script and exited the booth, smoothing her pink cardigan. Strolling to the counter, she sat at the marked stool and held still.

A makeup artist approached and touched up her foundation and lip-gloss.

Shirley strode behind the counter, dangling a coffee pot in one hand.

Her usual cheerful demeanor was marred by a wrinkled brow. Her hair was as firmly hair sprayed as ever, not a strand daring to escape the retro coiffure. When Kara first met the diner co-owner, she almost thought she'd stepped back into the late seventies. The diner's interior was pristine but trapped in the earthy colors favored half a century ago. Shirley's feathered bob and starched apron completed the feel. The diner was as successful for Ted's cooking as for Shirley's indomitable spirit.

Kara wanted to capture the woman's effervescence on film. Under the thick layer of cosmetics, Shirley looked pale. Her mouth frowned, hanging limp in a hang-dog expression better suited to a basset hound than the woman known for her one-liners and sassy retorts.

The makeup artist stepped away.

Reaching forward, Kara grazed Shirley's forearm.

Shirley jerked and lifted her gaze.

The wild-eyed look tightened Kara's smile. "You'll be okay. You're just doing what you do every day. Don't worry about the cameras."

Blinking several times, Shirley shook her head. "I can't forget with a bright light in my face. I can barely see. My eyes keep watering."

Kara patted her arm. She hoped the touch was instilled with enough sensitivity and confidence for the woman to absorb. "You'll get used to it. You'll be great."

"Quiet on set, please," Lydia said. "Places."

Shirley walked away.

Straightening on the stool, Kara angled toward the mark and nodded. The scene wasn't very complicated. She sat at the counter, and Shirley filled her coffee cup. The door opened, and her on-screen best friend strode toward her. The pair exchanged a few lines about hiring the brother to work for the theater, and Shirley interrupted to agree and get their order. Nothing too taxing.

"Action," Lydia called.

Kara sat at the counter and swirled notes in the pad next to the mug. She focused on the scribbles, feigning ignorance of Shirley's movements. Tension radiated off the woman like one of the heat lamps for an outside shoot.

Shirley knocked the empty mug. The clatter echoed.

Kara lifted her gaze, instilling every ounce of acting skill she had not to react to the first-timers flub.

Without glancing or turning away from camera, she righted the mug. "Thanks, Shirley."

Nodding, Shirley poured the coffee. With shaky hands, she jerked the pot. Coffee splashed over the rim and onto the pad.

Instinctively, Kara jumped back.

"CUT," Lydia called. "Reset."

"Oh, I am so sorry." Shirley shook her head.

Her gaze widened as big as the saucer holding the spilled liquid. Kara grabbed a napkin, wiping a dot of coffee off the tender skin above her wrist. "You're fine. Ignore the nerves and stick to muscle memory. You've served a customer at the counter a hundred thousand times."

"Not like this," Shirley murmured.

Several key grips approached, wiped the counter clean, and reset the mug.

"Let's try again," Lydia said.

Kara repositioned herself and studied the fresh pad replacing the coffee-stained one from the last take. With her pen, she swirled her hand in pantomime writing. From the corner of her gaze, she glimpsed Shirley. The woman moved woodenly, like her legs didn't have knees. At the counter, she grabbed the empty mug in a tight grip and poured the coffee. A perfect stream of dark brew filled the mug, stopping just under the rim.

Kara lifted her chin to meet Shirley's gaze and plastered on her movie-star grin.

Shirley frowned.

The wrinkled brow was startling in its intensity. Kara nearly recoiled. "Thanks, Shirley."

With a nod, Shirley spun on her heel and stalked

toward the kitchen door.

"CUT," Lydia said.

With a sigh, Kara slid off the stool and approached the director.

As always, Lydia's face was an expressionless mask, utilizing her card-playing skills to advantage on set. She didn't let anything faze her or throw her off her purpose. Kara nibbled the inside of her cheek. "So?"

Lydia pulled off the headphones, draping the device around her neck like statement jewelry. "Can you chat with Shirley? We can't use any of the film, and we're exerting a lot of effort."

*Don't be difficult.* Kara nodded, hiding the shudder in her torso. She wanted to include Shirley and Ted. Could she risk her reputation for another few takes? If she fought, would the impromptu sequence sabotage her reputation and future projects? Kara plastered on a smile. "I'll try." Spinning on her heels, she crossed through the restaurant to the last booth and her phone. She relied on Scott. He'd help her navigate the problem and soothe his aunt. He helped Kara achieve both, and she'd rather not dwell on the inescapable fact she needed him—in many facets—of her life.

****

Scott scrubbed the tile wall above the flattop grill. With the diner closed to customers, he didn't have to worry about accidentally burning himself. Instead of staying home, however, he and Uncle Ted joined Aunt Shirley for her big debut. Cleaning offered a chance to stay busy and out of the way while being near enough for moral support.

All weekend long, Aunt Shirley had spoken of little else but her minor role. Scott grinned. He was happy for his aunt to have an opportunity. He'd never cared about celebrity or appearing on screen. If he had, living in Los Angeles on the fringe of fame would be unbearable. Firsthand, he glimpsed how few talented people actually got a star-making chance. He settled in the West Coast for weather and career opportunities. He never once wanted to be on-screen.

What would dating a celebrity entail? Frowning, he applied pressure to a particularly sticky spot, the terry cloth catching in the raised stain. He wasn't likely to find out. Friday night, he had thought she'd discuss the relationship. She didn't. He stupidly misread the situation.

The rest of the night was fine. Together with his aunt and uncle, they decorated the tree, ate dessert, and laughed at old stories. At the end of the evening, he'd wanted to kiss her goodbye but backed off. Avoiding another awkward run-in, he didn't walk her to the door.

Instead, he waved from the kitchen sink as she left and submerged his hands in a sink of sudsy water. For the next two days, he analyzed every interaction. Was he sending her mixed signals or vice versa? He was so confused by the whole situation he couldn't remember who came up with the fake relationship idea and who followed. Did the particulars matter?

The swinging door from the diner crashed against the wall.

He dropped the rag into the bucket of cleaning solution and turned, drying palms on his pants.

Whiter than a sheet, Aunt Shirley stood inside the room as the door swung shut behind her.

"How's it going?"

Aunt Shirley stared at the ground.

*Is she feeling okay?* He took a step forward, forcing his heavy limbs to move.

Uncle Ted brushed past him, reaching his wife and holding her shoulders. He steered her through the galley to a stool near the back door. Lifting his head, he met Scott's gaze and nodded.

Swiveling on his heel, Scott approached the pair. He should be glad for Uncle Ted's fast reflexes. Truthfully, he was annoyed he hadn't responded faster. What if she had been having a heart attack? Would he be ineffectual in an actual emergency? Part of his argument for their retirement was that they couldn't manage on their own. He had just proved otherwise.

Uncle Ted filled a glass with water and handed it to his wife.

Scott cleared his throat. "Are you okay?" With his verbose aunt now mute, he tightened every muscle in his body, external and internal. Had she been yelled at by the director? Or worse, Kara? He knew Kara exerted control over every facet in her life, but she couldn't expect his aunt to be a seasoned pro. The treatment of his family was especially egregious after they welcomed her into their home.

But how much did he really know about Kara? If she chose to work over the holidays in lieu of spending time with her parents, she might not understand what family meant. When he first met her, he hadn't been bothered by her explanation that now seemed more like a waving, red flag.

If he exposed his aunt and uncle to pain while humoring his phony love interest, he wouldn't forgive himself. He rested a hand on Aunt Shirley's shoulder. "Let me go out and see what's happening."

She nodded and sipped her water.

Uncle Ted met his gaze, folding his arms over his chest.

Scott didn't need more than the solemn look. He'd right the wrong. Pulling back his shoulders, Scott strode through the kitchen and pushed the swinging door. Bright light assaulted him the second he stepped into the diner. Squinting, he raised both hands to shield his gaze and blinked rapidly, clearing his watery eyes. After a few seconds, he adjusted and scanned the vicinity, spotting Kara in the back booth.

Dressed in a pink sweater and dress, she looked beautiful and somehow older. Without her makeup, she was fresh-faced and approachable. In her full movie star get-up, however, he understood the truth. She was way out of his league. Standing up for his aunt shouldn't bother him. He wasn't risking anything real. He rounded the counter and approached.

Kara lifted her gaze. "Scott, hi. I didn't realize you were here."

"You didn't?"

She shook her head and waved to the opposite side of the booth.

Sliding across the bench, he interlaced his hands on the table top. He didn't want to have a serious talk but maybe a discussion was inevitable. Over the past week, he was thrown for a loop with every missed moment and mix-up. He needed clarity and answers. "Everything all right out here?"

"How is your aunt?" Kara sighed and dropped her shoulders. "She left rather abruptly."

*Because you yelled.* He held his tongue. Nothing he'd glimpsed hinted at Kara raising her voice. But she was the producer as well as the star. If she didn't stop someone from scaring his aunt, she remained culpable because of her powerful position. "Did she?" He arched a brow.

"We had a couple mistakes. Not a big deal." Kara nodded and leaned forward. "But she's so nervous. I can't imagine the stress is good for her heart."

Exhaling a sigh, he released the tightness in his chest and dropped his chin. She cared. He doubted her without a shred of evidence. "No, probably not." He circled his thumbs, his neck bent. "What do you want to do?"

"It's not what I want to do. It's the best option. I'm worried we're straining her. If something happened, I wouldn't…" Biting her lip, she sniffed.

He studied her.

"She's been so welcoming and so good to the entire production." Kara scrunched her nose. "Sorry. I really like your aunt. She's a sweet lady. I wanted to do something fun and spotlight the diner. I thought including a local business in the movie added depth. I wanted to capture her spirit and offer some free advertising."

He nodded and scrubbed a hand over his face. He trusted her. She hadn't set up his aunt for failure but wanted to include the woman in a special experience. "You're thinking about recasting her?"

Kara shrugged and nibbled her lip.

She looked so frank. For a second, he glimpsed past the layers of star to the woman underneath. He saw the woman he met on the plane and helped in a blizzard. Holding her gaze, he smiled at the woman he liked.

As a star, she very well might have control issues. She hadn't hidden or concealed others' opinions about her. But maybe he was unfairly projecting his problems because she was there, and he could. Maybe he was so wound up over the unknowns of a potential romance mixed with his family distress, he cast her as the villain. He wouldn't be the first, but he regretted the rash action.

He reached across the table and squeezed her icy fingers. If he wanted control, he had to start by speaking honestly to her and his family. Delaying both conversations was only hindering him from moving forward. "Kara, I want—"

"Almost ready?" an assistant dressed in all-black with a ponytail asked.

Kara turned her head to the side. "Oh, umm, another minute?"

The assistant glanced at her wristwatch. "We have to reset and wrap up the shoot in the next hour. You have sixty seconds max."

"Thanks," Kara murmured and faced him. "Sorry for the interruption."

"It's okay." He squeezed her hand and dropped his grip, flattening his palms on the table. "I have no experience, and please don't make me audition. I could play the role."

"Will you?" She leaned close.

He nodded. He'd do almost anything for a hint of her smile. *Even break my aunt's heart.* "Let me double check with my aunt."

"Of course, of course. What you're wearing is great. But you'll need makeup."

He stared down at his red-and-black, buffalo-checked flannel shirt. He'd probably regret the decision, but he had to give his aunt an out. Sliding from the booth, he turned. "I'll be back in a minute."

Grinning, Kara reached forward, grazing his arm. "Thank you, Scott," she murmured.

With his shirt sleeves rolled to his elbows, he felt her light touch brush his skin, and the hairs stood on end. He leaned close, tilting his lips and wrapping her back in both arms.

In a second, she turned her head and stiffened. "Sorry, but I can't smudge my makeup."

"Right. I forgot." He dropped his hands and stepped back. Were cosmetics a convenient excuse? Setting his jaw, he turned, shielding his burning cheeks from her gaze. He crossed behind the counter and pushed through the swinging door into the kitchen.

Aunt Shirley and Uncle Ted stood at the sink.

Scott wrinkled his brow. Dirty dishes weren't a two-person job. With the diner closed, no one had ordered any food. He cleared his throat and stuffed his hands in his pockets. Hard conversations weren't his favorite, but he needed practice for the even more difficult words to come. "Aunt Shirley?"

"Hmm?" She turned from the sink and rubbed her hands on her apron.

The sink was empty.

She acted with admirable skill in the back. Couldn't her abilities transfer in front of the camera? He shook his head. He wasn't here to judge. "I've spoken with Kara. She wants to include the diner in the movie but has a suggestion. Would you be okay if I take your role?"

Aunt Shirley heaved a heavy sigh and doubled

over. “Oh, thank goodness,” she murmured. Straightening, she wiped a hand over her brow. “Yes, honey. Please. By all means. I am not cut out for the movies.”

“Are you sure?” She’d been so excited. He hated to steal her once-in-a-lifetime opportunity.

Aunt Shirley approached and rested her dry hands on his shoulders. “A thousand percent. You’re far more camera-ready. Maybe you’ll get an onscreen kiss, too.” She winked.

*Not likely*. Lowering his head, he kissed Aunt Shirley’s cheek. He didn’t need her to glimpse his flaring nostrils and misinterpret the cue. Since he arrived, he’d been subjected to everyone else’s whims. He’d almost forgotten what taking charge meant. But he couldn’t back down with life-or-death stakes. He turned on his heel and pushed out the door. He’d had enough with delays.

## Chapter Thirteen

The next morning on stage at Holidays, Inc., Kara braced her hands on either side of her waist. After a rousing run through with the choreographer, she needed a moment to catch her breath.

A flashing light danced on the wooden planks.

She straightened and lifted her gaze to the rafters.

Movie crew worked alongside the theater's staff, securing additional lights and cameras around the room and backstage.

Finally, the long-awaited rehearsals for Paul's Christmas show began. With only one week to Christmas Eve, she was up most of the night worrying about another delay or setback. She refused to concede her unease and guilt over yesterday's filming.

Over coffee, she identified the emotion. She was unsatisfied. Typically, she operated with the mindset of the ends justifying the means. But when the feelings of people she'd gotten to know and grown to care for were involved, she had to rethink every old mantra she'd unknowingly ingested in her career. Scott carried his walk-on role admirably. After shooting wrapped, she met with Shirley and Scott. Neither expressed any regrets at the handling of the situation. But she admitted disappointment. Shirley was excited to be part of the movie. Kara wished filming hadn't scared the older woman. *I wanted to do something nice.*

"Kara?" Paul's voice echoed through the megaphone.

Squinting, she smiled in the general direction of the voice in the auditorium. She crossed to the front of the stage and spotted the director standing in the center of the room. "Yes. I'm ready. Where do you want me?"

"We're breaking for coffee. We'll pick up the number again in twenty minutes."

She shot the director a thumbs-up. Blocking was surprisingly fast. Neither the script nor the songs were overly taxing. The performances relied on elaborate costumes and set pieces to tap into a warm and fuzzy nostalgia. She clicked her character shoes against the wooden boards of the stage and picked her way over cords and cables to her tote bag in the corner. With a long hiatus from performing in plays, she was glad she remembered to dress in comfy fleece.

She kneeled on the ground, rifling through her bag. Grabbing a towel and her water bottle, she uncapped the drink and wiped her brow. Her tote started vibrating. Reaching inside the bag, she grabbed her phone and gaped. She unlocked the screen and pressed the device against her ear. "Mom?"

"Hi, Kare bear. Is this a good time?" Mom asked.

Kara smiled. Mom's sunny voice shone through the line. "Couldn't be better. We're taking a break from rehearsals at Dani's theater."

"Oh! How's she doing?"

"She's great." Kara sipped from the water. For years, Dani hadn't just played Kara's body double, she practically lived the experience. Mom and Dad were only too happy to include Dani in family moments. With her impeccable manners, Dani was often more welcome than Kara. Had she internalized some jealousy? When she replayed the events leading to the break in their friendship, she stopped justifying her actions and looked at the plain facts. She stole Dani's ex. Had it been a delayed reaction from years of suppressing her second fiddle worries?

"We need to make a trip to see one of her shows. I tried this year, but everything was sold out."

"I can put in a word for you." Kara chuckled.

"How's the movie?"

"We've had a few curve balls." Kara nibbled her lip. She wanted to say more. *I've met someone*. Would he still be her someone after they left town? She owed him the conversation first.

"Don't you always? We're so proud. You're taking charge like you should."

Sniffing, Kara scrunched her nose and blinked her watery eyes. She wouldn't break down on a phone call. "How are you enjoying Hawaii?"

"Warm breezes. Fresh seafood. Everything is blooming and smells gorgeous. We're heading to Hanauma Bay soon to watch the sunrise and snorkel."

Kara sighed and glanced at the clock. Quickly calculating the time difference, she shook her head. Mom had always been an early riser. Kara's heart squeezed. "I miss you."

Silence replied.

Cringing, she rubbed the base of her palm against her heart. But she couldn't ease the ache. At the holidays, she wanted her family.

"You do?"

Mom's voice was almost a croak. Something bittersweet and sentimental released inside. "Here, I've sort of joined in everyone else's traditions, and I'm missing ours. Remember those parties?"

Mom barked a laugh. "Those were such a nightmare."

Kara gasped. "They were?"

"Dad and I hated entertaining, but we had to for his accounting firm. We were strong-armed into it."

"Really?" Kara sat and pulled her knees into her chest. "I always liked the glamour."

"We know. But we had our own traditions. Don't you remember the snowball eating competition?"

"Oh, that?" Kara tipped her head to the side, nearly forgetting the coconut-covered, vanilla ice cream balls. Every Christmas Eve, after the party, Mom would set one on a plate for Kara, Dani, and Dad and stick in a lighted birthday candle. Whoever left the candle burning on the smallest amount of ice cream won. Dani nearly always did. One year, she kept the candle upright with only a drop of ice cream underneath.

"The snowballs were my favorite childhood memory." Mom sighed. "I never liked all the fuss about the big holiday parties. After every one, I needed a week to recover. But I loved being together."

A door hit the wall with a crash.

Lifting her gaze, Kara spotted a member of the crew, dressed in a heavy parka, tracking snow onto the carpet. Mom might like the confection but had no real experience with the actual icy weather conditions. Kara longed for warm trade-winds. "I have to admit Hawaii sounds nice."

"Is it freezing? Do your teeth chatter?"

Kara shivered. Mom and Dad would be better off coming to one of Dani's summer holiday shows. "Icier than you can imagine."

"Brr," Mom said.

Kara chuckled. "I've adapted. I think I will join you next year."

"Big Island?"

Images of hula dancers, palm trees, and tiki torches flashed in her mind. "Sounds great. I'm here until New Year's Ev—" Her phone buzzed. "Hold on, Mom." She pulled the device off her ear and glanced at the screen. Another shocking call in less than twenty minutes? "I've got another call. Sorry to cut this short, Mom, but I've got to take it."

"Of course. Love you, Kare bear. Bye."

"Bye." She ended the call and accepted the other. "Hello? Mrs. Winter?" Kara gritted her molars and clenched her jaw, darting her gaze.

Dani was nowhere close.

Kara released the pent-up breath from her dry throat. "Thank you for calling me back."

"You leave a persistent number of messages. Figured I better return your call so you'd stop hounding me."

Her voice was raspy and annoyed. Of course, Kara never knew the woman to be warm and kind. *Get to the* point. Kara cleared her throat. "Can I book your flights?"

"I don't… I'm not sure about coming."

"Why?" Kara knew asking served no purpose beyond adding to the discomfort, but she couldn't stop herself. Of all people, she was the last one Mrs. Winter would use as a confessional. She made no secret of feeling threatened by Kara and her family. But Dani deserved better than what the pair gave. Kara drew in a breath. *For Dani.* "If she's willing to give me another chance, she'd welcome you with even more open arms. She's built something amazing here. Let her show you. Please."

"You did mess up things."

At the callous tone and petty words, Kara winced. *No less than the truth.* "I did."

"Okay…"

"Great. I'll book you a flight for the twenty-second." She straightened, victory lightening the burden on her shoulders. She'd lift a fist to the sky if she wasn't worried about drawing attention. For once, she didn't want gazes on her. *Unless it's Scott.* "I'll email you the information."

She ended the call before Mrs. Winter could protest. Redemption required more crow-eating than she anticipated. But the prize was worth the price.

Until too late, she hadn't understood what she lost in her closest friend. She hadn't realized how much she'd miss her parents. She knew she didn't want to miss him, too. Would a conversation with Scott only speed up the inevitable end?

He didn't seem interested in the celebrity lifestyle. Back home, fame was just about the only thing she had. What else could she offer? Dropping the phone and towel into the tote bag, she pushed to standing. Lifting her chin, she scanned the stage and spotted him. Whether or not she was ready, he was heading her way. She could only hope her improv skills improved.

****

At one of the tables near the doors leading to the auditorium lobby, Scott hung back. He'd popped into the theater with a question for Kara. He could have asked Dani or a member of the movie crew, but he wanted the excuse to see her. He regretted questioning her motives at the diner. After the shoot, Aunt Shirley thanked him profusely, her relief palpable. He'd been worried first and foremost for her health and hadn't minded the quick scene. Aunt Shirley was still excited the diner would be included in the movie, even if she hadn't felt up to the task. His instinct to accuse Kara of something nefarious, however, bugged him. Was he searching for a reason to end their fake relationship before his real feelings developed any further? Rubbing a hand over his face, he leaned back in the chair and studied the stage.

Dressed in workout clothes, Kara held a script and a pencil. With her hair in a messy bun and her brow wrinkled, she stared at the director, Paul, and nodded. Deep in concentration, she'd never been more beautiful. Every day, he appreciated more how her appearance shielded her. He'd watched her turn on the movie star charm. As much as feeding into the public's perception, she separated the real, raw woman underneath with the veneer of a broad, toothy grin and sparkling blue eyes. People wanted the celebrity. *I prefer her.*

"Five-Six-Seven-Eight." Paul clapped on the stage.

Scott observed the musical number with an awed detachment. In a second, the actors set their scripts to the side and danced around the stage like a power switch flicking on. She perfected her posture and beamed. His mind erased the bare stage and inserted sets and costumes. The show was sure to be a festive hit. He returned her contagious grin.

With a hand, he covered his mouth. Smiling felt nice, light, and natural. Finally, he could grin without feeling like a fraud. Last night, after dinner, he had addressed his ultimate motive for the holiday visit. As hot emotion bubbled up his dry throat, and his eyes burned, he began. "I worry about you. You're giving too much."

Aunt Shirley rolled her eyes and slapped the table. She pushed her chair back, scraping the floor.

"Please don't leave. Can we talk?" He covered her hand with his and met his uncle's gaze, imploring him for help.

"Shirley," Uncle Ted said.

Heaving a sigh, she pulled back her hand and scooted the chair closer to the table. "Honey, you better start making sense."

"I appreciate and respect what this community means. But they aren't family."

Aunt Shirley snorted.

Scott scrubbed both hands over his face. How could he voice his concerns if he choked on the sentences? How could he put into words the fear gripping him in an awful, clammy embrace? "What I mean to say is you aren't giving the people you care about a chance to help. You can't do it all anymore. You've hired workers, and I applaud that move. But it's not enough. I have seen how much you still do on your own. And I'm scared. You could hurt yourselves in a hundred different ways by insisting on taking charge."

"Give me an example," Aunt Shirley said.

"You open and close every day. You are the first to arrive and the last to leave. Since I've been here, I've noted many times one of you goes home and the other is left alone. What if you had a health scare? What if you fell and couldn't reach the phone to call for help?"

“So what’s your alternative?” Aunt Shirley folded her arms over her chest. “Move us into some retirement center in Los Angeles? We love living here. Best choice we ever made.”

Uncle Ted grunted.

She hadn’t raised her voice, but her tone dripped with frustration. He fought against rolling his eyes or heaving a sigh. She wasn’t the only one discontented with the situation. If he showed his emotions, however, he’d lose his argument.

“You can’t leave us in some box and control the rest of our lives for your desired outcome.” Aunt Shirley dropped her arms to the table. “We need to be here.” She tapped the top with one finger. “With our friends, living our lives.”

Of course, Scott knew that. But he couldn’t escape the biggest sticking point. If something bad happened, he was a several hours plane ride away. “But…”

“Honey, Uncle Ted and I have talked about this before.” She turned her head to her husband.

Uncle Ted nodded.

“We have been thinking about the future, too. We miss you. But we aren’t pressuring you to move here, and we’d like the same in reverse.” Aunt Shirley interlaced her fingers on the table, gripping until her knuckles whitened.

“And if the worst happens?” Scott’s voice cracked.

“We can’t live the rest of our lives in fear. We are considering bringing on a partner and scaling way back on our civic obligations. But we aren’t leaving.”

Scott dragged in a shaky breath. Understanding their position couldn’t stop his emotions.

Aunt Shirley covered his hand and gently squeezed

his fingers.

"Let's keep talking. We'll never reach a perfect compromise. I think there is some middle ground so we can all feel comfortable with the result. I'm glad you finally talked."

Scott stood then and embraced both in a fierce hug. For a moment, he leaned into the touch. He would never get to hold his parents again. Some nights, he swore he felt Mom's famous surprise hug, grabbing him around the waist from behind and burying her face into his back. She'd started the sneak embraces when he shot up past her height back in high school. He'd give anything for another moment with those he lost and wouldn't waste any with his mom's sister or her husband.

"Hi, Scott. Everything okay?" Dani asked.

Lifting his gaze, he blinked. The theater owner stood next to the director, both frowning in his direction. Scott scrambled to his feet, knocking over the chair in the process. "Yeah, great. Sorry." He bent and righted the chair. Straightening, he dried his wet palms on his long sleeve shirt. "Had a question for Kara but didn't want to interrupt."

"We're taking a break," Paul said. "Any chance the kitchen still has leftovers?"

Scott shrugged. "Very doubtful. Nora hates waste of any kind."

Paul's stomach growled. "Guess I'll run to the diner while I can." He leaned over and kissed Dani's cheek. "I'll be back soon." He jogged off, the lobby door crashing shut behind him.

She rolled her eyes. "I hope your aunt has enough food."

Scott chuckled. “She’ll find a way to feed him. She’s been doing it for years.”

“True.” Dani nodded and folded her arms over her chest. “Since you’re here…”

He arched a brow. The sudden seriousness was so unlike the effervescent theater owner he’d gotten to know. She ran her business with a contagious enthusiasm, giving her all to everyone. She received the same in return.

“Thank you. I appreciate you leaping into action and saving the day. I’m sure you planned on enjoying time off and instead jumped into work.”

“If I hadn’t, my aunt and uncle would have. You wouldn’t have been stranded.”

“I know.” She met his gaze and lifted her chin. “They have saved me more often than I can count. But I don’t want to burden them. I would have called in other favors before asking them to take on the workload.”

Did Dani sense the health issues? Could he trust the community to look out for his family’s best interests as well as their own? He set his jaw, processing the new information. Maybe he was just as bad about needing to exert control as he thought of Kara. Perhaps they were two of a kind. If he wanted her to lean into others, he ought to follow the advice, too.

“Thank you for partnering with Nora. I know she has exacting standards and rules. But she is running an exceptional kitchen. I have no complaints.”

“Me, neither.”

“Good.” Dani grinned. “So…any way I can segue into a personal conversation?”

He shook his head and chuckled. “That’s just about the worst transition I’ve ever heard.”

"How about I don't ask?" She widened her stance. "Let me"—she pointed a finger to her collarbone—"tell you." She held her index finger straight at his chin.

He rolled his neck. He wasn't getting out of this situation.

"I haven't seen her smile in a long time."

Knitting together his brow, he stuffed his hands into his front pockets. Kara smiled instantaneously. She could brighten on command.

Dani held up a hand. "Before you argue semantics, I'm talking about a genuine can't-help-but-show-her-happiness smile. I've known her forever, but I think she's finally getting the chance to get to know herself."

Raising his gaze, he scanned the stage.

With a phone pressed against her ear, Kara sat cross-legged on the corner of the stage. Her hands moved constantly, and her mouth lifted with quirks and laughter.

She radiated happiness. Was the condition only temporary while on vacation from her real life? Or could they stay on a sort of reprieve from the burdens of external opinion indefinitely? He faced Dani, but she was gone. He strolled through the theater toward the stage and jogged up the steps.

Kara hung up a call.

"Hi." He grinned, and his mind blanked. He forgot his made-up question.

"Hello. Were you watching the whole morning? What a chore." She wiped her brow and the back of her neck with a towel.

"Not at all. The process is fascinating."

"Like the movie?"

He sat on the stage and covered a hand over his

mouth shielding his words from any curious ears. "Actually, if I'm honest, the stage work is more entertaining. Did you really just start today? Everyone seems so rehearsed."

She chuckled and dropped the towel into the bag. Extending her legs in front, she bent at the waist and folded over her knees. "We're actors. We're used to last minute."

"I don't think I could remember everything."

Turning her face, she rested a cheek on her knee. "If it's your passion, you would. I'm sure I couldn't open some random refrigerator and whip up the best pancakes and from-scratch cocoa ever."

He shrugged. "I'm a chocolate snob. If I'm indulging, I need the good stuff."

She pushed up her torso and bent one leg over the other, twisting in the opposite direction. "Me, too. But I'd take anything in a pinch."

"Were you the kid with a sweet tooth sneaking cookies from the kitchen at Christmas?"

"If we had them, sure." She unhooked her legs and twisted the other side. "Typically, we didn't keep treats in the house. Sweets belonged to special occasions, and on those instances, I did go overboard. What about you? What was your Christmas like growing up?"

"Family." *What about your parents?* He didn't push for more details. She was here for work. Why would she answer questions about her personal life? When she left town, she headed back to a life he couldn't fathom.

He stood. "Better head back to the kitchen. See you later?"

"I'll look forward to it." She smiled.

Striding away, he willed himself to focus on his direction and not get one more glance. If he pushed, he risked losing another week of enjoying the surprisingly happy moments of fake couple-dom. He had to accept her at face value. She never pretended she had other motives. She was like a fine dark chocolate, smooth and rich. The bitter undertones only enhanced the sweet. Knowing how precious each one was, he'd enjoy her smiles and stave off the inevitable pain in the coming days following goodbye.

# Chapter Fourteen

Kara tightened her grip on the steering wheel, locking her jaw in an approximation of a smile. On alert for any potholes, she narrowed her gaze and studied the salt-covered road. With only the minivan's lights illuminating the asphalt, she leaned forward on the seat. A flat tire was one more complication she couldn't take today.

When she answered the call from Dani's mom five days ago, she figured she was over the highest hurdle. She forgot what dealing with the woman in person entailed. In her excitement at finally starting rehearsals for the stage show, she glossed over any other difficulties, blocking her history with Mrs. Winter. Up close in the minivan, however, she couldn't escape the woman.

"Are you sure this is the right town?"

The acerbic tone lashed from the second row. Mrs. Winter always treated Kara with a cool disdain and tinged every sentence with condescension. As a child, Kara witnessed the woman's callous treatment of her daughter and vowed to be the family Dani deserved. For two decades, Kara kept her word. When she felt desperate and trapped by her career, however, she betrayed Dani's trust. Kara shook her head. Dealing with Dani's mom was the ultimate proof of the lengths Kara would go to restore the friendship.

"Because the house was empty. Did you get turned around?"

If Kara stuck to the facts and maintained an even tone, she might last the entire car ride without yelling at the passenger. The drive from the Milwaukee airport was silent and dark. The sun set as Kara pulled alongside the curb of arrivals.

Mrs. Winter hopped in the second row, leaving her luggage on the pavement.

Holding in a sigh, Kara flashed the hazard lights and retrieved the pair of heavy suitcases. After she hauled both into the trunk, she returned to the driver's seat and almost insisted the woman sit shotgun. But once she pulled onto the highway, she forgot Mrs. Winter's presence.

The drive had been smooth until the planned surprise at the house didn't stick to plan. Of course, Kara hadn't cleared Dani's plans ahead of time. More likely than not, she'd stayed late at the theater and grabbed dinner in town before coming home. Mrs. Winter's nerves showed in her increasingly short questions. The woman dared Kara to a challenge of who knew Dani best. The outcome wouldn't suit Kara's purposes. "Yes, ma'am. If she's not home, she'll be eating at the diner."

"Do you know where that is located?"

Kara glanced in her rearview mirror at the sixty-something year old in the back. With her dark blonde locks smoothed into a low ponytail and minimal makeup, Mrs. Winter looked almost young. For years, she dressed in skirts a little too short and tops a little too low cut. She played up her resemblance to her daughter for attention. Dressed in a turtleneck sweater and jeans, she never looked better. Not that Kara could compliment the woman.

Mrs. Winter stared out the window, fingers tapping the armrest.

*She's nervous*. If Kara focused on the emotions, she could commiserate and find a middle ground. Empathy was a requirement for any good actor. Rewinding her past year, she knew Mrs. Winter's feelings firsthand. Kara was in the same position only she hadn't received help. Working back into Dani's good graces required every ounce of groveling and apology Kara mustered. Add in a heaping helping of fake boyfriend, she almost returned to being counted as a friend. She hoped.

In nine days, Kara left for Los Angeles. When production wrapped on her big comeback, she had no reason to linger. Was asking for the restoration of her best-friend status before flying home too much? Try as she might, she couldn't bring herself to compete with Dani's new best friend, Jill Howell. The mayor dealt fairly and honestly with everyone. Kara would be lucky to count Jill as an ally. Her usual tricks of attacking a rival wouldn't work because she liked the mayor.

*What about Scott?* Kara couldn't figure out his motives. Not knowing what drove a person made identifying their weakness and preying upon them impossible. A bitter taste filled her mouth, and she swallowed. She'd used her instincts about people to propel herself up the ladder. She was tired of her old tricks and her old self. Scott lured her with a puzzle. She wanted to know him better and spend more time together. Did she dare admit she liked whoever she was in his company? She sighed. Her feelings probably didn't matter. When she headed back to L.A., she wasn't likely to see him again. More the shame.

"Are you lost? What's with all the noises up there?"

"Sorry. Just thinking." Kara flashed her signal and turned onto Main Street. "Here we are. Downtown New Hope."

"Hmm."

Kara stared straight ahead, not allowing her eyes to roll. Slowly, she drove around the corner and parked on the street in front of the diner. Under the black sky, stars lit up the night, competing with the strands of holiday string lights.

For a more amenable passenger, she would have driven around the looping street and stopped at the former hardware store opposite the diner, providing the full New Hope tour. The small town was better than any seasonally decorated soundstage. Warmth spread through her. A little bit of pride in this town? Strange considering she never imagined having a tie to anyplace. The little town handed out second chances like candy, and she gladly grabbed hers. Cutting the engine, she pulled the keys from the ignition and unbuckled her seatbelt. She turned in her chair.

Mrs. Winter sat still as a statue, mouth agape, sweat beading on her brow.

"Mrs. Winter? Are you feeling well?"

Taking in a deep breath, she shook her head and shuddered.

Kara understood the situation better than anyone. She leaned toward her passenger and willed the woman to meet her steady gaze. "I wouldn't have brought you here if I didn't know she wanted to see you. I am certain she will be thrilled."

Mrs. Winter faced Kara, her chin trembling.

"It's okay to start fresh. She came here for a new beginning. Now, you get the same chance."

The older woman scrunched her nose and sniffed.

Niceties were the wrong angle. "Or maybe you're too scared? To see your daughter?"

Mrs. Winter rolled her eyes and huffed. "Fine." She unbuckled her seatbelt and opened the side door, hopping to the curb.

With a grin, Kara exited the car, shut the door, and followed Mrs. Winter up the stairs to the diner. Kara reached around Mrs. Winter and opened the door.

The bell jingled overhead.

Mrs. Winter stopped just inside the threshold. "Where now?"

Clinking utensils, low laughter, and murmured conversations welcomed the newcomers. Kara breathed deep, inhaling the scent of the fryer. She scanned the room and widened her gaze. Everyone wanted a night off from cooking.

The counter was lined with patrons seated shoulder to shoulder. Every booth was occupied.

She leaned close. "Last booth."

"You coming?"

Kara nodded. "I'll follow."

Pulling back her shoulders, Mrs. Winter strolled past the booths.

Taking her time, Kara ambled. As much as she loved a perfect entrance and dramatic exit, this time she was happy to give someone else center stage and observe from the wings. She slowed her steps and rose tiptoe, peering over the top of the last two booths to spot Dani and Paul.

Dani chuckled at something Paul said, her head tipped back. Shaking off the giggles, she turned her head. Her skin lost its color, and her jaw slackened. *Mom?* she mouthed and rushed out from the booth, embracing her mom in a hug, tears streaming down her face.

Kara rocked back on her heels and stopped. Her body felt limp, drained of the anxiety of orchestrating the surprise, and she could barely stay upright. Her knees buckled. A strong arm snaked around her waist, lifting her.

"Are you okay?" Scott asked.

"Oh, I'm fine." She sighed. Catching her before she could fall? He was too good to be true. If she stayed in his arms, she couldn't pretend she remained in command. With every encounter, she faltered a little more in keeping her heart out of the arrangement. She needed to break contact but didn't want to step away. She liked the safety in his warm embrace. Reluctantly, she stepped back and faced him.

He tipped his head, wrinkling his brow.

*He really is concerned.* A reassurance dangled on the tip of her tongue. But she didn't say a word. Having someone worry about her felt oddly nice.

"Kara?" Dani asked.

With a start, Kara turned.

Dani lunged forward, wrapping her in a tight hug. "Thank you so much."

"Merry Christmas," Kara murmured and blinked her watery eyes. She stepped out of the warmest hug she'd had in a long time. "Go with your mom. Show her the theater. I pulled in front of the house and then came here. She hasn't seen anything yet."

Dani grinned and nodded, spinning toward the booth.

Scott cleared his throat.

Kara met his widened gaze.

He arched an eyebrow and lifted his chin. "You did that? Impromptu family reunion?"

Was the surprise gift so shockingly out of character? She shrugged.

"You gave her a pretty special gift. A lot of planning." He grinned and leaned close. "You might be the most thoughtful person I know."

His smile warmed her faster than his hot cocoa. "I don't have a heart of gold. But I do have a heart."

Nudging with his shoulder, he leaned close. "Tell me something I don't know."

"I like you," she muttered.

He opened his mouth.

Had he meant the words rhetorically? Heat crept up her cheeks, and she pressed together her lips, crossing her arms. When she controlled the narrative, she didn't mind drawing attention. With Scott, she was never in charge, her fast-beating heart heightening every second of silence. Could she run outside without causing a scene?

****

Scott opened his mouth. He could either pretend he hadn't heard her murmur, which he was sure was her intention with the soft uttering of her comment. Or he could address it. Hadn't he been looking for the perfect opportunity to discuss them for the better part of the past five days? He shook his head. More accurately, he wanted to talk about them since Thanksgiving.

A shove pushed him forward.

Straightening, he twisted his head over his shoulder.

Paul held up a hand. “Sorry. I think we’re heading out. Back booth is free.”

Scott turned to the side, allowing the group to pass. “Have a good night.”

“Thanks, Kara. This family moment means a lot.” Paul reached out a hand. “To both of us.”

Kara shook his hand, dipping her head.

Her smile was stretched taut. If she held the expression longer, she’d crack. She was not in control. The thought slammed into Scott like one of the food delivery trucks hitting the brakes behind the diner. He accused her of micromanaging every scenario. Her red cheeks proved him wrong. Hovering a hand over her lower back, he leaned close. “Let’s sit in the back booth.”

Nodding, she strolled forward.

He uttered farewells to Dani and her mom and followed Kara to the last booth. A light rose scent wafted past him. Warmth spread through his chest. When he first met her, he likened the perfume to a silver screen star long before he understood her identity. Was his subconscious far more in tune than his waking brain? If he quieted his mind, what would he know?

At the very last booth, she slid across the bench seat and grabbed a napkin, dabbing her eyes. “I didn’t think I’d get so emotional.” She sniffed and blinked, shaking her head. “I don’t even like Dani’s mom.”

*What about us?* Scott coughed, forcing his dry throat to open and shut. He missed his moment.

"I guess talking to my parents the other day just kind of has me thinking of family."

He wanted to know more of her personal life. If he wanted a chance with her in the New Year, he needed to jump on the opportunity now.

"I didn't think I'd miss them at the holidays. They aren't even home." She lifted her gaze and quirked the corner of her mouth. "Did I tell you my parents are celebrating Christmas in Hawaii? On Oahu."

"Really?" *If I stuck to the original plan, I still might have met her this year.* Dropping his shoulders, he rested his forearms on the table. He had no guarantees a chance encounter could have happened. But he couldn't stop the surge of adrenaline electrifying his skin.

She laced her fingers and stared at the table. "In the past decade, we haven't spent more than a few hours together on Christmas Eve or Christmas morning. I've been busy."

"What are they like?" His voice cracked. "Your parents?"

"My mom and dad are not show business people." The corner of her mouth lifted. "On a whim, Mom signed me as a baby model. She had no idea I'd make a career out of performing. I was very precocious. I handed her contracts for her signature and started my career before Mom understood what was happening."

He grinned. Once again, her contagious smile sparked joy. He could picture a tiny girl with golden curls sweet-talking her parents into any demand. "I can imagine."

Exhaling a heavy breath, she rested her chin in a palm. "I booked this job out of desperation. I didn't stop to think it through all the way. I've focused on the work. If I can't make a comeback with a feel-good project, I'm done, and my new production company is finished."

A busser approached and grabbed the used plates and cups. The pimply teenage boy wiped down the table, gazing at Kara.

Her features assumed a pleasant, but unengaging, expression. The youth was undeterred.

After the third scrubbing of the surface, Scott flattened a hand on the table. "We're good. Thank you, Aidan."

With a nod, the kid backed away.

She leaned forward, resting her forearms on the table. "Next year, I'm not working. No matter how bad is the state of my career."

"Only a fool would bet against you."

She nibbled her bottom lip and lifted her chin.

Her blue eyes flashed like an emergency light. What did she want to say? If he pushed, and she backed down, he'd regret wasting a nice moment on an answer he already knew. The time together served a purpose. At the end, he'd have a great story for any dinner party. His chest tightened, an invisible vise squeezing his ribcage. If he stopped the war of his head and his heart, maybe he could make it to New Years without suffering a heart attack. He wanted to focus on the nine days left in town, and he wouldn't squander any. "What will you do next Christmas?"

"Take them up on their idea of another Hawaiian holiday. They want to visit the Big Island next year."

*I like you, too.* He wanted to circle back to her statement. Should he blurt his feelings? She was so much braver than he was. She stared expectantly. "Hawaii sounds perfect."

She shrugged. "You should join us."

*Really?* Under every joke hid a kernel of truth. He wanted to believe they could exist outside of the small-town bubble. Back in their real lives, how would she react to a boyfriend with limited days off? He was and always would be a working stiff. A solid day's labor defined his hours. Even when he wasn't on the clock, he stayed occupied with projects. She wasn't the only one on sabbatical from real life. "What are you doing this Christmas? Would you want to join me at my aunt and uncle's? It's the only morning of the year the diner is closed."

Kara widened her gaze. "They only stay home one day a year?"

He shook his head. "Only the morning. They open at noon and work until closing."

"Wow. Your family must be the definition of dedication."

"Or tradition." He shrugged. "But if you come over, I can promise it'll be worth it. Uncle Ted bakes cinnamon rolls from scratch."

She licked her lips. "Does he put pecans in any?"

"If you are offering an official request, I can submit it." He winked, liking her playful tone. "The frosting is about an inch thick."

"Don't threaten me with a good time." She sucked in a breath. "I suppose I can indulge once this year. Okay, you're on." She clapped a hand over her mouth and shook her head, eyes wide.

He frowned. "What's wrong?"

"Oh, I have to be at Dani's house on Christmas

morning."

*Of course*. He should have known she had better plans. Swallowing, he ignored his swirling stomach. "Never mind. It's not a big deal."

"Maybe we could do both?"

Lifting his gaze, he studied her brows arched over sparkling sapphire eyes. With the corner of her lips in a half-smile, she mirrored him. He reached across the table and flipped up his palms.

She lowered her hands.

He squeezed her fingers four times. *I like you, too.* The feeling of warmth and satisfaction oozed out from deep in his soul. He hadn't talked about a real relationship and sensed she was equally out of her depth. If they both backed off from controlling the narrative, they'd forge a new path. Enjoying every moment together and not taking any second for granted was a dream. Could a future with her be so simple? He hoped so. Because he slowly named the sensation coming over him every time he saw her as love. He'd fallen for a star. If he put her in his pocket, he'd never let her slip away.

A crash shook the table.

With a jerk, he withdrew his hands and turned toward the sound.

The kitchen door swung back and forth.

"I'd better check and see if I'm needed." He scrubbed a hand over his face and sighed. He didn't want to interrupt a good moment with emotional heavy lifting. Time wasn't on his side. He faced Kara.

"Of course. I'm heading home now." She smiled and slid from the booth.

He followed her progress toward the front door.

She floated through the restaurant. He breathed deep. On his exhale, he released the dull twinge in his neck and shoulders. He came to town with purpose and discovered so much more. For the first time in years, he shared a connection with someone and the calm of mutual understanding. He needed to earn the reward by doing the difficult work. Sliding from the booth, he slipped along the wall behind the counter and pushed the door.

Aunt Shirley stood near the cooktop, wrapping her arms around Uncle Ted.

Uncle Ted faced the grill, hunching his back.

The night crew, consisting of one dishwasher and two cooks, continued their work. The cooks flipped patties and doused potatoes in the fryer. The dishwasher scrubbed plates in the sudsy sink.

In three, broad steps, Scott reached his aunt and uncle. “What’s wrong?”

“Nothing,” Uncle Ted said.

The low tone was a growl. Scott recoiled, stepping aside.

Aunt Shirley lifted her chin, meeting his gaze over Uncle Ted’s shoulder. She shook her head. “Ready to go home, Scott?”

Under the steady gaze, he nodded.

Dropping her hold, Aunt Shirley strode to the back door.

Uncle Ted followed, grabbing his coat and hers off the hooks on the wall.

Scott hung back, analyzing the scene. The stovetop was in working order. He spotted nothing on the ground. No obvious clue jumped into prominence. A blast of chilly air snaked through the kitchen. He shivered and raised his gaze, watching the door shut.

"He got dizzy."

Frowning, Scott turned toward the grill.

The broad-shouldered man hadn't stopped moving.

"Did anything happen? Did he fall? Is he often dizzy?" *Why didn't anyone tell me?* Blood coursed through Scott's veins, pumping double-time. He clenched his hands into fists.

The cook shook his head and backed away.

"Thanks." Scott set his mouth in a flat line and strode toward the exit. He knew better than to direct his frustration at an unsuspecting bystander. Reaching for his coat, he pulled on the outerwear and slipped outside, slamming the door. Under his boots, he crunched the road salt against the asphalt alley. If he restricted his emotions to the satisfying grind of heavy steps, he held himself in check. While he'd been hyper-focused on Aunt Shirley's health, he ignored every sign of his uncle's aging. He dropped his chin to his chest and studied each slush-filled pothole, navigating around the in-need-of-repairs roadway toward the truck parked on Main Street.

"Stop muttering," Aunt Shirley called. "Speaking under your breath is not helpful."

Frowning, Scott lifted his gaze. He hadn't made a sound, but he had a lot to say.

Aunt Shirley stood on the driver's side, rolling her eyes.

Uncle Ted held open the passenger door, motioning Scott inside.

Scott swallowed the sigh building in his chest. He hopped inside the cab and assumed the center seat, buckling himself in position. His companions joined him, jostling on either side.

Aunt Shirley turned the key in the ignition, and the truck rumbled to life. She buckled her seatbelt and signaled.

For a few minutes, the repetitive click echoed in the silent cab.

Each beat thundered in his ears, and he tightened his chest. How many times had his uncle experienced sudden dizziness? When was his last physical? “What happened?”

“Nothing,” Uncle Ted muttered. “I bent and stood too fast.”

“Your uncle has low blood pressure. The situation isn’t new,” Aunt Shirley said.

Positioned between the pair, Scott couldn’t study either for inconsistencies in their respective expressions. He stared at the snow-covered road. The headlights illuminated only a tiny stretch of oncoming road at a time. In the conditions, a driver could deal with what lay directly ahead. Looking too far forward, the rest of the landscape hid in darkness. He’d missed the signs by narrowing his gaze on the present. He couldn’t lose them. “What if something happened?”

Uncle Ted snorted and crossed his arms.

A sharp elbow dug into Scott’s right side. He couldn’t leave the situation undiscussed.

“We have help,” Aunt Shirley said. “We aren’t feeble.”

At the stubborn tone, Scott cringed. Implying his aunt and uncle were anything other than supremely capable wasn’t his goal. “But don’t you think—”

“We should go home and have cocoa? Yes, I agree,” Aunt Shirley said. “After a long day, I want to curl up on the couch and watch a movie. Only a few more nights until Christmas. I want to enjoy each one."

Her chipper tone left a sour taste in Scott's mouth. If he persisted, he risked stressing her to keep up the cheer. He wouldn't push her. Since his arrival, he'd been reactive instead of proactive and jeopardized both. If he approached them calmly with facts, he had a better chance. He nodded. "Sounds great. I'll make the popcorn." After two poor attempts to discuss a serious issue, he had one last opportunity before striking out.

# Chapter Fifteen

Seated at the end of the folding table, backstage on Christmas Eve at Holidays, Inc., Kara adjusted the light on the vintage portable vanity. The faded, yellow plastic shell opened, revealing three mirrors. A wheel controlled the fluorescent light shining on the reflections with settings ranging from daylight to office. She smiled and scrunched her nose. Mom had one on her bathroom counter. During her childhood, she spent hours playing with the mirror in fascination. She hadn't thought about it in years. How many similar tabletop vanities had she used without a second thought?

Dragging in a shaky breath, she shifted forward and widened her gaze, holding the mascara wand to her lashes. Her hand shook, wobbling the wand. She dropped the mascara back into the tube and braced her hands on her waist, steadying. Her stomach fluttered, gently roiling. She never dealt with stage fright. If she could blame the sudden pang of nostalgia for the awkward feelings, she would. This sensation was nerves. Tonight, in ten minutes, she'd sing and dance for the crowd and the cameras. Tomorrow, she couldn't hide behind the trappings of her glittery costume or over the top makeup.

She'd be just herself celebrating Christmas morning with the man she loved. The scenario seemed almost impossible. In her life, she was the boss. Love left a person out of control and vulnerable. Besides, she was probably crazy to hope he'd want a relationship in her real world. L.A. was fast-paced. They were both career-driven. Could they save time for each other? Without knowing she'd see him at the end of a long day, she couldn't focus on the job.

Tomorrow was the perfect moment. She'd mark their first Christmas as an official couple. When she suggested they pretend to date, she never imagined she'd fall for him in the process. But maybe, deep down, she had. The connection sparked on a red-eye flight deepened every day. She didn't want to go back home without him.

A throat cleared.

Straightening, she studied the mirror, spotting Paul behind her shoulder. He wrinkled his brow and frowned so deeply he aged twenty years. *No more setbacks, please*. She turned and faced him, assuming a relaxed expression. "Hi, Paul."

He darted his gaze side to side.

Clenching her jaw, she locked her mouth into a tight smile and ignored the spiral twist of her stomach. Her middle felt like a wrung towel. She'd never seen him operate with such paranoia. During their brief cohabitation, he'd been slightly jumpy but nothing like this.

Dragging over a folding chair, he sat and rested his arms over the back.

At the loud scrape, she cringed. If he hadn't wanted to be noticed, he could use a bit of finesse. From her vantage point, she faced the stage. She'd trust Paul's stony expression to hint at any impending interruption from a crew member.

"I need to talk," he murmured. "Will you listen?"

Straining to hear the barely audible words, she scooted to the end of her chair and turned her head. "Yep. Go for it."

He exhaled a heavy sigh. "I'm proposing to Dani."

She gasped. *And you're telling me ahead of time?* Joy for her friend bubbled inside her chest, making her lighter than air.

He frowned.

With a nod, she clapped a hand over her mouth. Unshed tears blurred her vision, and her nose tickled.

"I thought about waiting a little longer. But the timing seems perfect. Her mom is here. You're here." He shrugged.

*I still count.* Her throat clogged, emotion lodging above her windpipe. When she arrived, she had a clear understanding of how far she'd fallen with her best friend. Every day since, Kara struggled to prove herself changed. She feared she'd never earn Dani's trust again and would be pushed out forever. Being included in one of the biggest moments in her friend's life, however, sparked hope. Blinking, she held back the tears filling her eyes. She didn't have time for a complete breakdown. She needed her composure and makeup in order.

Slipping a hand into his pocket, he slowly extended a small box in one palm. Leaning close, he opened the lid.

Again, she gasped. An emerald cut diamond solitaire, centered on a slim gold band, rested in the box. The ring was a throwback to another era like the intended recipient.

"I need to know the best way to do it."

She arched her brows into her hairline, pressing

together her lips.

"You can talk now."

With a heavy sigh, she dropped her shoulders. "The ring is perfect. Dani will love the setting. Why do you need my input? Seems like you're already well under way on your plan."

He darted his gaze side to side. "I want to ask her during the show."

"What?" She shook her head. "You'll screw up the timing and the camera work. You're not even in the musical." She crossed her arms over her stomach.

Annoyance flared inside her, increasing her pulse. Couldn't she have been informed earlier? Yes, Dani's mom was in town. Because of Kara. Holidays, Inc.'s Christmas shows sold out before Labor Day. Thanks to the announcement Kara and her cast would perform and film a movie. "How is Dani supposed to be involved? We can't just re-write the script. We needed to film tonight's show from start to finish. The proposal will ruin the curtain calls."

She shook her head and shut her eyes. Of course Paul felt odd sharing details with her ahead of time. Her presence was a touchy issue, bringing up a mix of confusion and frustration for Paul, Dani, and Kara. Dani loved Paul and deserved to be happy. But once again, Kara was the odd person out, thus the initial idea for a fake relationship to calm the situation. Dani built something real for herself out of courage and moxie. Could Kara find a meaningful future with Scott?

In New Hope, she enjoyed a sabbatical from her real life and relaxed, discovering a new side to herself. The person she was with Scott was how she wanted to live going forward. Smoothing her clammy hands over her sequin dress, she breathed through her nose and dipped her chin to chest. Dani deserved everything she worked hard for including a happily ever after. By keeping up her guard, she almost lost him. Kara could learn from her friend. She lifted her chin.

The stage door crashed, slamming against the wall.

Paul stared at something behind her and quickly dragged his gaze into focus.

"Paul, we'll figure it out." She shrugged. "The movie cast and crew committed to staying through the Christmas Day and Boxing Day shows. We can film all three and splice it together somehow."

Paul rubbed the back of his neck. "You're sure?"

"I am."

"Thanks, Kara." He shut the ring box and slipped it back into his pocket. Pressing a finger to his mouth, he stood and walked away.

A public declaration of love. She shook her head and turned back toward the vanity. The plan wasn't exactly her ideal proposal, but she wasn't involved other than getting out of the way. Narrowing her gaze, she studied her makeup and didn't need to touch up. A scrap of paper on the table caught her attention. Dragging the sheet with her fingertips, she squinted.

*Meet me outside. Now. Scott*

Rising, she smoothed down her gown. She hadn't wanted to address the subject of a real relationship until the morning. But nothing about the evening stuck to the plan. Maybe this unexpected meeting was for the best. If she expressed her feelings, she'd have an answer. Whether or not it was the one she wanted, she couldn't predict. But at least she wouldn't be stuck waiting for something to happen.

Heading toward the door, she glanced at the clock on the wall. She had five minutes and still needed to discuss the change in plans with the movie crew. She couldn't put off the conversation with Scott. *Now or never.*

****

On Christmas Eve, dressed in the nicest sweater and slacks he packed, Scott strode down the employees-only hallway at Holidays, Inc. toward the stage. He never imagined he'd need to wear anything besides jeans on his trip to New Hope. But from the moment he took his seat on the plane, nothing about his journey was typical.

With his mind made up, he had a difficult time delaying an action. Of course, realizing he was in love with a celebrity wasn't his usual pattern of behavior. Was he overdressed? Was bringing her an opening night bouquet too cliché? *What if she doesn't want to continue dating at home?*

A few yards from the backstage door, he adjusted his grip on the roses and swallowed, forcing every doubt down his throat. He couldn't hold back how he felt. If it made him a fool, at least he tried. He refused to regret what could have been but for a lack of courage. He never expected he'd find love while working to convince his aunt and uncle to retire. Where he'd been frustrated with those attempts, he was strengthened by the connection with Kara. He had to trust.

Opening the backstage door, he blinked, clearing his vision. The knob slipped from his damp grip, and the door hit the wall. Pressing together his lips, he carefully shut the door in the frame and turned, surveying the vicinity. No one seemed to notice. Actors rehearsed their lines, crew set up cables, and a cameraman prowled with his equipment. He raised a hand, shielding his face from the lens. He didn't want to be caught and used in the movie.

Maybe this wasn't the right time. Scanning through the crowd, he spotted Kara to the left. Seated at a table, she had her back toward the door. She spoke with Paul, who moved with sharp, jerky motions. He slipped a hand into his pocket.

On instinct, Scott rushed forward. If the man harmed Kara, he'd be lucky to walk away from Scott. Raising a fist, he neared and froze.

Paul held open a ring box.

Scott inched forward, straining his ears. Wasn't that the guy she was involved with for a reality show? She'd explained the relationship was invented for TV cameras. Maybe he caught feelings? *If he proposes to Kara…*

"I need to know the best way to do it," Paul said. "You can talk now."

"The ring is perfect," Kara said. "Dani will love the setting."

At the wistful lilt in her voice, Scott smiled and dropped his shoulders. Flattening his hand against his thigh, he relaxed his muscles. He hadn't seen Kara and her previous, make-believe ex in such close proximity. Now he understood the man was truly in love with someone else.

"But why do you need my input? Seems like you're already well under way."

"I want to ask her during the show."

"What?" Kara gasped. "You'll screw up the timing

and the camera work. You're not even in the musical."

The sharp edge scraped Scott's heart. Was she still more concerned about herself than her friend? He frowned. The woman he'd grown close to wouldn't begrudge her best friend a happy moment. Didn't she have empathy or feelings? She told him her greatest skill was smiling through anything. Why wasn't she accommodating a request and gritting her teeth?

"How is Dani supposed to be involved?" Kara asked. "We can't just re-write the script. We needed to film tonight's show from start to finish. The proposal will ruin the curtain calls."

Her voice pitched and cracked. Frustration oozing from every syllable, and he dropped his heavy arms to his sides. First and foremost, she valued herself and her career. Her best friend needed a favor, and she refused.

He'd been conned. She wasn't the woman he thought she was. She played a part and nothing more. He shook his head, fighting the chuckle building in his throat. He'd been a fool. At no point had she deceived him. She suggested the fake relationship and never hinted at more. He imagined a connection because he couldn't see or listen to the truth. She carried a little scrap of fabric to remind her to keep up her façade.

He scrubbed a hand over his face, turning toward the exit. From the corner of his gaze, he spotted a clipboard with a sheet of white paper and a pen on the ground. Bending, he retrieved the set. He dashed off a note and set it on the edge of the table, returning the clipboard to its original spot. He couldn't get nearer to Kara without making a scene. For self-preservation, he needed escape. Shaking his head, Scott turned and stalked toward the door.

At the stage exit, he spotted a trash can and threw in the roses. Several blooms hit the lip of the receptacle. The petals fluttered to the floor in a fragrant burst of a killed dream. He grabbed the knob and swung open the door. Too late, he lost his grip, and the metal panel crashed into the wall with a loud slam. He stepped over the threshold and paced the hall, sticking to the edge. Lost in the repetitive motion, he circled his thoughts and strode the threadbare carpet in long steps. He should leave. But he couldn't.

"Scott?"

He turned, and his traitorous heart leapt into his throat. In a gold sequin gown, she shimmered and shone under the dim lights of wall sconces. Her smile brightened her whole face. She nearly convinced him of her genuine happiness. But at what cost?

She stopped a few feet away. "Hi. I only have a few minutes until curtain."

"I…" He raised a fist and coughed. "Fine. I'll be brief." He widened his stance and crossed his arms, gripping his biceps. "Are you seriously more concerned with yourself than your friend?"

Tipping her head to the side, she frowned. "What are you talking about?"

"What are you doing?" He clenched his jaw. Rage bubbled up in his throat, choking off his words. "Is everything a game? An angle?"

"Calm down." She held up her hands. "I don't understand what you're talking about."

"You and your need to control everything. You operate in a constant state of spin. Every moment is calculated and manipulated. You're not real."

She arched a brow. "If I was in command, this

moment wouldn't be happening. I only have a few minutes until curtain. Can we talk later?"

Gritting his teeth, he clenched his jaw. No, he wouldn't be sticking around. "I'm talking about us. I don't fit into your life outside of what you can micromanage."

She gulped. Her blue eyes turned misty, and her nostrils flared.

"We never had a chance. This thing was all a game?" He shut his eyes. He hated the crack in his voice. If he focused on his anger, he claimed the upper hand in what he desperately realized was a fight for everything.

"I'm confused. We agreed to pretend to be dating. We both had reasons." She folded her arms over her chest, narrowing her gaze. "Did you speak to your aunt and uncle? Are you picking a fight because you're frustrated?"

He shook his head. She hit a bull's eye on target. He failed on his can't-lose mission. Why not declare the entire endeavor a bust and save a shred of his pride? "We're not talking about my situation. I thought…" He pinched the bridge of his nose, staving off the pounding headache of hot emotion. "I'm an idiot," he murmured.

With a blank expression, she neared and reached out a hand.

Her perfume tickled his nose, teasing him with the same scent he just threw in the trash can. With a featherlight touch on his shoulder, he shuddered and bucked. He stepped back, breaking the contact. He couldn't be undone. He came to town under highly charged emotional circumstances, and he let all those feelings undermine his own best interests.

"No, you're not an idiot." She tilted her head to the side and pursed her lips. "I have to be on stage. Can we talk about why you're upset later?"

"You know what?" He dropped his hands to his sides and lifted his chin. She stood a few inches away. He hadn't expected her to draw close. *Like our whole relationship.* "I'm good. Have a great Christmas."

Without a backward glance, he strode away on weak legs. In a single, overheard conversation, he realized the depths of deception. Was he mad at her or at himself for believing in the lie they created? He almost told her he loved her. He nearly gave her everything he had. More fool him.

****

*Shuffle-flap-hop-step. Shuffle-flap-hop-step.*

Under the bright stage lights, Kara focused on the meditative rhythm. During rehearsals, she practiced until her bones absorbed the choreography. On opening night, she performed the final number in front of the crowded room without missing a step. While her night started with emotional upheaval, she found balance in what she did best. With a final twirl, she struck a pose, extending her arms and grinning. Her chest rose and fell with her shallow breathing, but she didn't blink.

The audience roared with cheers and claps.

Years of training, weeks of practice, and hours of costuming culminated in one perfect moment. Inside her skintight, skirted, sequin leotard, she felt the outline of her star against her ribs. The rush of a good performance was better than anything else. *Except a good kiss*. She shook off the thought, dropping heavy arms to her sides. She hadn't found Mr. Right. If Scott couldn't understand her survival in the business depended on compartmentalizing her feelings, he wasn't the man she needed. In her disappointment, however, she wouldn't begrudge someone else's happy ending. Taking a few steps back, she darted her gaze to the wings.

Behind the curtain, Paul and Dani stood side by side.

He tipped his head.

Kara nodded and faced the audience. Strolling in a slow circle, she winked at her movie co-stars. She was greeted with nods and thumbs-ups. With only a few minutes to spare before starting the show, she called a quick, emergency meeting of the entire movie crew and explained the changed circumstances. For the most part, she heard positive feedback about the new plan.

Lydia resisted the *cameras off* directive.

Kara held firm. She'd already monetized so much of Dani's life and wouldn't take another moment.

Two black-clad stagehands ran from the wings, setting up a pair of microphone stands in the center of the stage.

Approaching the microphone on the right, Kara angled into the spotlight. "Ladies and gentlemen." She paused and scanned the crowd.

The noise dimmed from the thunderous applause to a low rumble.

Before her, she smiled at a faceless crowd and narrowed her gaze, squinting toward the back of the room. She had a sixth sense about cameras and knew the moment she was "on." Growing up on a soundstage, she honed a particular set of skills and prided herself on her work. Typically, accusations about deception didn't sting. Actors endured the same complaint since the profession began in ancient Greece. When she'd shown her real self with candor, however, she couldn't shrug off Scott's cheap jibe.

With a squint, she spotted a thumbs-up from the cameraman. She cleared her throat and interlaced her fingers. "Good evening, once again. Ladies and gentlemen, you have been a truly marvelous crowd. Thank you for your patience tonight. Filming before a live audience can have its share of unexpected moments. And…if you haven't guessed…" She wiggled her shoulders and turned her head side to side. "I'm stalling right now, so we can set up a huge surprise."

Chuckles and guffaws echoed in the cavernous space.

She grinned. "I have the honor of welcoming to the stage the owner of Holidays, Inc. and my dearest friend, Dani Winter. Accompanying her is talented showman extraordinaire, Paul Howell." Holding wide her arms, Kara stepped back and turned toward the wings.

Wide-eyed and mouth agape, Dani pressed a finger against her chest.

Kara nodded and waved a beckoning hand.

Paul wrapped an arm around Dani's shoulders and steered her onstage.

Dressed in a suit, he was outfitted for his mission like a star. The couple passed. In the light, Dani's knee-length, forest green dress glinted. Kara smiled. Her friend wasn't expecting to be on stage and arrived in jeans. Kara couldn't imagine the pretense concocted to get Dani glam and camera-ready, but she'd be glad for the white lie. Kara strode toward the curtain. In her sequins, she caught every light and sparkled. This moment wasn't hers. Slipping behind the red velvet, she stood backstage and faced the couple.

"Merry Christmas and thank you all for coming," Paul said, his voice booming over the sound system. "The cast did an amazing job, and we still have a grand finale song. I won't take up too much time, but I couldn't let the night slip past without a few words." He turned to Dani and extended his hands.

She tipped her head to the side and reached for him in return.

Kara scrunched her nose. She wasn't an overly sentimental person. *Except with the people who matter.*

"A year ago, I followed my heart and returned to my hometown. Thanks to this remarkable woman, I found more than I dreamed in the place I least expected." He raised her hands, kissing both.

Dani blushed and pressed together her lips.

"Dani, from the moment I met you, I've been searching for the strength and courage to be the man you deserve. You are gutsy, determined, and a dreamer. You have opened my eyes to possibilities I couldn't see. You truly make every day a holiday, and I want to share all of them with you." He dropped her hands and knelt on one knee, reaching inside his suit coat.

Gasping, Dani covered her mouth with both hands.

Paul cleared his throat. "Will yo—"

"YES," she shouted. Launching herself into his arms, she knocked him to the stage.

A whistle rent the air followed by cheers and applause.

The noise was louder than only moments ago, as if every nail and floorboard in the building joined in the exultation. Kara rubbed the back of her hand over her nose.

"You did good," a woman said.

With a start, Kara turned and faced Mrs. Winter.

In a red and white angora sweater, the older woman coordinated with bright lipstick and a smile. She shrugged. "For once."

Kara sighed and strode back across the stage.

The cast and crew spotted her cue and followed. With the stage filled to capacity, the collective unit started a Christmas carol.

Kara faded into the group and moved her lips without singing. Dani's mom wasn't wrong. Kara got one moment absolutely right. After an evening of stellar performances, she helped be part of Dani's happily ever after. Too bad she couldn't seem to fix her own problems. With one holiday miracle under her belt, she didn't have enough luck for another.

# Chapter Sixteen

On Christmas morning, Kara leaned against the doorjamb dividing the living room from the front hall in Dani and Paul's house. With only a few feet to the door, she could slip from the festivities without notice. But she had nowhere to go.

"One more kiss. One more kiss," Mrs. Winter said.

Her delighted cheers were met with claps and murmured encouragement.

Dani and Paul sat in the center of a low-backed sofa. Broad grins stretched their cheeks taut. Mrs. Winter, Jill, and Rob sat on dining room chairs, soaking in the couple's resplendent joy.

Stifling a cringe, Kara straightened. She didn't need to look under the tree. She'd been up all night, giving Santa no opportunity for a clandestine last-minute holiday surprise. All she wanted was a chance to talk to Scott. How had everything gone so sideways? She accepted her blame in the mess of a situation.

Under different guises, she hid the truth from herself until too late. While she rationalized the time together as mutually beneficial, she ignored the deepening emotions from caring to love. To protect her fragile heart, she avoided a tough conversation.

In the end, he spewed misconceptions and judgment.

What would she gain from another conversation?

*Everyone has a price*. She couldn't pay without risking her heart. Maybe his out-of-character blow-up was for the best, saving pain from a lengthy relationship with the same outcome.

Her modus operandi would have her cut ties now and move on. She wasn't one to cling to a failing project. Nothing about her time in New Hope stuck to a typical routine. From the moment she met him, she'd dropped her guard. By showing her mess, she included him and relaxed into a softer person. She adapted to the subsequent changes with more grace. Last night, he accused her of being too controlling and slashed her to shreds. Didn't he see, since arriving, she relinquished her power? She pressed a hand against her locked jaw and lifted her gaze.

No one noticed her.

She should leave. Her mood threatened everyone else's. Dani deserved better.

A loud *beep* echoed down the hall.

"I'll get more coffee," Kara said, her words almost a whisper.

"Let me help." Dani scrambled from the sofa and crossed the room, linking her arm through Kara's. Dani steered them through the entry and down the hall.

"You don't need to follow me, doll." She shook her head.

Inside the kitchen, Dani dropped her hold.

On the stretch of counter between refrigerator and sink, Kara spotted the coffee maker. A row of seasonal, character-shaped mugs flanked the appliance. The bright colors of a cheery Santa and his elves mocked her. She grabbed a white and black snowman, filling to the brim of the top hat.

"Everything okay?" Dani tipped her head to the side.

"Of course, doll. Don't worry about me." Kara raised her drink, taking a long sip.

Dani rolled her eyes and grabbed an elf-shaped mug. "Of course, I worry about you."

"Why?" Kara murmured.

Dani turned. "Sorry?"

Lifting the mug, Kara sipped her coffee and ignored her scalding cheeks. She hadn't meant her under-the-breath mutter for Dani's ears. Kara drew in a sharp breath, her rib cage squeezing, and wished for her little star. She needed the smile through anything reminder now more than ever. After being emotionally split in half last night, however, she couldn't maintain the charade anymore.

"What's wrong? Please tell me."

Scooting closer to the wall, Kara wedged herself in the corner. Preparing for an honest conversation, she needed all the physical support she could find. "Didn't you want me subdued? Since I came to town, I've been pushed to the side time and again."

Dani widened her gaze. "Is that what you think?"

*It's how I feel.* Dropping her chin, Kara stared into the mug. With her throat tightening, she couldn't respond if she wanted. She had no eloquent way of phrasing her pain and fear.

"I'm sorry I've been so unforgiving." Dani shook her head. "Actions speak louder than words. Since Thanksgiving, you've done nothing but prove your loyalty. I haven't given you a chance."

Kara sighed. When she came to town, she wanted to restore her friendship. In her wildest dreams, she never expected to hear such groveling words. She couldn't enjoy the moment. "I probably don't deserve one."

Standing in front of the coffee maker, Dani set her mug on the counter and leaned against the lower cabinets. "Of course you do. I've always admired your strength. For our entire friendship, you grin with your megawatt smile and get through anything."

"I'm emotionally stunted. I push aside everything because I don't analyze my feelings."

Dani rolled her eyes. "Where's Scott? He might disagree with your personal assessment. Isn't he joining us?"

Scrunching her nose, Kara set the coffee on the counter and leaned back, crossing one leg in front of the other. "We had a fight."

"What?" Dani gasped, dropping her jaw. With a shake, she shut her mouth. "When? Why?"

Kara studied the toe of her purple velvet slippers. When she received the wrapped box from Dani, she'd been shocked speechless. With tears welling, she scrunched her nose and opened the present. The one item Kara forgot and never added to her online shopping cart was a pair of slippers for the chilly mornings at the cottage. The pretty pair touched Kara's heart. Dani remembered Kara's icy feet. Once Kara divulged the truth about Scott, she ruined all good feelings. "Don't you want a coffee?"

"Hey, talk to me."

Kara lifted her gaze.

Crossing her arms, Dani wrinkled her brow.

"Last night." Kara croaked. "He ended things…"

Dani covered her mouth with her left hand. "Why

didn't you say anything?"

At the muffled words, Kara glanced at the sparkling engagement ring. She was right not to ruin Dani's big moment. She hated to impact Dani's first morning as a fiancée. Lifting one shoulder in a shrug, Kara dropped her gaze to the floor. "There wasn't really a moment. It happened right before the show and then afterward…"

The cast performed the musical with aplomb, infusing the songs and script with a playful, lively spirit. Or maybe holiday magic was real. One minute, Kara wanted to curl up in a little ball alone at her cottage. In the next, she had reapplied her lipstick and strolled across the stage. The enthusiasm of the crowd carried her through her performance. With a quick adjustment to the last scene, Paul proposed to Dani during the finale. The entire auditorium erupted into cheers. Sharing in the thrill of the moment, Kara blocked out the hurt of Scott's accusatory words until she had snuck out of the theater and driven herself home.

"Bad timing, but you'll get over it and move on." Dani swatted the air with a flick of her wrist. "Maybe I should congratulate you. Have you ever had a boyfriend you cared about enough to argue?"

"Not that I can remember." Exhaling a heavy sigh, Kara scrunched her face. At the first hint of trouble, she always moved on alone. She didn't mind solitude. Until meeting Scott, she never wanted company.

Dani grinned. "I like you two. You have a spark."

Shutting her eyes tight, Kara winced. Her friend's hopeful words cut to the core. If she let Dani continue in ignorance, Kara endangered the truce with more lies.

"We weren't really together."

Dani stiffened, drawing her arms in and raising a brow. "What do you mean?"

She heard the frown in the question and lifted her gaze to meet her friend's stare. Hiding from the truth nearly cost them a friendship eighteen months ago. Would admitting to another lie be the official end? She had no will to exert over the situation. Scott accused her of wielding control like a shield. If she could, she wouldn't hurt so much now. "When I first arrived, I wasn't… You weren't…"

Dani sighed. "After everything last year, I was on edge before I said hello. I was nervous. I'm sorry."

Kara held up her hands, facing out her palms. "I created my own set of problems. I didn't realize how hard regaining your trust would be. I didn't want to make you uncomfortable. When you caught me talking to Scott…"

Widening her gaze, Dani nodded. "I made an assumption, and you didn't correct me."

Kara pressed together her lips and locked her knees. If she ran away, she'd lose her friendship forever. For once, she'd stay in place and absorb Dani's heated stare. She earned every bit of Dani's frustrated scorn.

Dani arched a brow. "Why do I have déjà vu? When we were kids, didn't we act out a similar scene on the TV show?"

"You're probably right. I can't even script a successful, original plot for my life. I have to recycle someone else's." Kara dropped her chin to her chest. "Do you hate me?"

Dani crossed to her side and wrapped an arm

around Kara's shoulders, squeezing. "Why would I?"

"Because I lied. Again."

Dani hugged tighter. "I don't think you did."

Kara stiffened.

"I watched you light up. You two are always laughing and talking. I think you are in a relationship."

*We were.* Kara gulped. Shaking her head, she slid her shoulders loose from Dani's light hold.

"Is the coffee coming?" Mrs. Winter yelled, her voice carrying down the hall.

Swiping her watery eyes, Kara then wiped her hands on her pants. She grabbed the carafe and filled the mugs.

Dani grabbed a wooden tray and loaded the mugs, napkins, and sugar.

Following her lead, Kara opened the refrigerator and retrieved the already filled pitcher of creamer. She added the jug to the tray and stepped back.

"Thanks for everything. For the movie. For last night." Dani lifted her chin. "For caring so much about our friendship."

Kara sniffed and scrunched her nose to the side. "You've always been my sister."

"Then let me take a moment for a rare piece of sisterly advice." Dani wiggled her eyebrows. "Don't let him go without telling him how you feel. Be honest about everything, and don't hold back because the truth hurts. I almost ruined my life by making things easier and ignoring my feelings."

Both chastened and warmed, Kara considered her friend's words. Dani had to care enough to offer advice and hadn't done so in the last five years. "Okay," she murmured.

With a nod, Dani swept past, carrying the beverages.

Kara trailed behind. She'd come to town to fight for a chance to get her career back on track. She'd leave with more than she could have hoped for. The community adopted her and changed her forever with their easy-going, warm-hearted ways. If she only gained the town's support, she'd be eternally grateful for their guiding force into the next phase of her life. But Dani was right. Kara couldn't leave without telling Scott how she felt deep in her soul. All she needed was one moment, and she'd explain everything. If her feelings weren't reciprocated, she had an answer.

****

Slicing his fork through the cold cinnamon roll, Scott focused on the satisfying task of cutting through layers of flaky pastry and sugar. If he honed all his attention on the last Christmas morning cinnamon roll, he accepted a reprieve from his self-directed anger. He snorted. His efforts to tamp down his internal dialogue hadn't worked so far. After storming out of the theater last night, he headed to the diner and helped his family close the restaurant. He thought work would soothe his unease. Cleaning the grease traps and mopping the floor twice, however, only strained his back.

Kneeling on the tile floor, Aunt Shirley and Uncle Ted heaved him to his feet. From there they trudged out of the building and drove home. Following their tradition, Uncle Ted drove ten miles per hour on every residential street, giving his passengers plenty of time for oohing and aahing at the lights and decorations. Instead of sharing the infectious joy, he sat squished in the middle and stewed. He wasn't wrong about her. But he hadn't been entirely right either.

He blocked her chance for offering anything in the way of an explanation. Because if she talked about her feelings, and she didn't share his, she'd ruin every moment of their time together. He'd rather pull the plug on their fake relationship quicker and save himself the slow burning ache of what he'd never have. *Her*.

"Scott, I spot one more gift under the tree." Aunt Shirley's voice carried from the family room through the open doorway to the kitchen.

"Leave it," he called, his voice breaking. He speared the too-large bite and stuffed it in his mouth.

Less than a second later, Aunt Shirley poked her head around the doorway, rollers covering her scalp. "Excuse me?"

Her voice held an edge of warning. He hadn't intended to be short and rude. But he couldn't get into much more of an explanation without a full break-down.

Without waiting for an invitation, Aunt Shirley sashayed into the kitchen and poured herself another cup from the second batch of coffee. She turned and faced him, squinting over the top of her mug.

He couldn't hold her gaze. All morning, he pretended he was fine. With the gifts opened, he shoved his present for Kara under the tree skirt. Out of sight was almost out of mind. He showered and cleaned the kitchen, starting the next batch of coffee in a house full of caffeine-addicted adults. He only had a little bit more unstructured time before his aunt and uncle left for the diner. He almost made it through.

"Ted?" Aunt Shirley leaned back and called over her shoulder. "Get in here. He's ready to spill."

Scott scrunched his face, his mouth pursing like he bit into a lemon. He stuffed another bite of cinnamon roll in his mouth, but the sweet flavor left a bitter taste on his tongue. Swallowing, he crossed his arms over his chest.

Aunt Shirley widened her gaze. “What? You think we can’t read your moods?”

Uncle Ted trudged through the door, gazing from Scott to Aunt Shirley and back again. With a shrug, he crossed to the table and sat in a chair at Scott’s right. He frowned. “Are you eating the last roll?”

Scott nodded.

Aunt Shirley filled another coffee mug and brought both over to the breakfast nook. The circular table held four chairs, leaving everyone in close quarters. She slid a mug to Uncle Ted and held hers in both hands. “I’m guessing the gift is for your lady. Where is she?”

“I don’t know.” Scott squirmed, shifting on the chair. With long distance from his family, he never discussed his relationships with his aunt and uncle. He hadn’t dated anyone seriously in a few years and hadn’t considered introducing them to anyone on their occasional trips out west. How did he broach the truth of his current situation?

“Real answers, please, Scott Arthur.” She set her mug on the table, folding her arms over her chest. “I need more than three words.”

He’d reached the first and middle name level of reprimand on Christmas. He’d only brought the negativity to himself, but he couldn’t look into his aunt’s eyes as he divulged the truth. “We weren’t dating.”

“Huh. ’N so?”

He shrugged, arms hanging limp and useless at his sides. He wanted more but was foolish to imagine she did, too.

Uncle Ted clapped a hand on Scott's shoulder and squeezed.

"She suggested pretending to be a couple, and I agreed. It wasn't real. We were never together."

"You sure?" Uncle Ted stroked his jaw.

Lifting his chin, Scott met his uncle's solemn gaze and nearly cracked in two. Admitting the truth was hard enough. The hopeful, lilting tone in the simple question threatened his composure. Slowly, Scott nodded. "We weren't a real couple."

Aunt Shirley snorted. "If I replayed every conversation this year, I'd rank your comment as the stupidest thing I've heard."

Turning, he frowned. His aunt was honest but not cruel. Her words were unnecessary.

Drawing back her chin, she rolled her eyes. "I'm serious. But first, I wanted to add something to our previous discussion. Remember, the one about us retiring and moving?"

Scott pinched the bridge of his nose. "You guys are all I have."

"Sweetie, we feel the same." She reached across the table, flipping up her palms. "Next year, we're taking vacations, and you need to do the same. Let's spend good time together. More than trips, I'm asking you to trust. If something happened, we'd reach out and maybe change our opinions and our plan then. I promise, if I'm told I have to stop completely, I will."

Dropping his hands to the table, he reached across and rested his palms on Aunt Shirley's. He lifted his chin and glanced from his aunt to his uncle and back again. "I trust you."

"Good." Aunt Shirley patted his hands and drew back, tipping her chin. "Now what about Kara? Why don't you go to the theater and give her the gift?"

Drawing up his shoulders, Scott bristled. "Why? I told you we weren't dating."

"I'm not so sure your opinion's accurate. What do you think, Ted?"

Uncle Ted stroked his chin. "Tell her the truth."

"What's the truth?" Scott wrinkled his brow. "She suggested a fake relationship, and I agreed."

Uncle Ted shook his head and stood.

Aunt Shirley pushed back her chair. "We're heading into town. You know what you need to do?"

*Be honest*. Scott lowered his chin to his chest and interlaced his fingers over the back of his burning neck. He came to town with a clear mission and was almost immediately thrown off-course. Kara surprised him. After years in L.A., he thought himself immune to movie stars. When he least expected, he fell in love. With less than a week left in his trip, he reached a solution for his family. But was even more lost about his heart. *Be honest.* The mantra simplified his complications with his family. He owed himself a chance. Scott drew in the first easy breath he'd had in the past week. Since he realized he loved Kara and allowed his fears to twist him. He met his aunt's gaze. "I do. Thanks."

With a nod, Aunt Shirley left, followed by Uncle Ted.

Scott cleaned his plate, grabbed his keys and the gift, and drove the rental hatchback to Holidays, Inc.

Though the evening show was still several hours away, string lights and street lamps illuminated under the heavy gray clouds hanging overhead. He turned behind the diner and navigated down the tight alley toward the theater. Hopping out of the car, he tucked the gift in his coat pocket and locked the door. A hint of snow hung in the air, the slight rise in humidity scented the afternoon with damp.

Carefully, he picked his way over the broken asphalt to the loading dock and climbed to the landing. He slipped through the open door and squinted. He'd never entered the building from the alley, preferring to use the side door near the kitchens. Narrowing his gaze, he adjusted to the light and processed his surroundings. He was in a storage room behind backstage. Slipping through the row of metal shelves, he reached a door and opened, twisting the knob.

"AAHH!" a feminine voice shrieked.

Quickly stepping over the threshold, he frowned and turned.

Kara held both fists under her chin, eyes wide.

She looked like a nineteenth century pugilist. He ducked and swerved, narrowly missing her right hook. "Whoa. Sorry. It's me, Scott."

"Scott?" She panted, her chest rapidly rising and falling. Lowering her hands, she squinted. "What are you doing here?"

He straightened. "I came to see you and give you this." He pulled the box from his pocket and stuck out his arm.

"Oh." She reached for the box. "Thank you." She met his gaze, opening and shutting her mouth.

Her blue eyes flickered, the dark color almost

lightening. He coughed and shrugged. "You can open it."

With a nod, she ripped the wrapping paper, balling it in one hand. Lifting the lid off the small box, she removed a small silver frame tied with a ribbon and dangled it in midair. The frame glinted in the light, catching the engraved message. "Our first Christmas," she read.

He clenched his stomach. Her tone was flat. He'd missed the mark. "Our *first,*" he moved his fingers in air quotes, "Christmas." *Hopefully not our last.*

"I've never owned an ornament. Thank you." She swiped at her lower lashes.

Could that be true? He was glad to give her the ornament. He wanted her to remember him. "You can change the photograph. I thought we looked pretty good."

"It's us?" Wrinkling her brow, she stared at the image. "I figured it was a stock image. Where did you get the picture?"

He couldn't read her expression with her focus on the photograph in her hands. When he searched through his phone, he hadn't found a single snapshot or couple selfie. He almost conceded defeat and resigned himself to the peculiar holiday season living only in his memory without evidence. On a whim, he asked her friend. Dani shocked him with several pictures of Kara and Scott. He selected an image taken from a distance. Side by side on the Holidays, Inc. stage, Kara beamed, and he threw back his head in a fit of laughter. "Dani." He stuffed his hands in his pockets and rocked back on his heels. "Something to remember me by."

"About that…" she said.

"Kara, I…" he joined in sync.

She shook her head. "Sorry. You were saying?"

"Well, ladies first," he demurred.

Arching a brow, she narrowed her gaze. "Oh, I insist you continue."

She tried so hard to look fierce and in command, but she couldn't hide the sheen in her eyes or the wobble in her chin. He understood now that control was an illusion built on need. No one could ever run a situation to the best advantage at all times and shouldn't want to. When he stopped micromanaging and accepted honesty, he experienced the best moments in his life. She deserved the same. "I'm sorry. Everything I said last night." He exhaled a heavy breath and stroked his tight jaw. "I didn't mean it about you. I was scared, and I lashed out."

Her chin quivered. "Why?"

"To protect myself."

She crossed her arms. "The real answer."

Dropping the arm to his side, he locked his knees so he wouldn't buckle under the weight of heavy limbs. After his angry words, he was a hopeless idiot, imagining she'd give him another chance. But he owed them both the truth. "Because at some point, I fell in love."

Nodding, she strode past him, setting the box, ornament, and wrapping paper on a table.

He caught his breath. She approached the same table as the night before. Every second was burned into his mind with piercing clarity. If she yelled here, she closed the open circle. He deserved no less and turned.

She crashed into his chest.

Stumbling backward, he grasped her waist, and he

regained his footing, dragging her along. “Kara? What?”

“I love you, too.” She stretched on tiptoe and interlaced her hands behind his head, tugging his head close.

He pressed his lips to hers and knew, deep in his bones, he’d come home. The physical geography didn’t factor. As outsiders, they enjoyed an unexpected, perfect meet-cute. They connected here in New Hope and would always have a tie to a special small-town. Real life mirrored the plot she explained on the red-eye flight. An almost unbelievable love story sparked by taking a chance.

# Epilogue

*One year later*

Kara buried her feet in the warm sand and leaned back against her beach chair. As the sun began its descent into the ocean, she adjusted her sunglasses against the glare. *Everyone has a price*. She smiled. Her costs weren't too high. All she needed for a happy holiday was family and a Hawaiian vacation.

"Your tropical drink, Miss Kensington," Scott said.

Turning her head, she held onto her floppy hat with a hand and reached for the icy glass topped with a paper umbrella. "Oooh. Thank you."

He sank into the chair at her side. "My pleasure. Anything for the best star."

She chuckled and swatted him on the arm. "Stop." She sipped her drink, a fruity concoction of passion fruit, pineapple, and coconut danced on her tongue. "Yum. This drink is so good. I have a new favorite. What's it called?"

"A merry Christmas?" He arched an eyebrow.

"Save me from your terrible jokes." She took another sip and set the drink in the cupholder attached to the armrest.

"I have to test them out before I meet with the screenwriter."

She pulled off her sunglasses and met his gaze. During the past year, she treated show business as a career and not a lifestyle. When she left a set or a meeting, she shed the star persona like leaving behind a costume. She didn't want to blur the lines again with a boyfriend dabbling in production. "No, Scott. Please. Don't."

He chuckled and reached for her hand, kissing her knuckles. "I'm teasing. I promise." Interlacing their fingers, he stroked a thumb over the back of her hand. "I am curious about the process."

"And a little uncomfortable?"

Lifting one shoulder, he shrugged and stared at the ocean.

She followed his gaze and squinted. A few figures paddleboarded near the shore of the Big Island's private resort. She didn't spot her parents, but they probably returned to their room to change for dinner. Glancing at her watch, she had twenty minutes before she'd need to get ready for the Christmas Eve luau.

Aunt Shirley and Uncle Ted were finishing up the couple's massage and would meet them.

She never had so much family time, and she loved every second. When she had flown into town with her parents and Scott for the Holidays, Inc. Valentine's Day show, she introduced her folks to Aunt Shirley and Uncle Ted. She nervously anticipated the meeting for weeks.

From the first hello, the foursome instantly clicked.

Without relying on any of her usual tricks, she found a place she belonged. "You'll be great." She squeezed his hand. "Just…be normal."

He tilted his head and arched a brow.

She nibbled her lip. For someone who only just discovered her real self, she definitely couldn't hand out expert advice. She was still learning. But the screenwriter would respond better to the actual Scott and not the man of a thousand corny jokes. "Do you want me to cancel the project?"

"Never." He squeezed her hand. "I'm so proud. The highest-rated Christmas movie premiere on TV ever? You have to follow up with a sequel."

"I wasn't so sure about getting back on screen." She sighed. Her production company slowly took off. With the Thanksgiving debut of *Holidays, Inc.*, the movie based on Dani's life, she fielded more professional calls in the past three weeks than the last three years. Only one offer included a pitch to bring her back onscreen. She liked playing a part. But how would she feel only a few feet away from another actress reenacting the events of the past year?

Would the audience realize the film portrayed a fictionalized version of Kara's love story and cheer? Or would critics tear her apart for her mistakes in the course of finding her happily ever after? *I'll understand how awkward Dani felt, which I deserve*. After this project, she officially paid the debt owed to her best friend. "The writing process won't be as painful as you imagine. For consistency, the story can't be a true remake of what really happened. The screenwriter wants to chat and meet with us to get a sense of our relationship and include realistic moments for the characters."

"Production starts in September?"

"Hopefully, yes." She sighed and reached for her drink. Taking a long sip, she savored the sweetness on her tongue. She set the drink into the cupholder and interlaced her hands in her lap. "Delays can happen.

The original cast might be unavailable. I reached out preemptively to everyone, and they agreed."

Reaching for his drink, he raised it in salute. "You have food service secured? I'm not needed?"

She rolled her eyes. "Never say never. Catering worked out okay last time."

"Yes, but I had something different in mind for our next visit to New Hope." He sipped his drink and returned it to the chair's cupholder. "I thought I'd be a private chef at a little cottage on the outskirts of town. In fact, I already paid the deposit."

"You did?" Warmth spread through her. She curled her toes, cracking the fine web of sand mounded over her feet.

He nodded. "Figured we'd want to celebrate our first fake Christmas in a place with memories."

She scrunched her nose. "Didn't we already have a fake Christmas last year?"

With a hand, he stroked his chin. "No, that was our first, accidental Christmas. Fake Christmas is in September during filming."

Knitting her brow, she tugged her hand and crossed her arms, angling toward him. "So what on earth will you call December twenty-fifth this year?"

With a wink, he slid out of his beach chair. On his knees in the sand, he held out his hands.

She darted her gaze. No one nearby spared them a second glance. Readjusting on the chair, she leaned forward. "What are you doing?" She kept her tone light and nibbled her lip. Was he teasing her by pretending to be a starstruck fan?

Reaching for her hands, he squeezed her fingers. "Isn't this what I do?" He dropped his chin, frowning at the sand. “Yep, I’m doing this wrong.”

She widened her gaze and pulled back her hands. “I repeat. What are you doing?”

He lifted a leg, bending the knee and pressing his foot against the sand.

Behind him, the sun dipped below the horizon. The sky was washed with pinks and oranges, like an elaborate background painted for an old movie musical.

“Kara Kensington.” He gazed into her eyes, lifting the corner of his mouth in a lopsided smile. “You inspire me to spend every day being my best self. You dropped into my life like you always belonged. I want to keep you there, forever.”

Her heartbeat thundered in her ears, and her eyes filled with tears. In all her daydreams, she never fantasized about a wedding. Depending on another person so completely she vowed to cherish them forever? The concept never fit in the world-view of a woman who worked hard and doubted everything. But then she got on a plane, and she unexpectedly met someone.

“I call this Christmas the start of our lives.” He pulled a box from his board shorts pocket.

She launched herself into his arms, knocking him backward. She didn’t need to see the ring. She didn’t care about the jewelry. Pressing her lips to his, she kissed him with every ounce of her being. An electric surge sizzled along every nerve ending. Every kiss was like coming home after a decade. The thrill never diminished. When she was with him, she knew exactly who she was.

He rolled sideways.

A bubble of excitement rose in her chest. She

landed on the sand, smashing her hat against the ground.

"Is that a yes?"

"Absolutely." She laughed and traced the side of his face with a hand. She adored him.

Grinning, he lowered his mouth, touching his lips to hers.

She understood then how marvelous he'd make the rest of her life. He'd come up with new ways to make every moment as special as the first. And she couldn't wait to celebrate each one.

## A word about the author...

Rachelle Paige Campbell writes contemporary romance filled with heart and hope. No matter the location—big city, small town, or European kingdom—her feel-good stories always end with a happily ever after. She's grateful for the support of her family, her robot floor cleaner, and her reluctant writing partner (her dog). http://rachellepaigecampbell.com

Other titles by this Author
*A Perfect Picture of Us*
*Love Overboard*

Finding New Hope series
*Holidays Inc.*, book 1
*Hope for the Holidays*, book 2

Thank you for purchasing
this publication of The Wild Rose Press, Inc.

For questions or more information
contact us at
info@thewildrosepress.com.

The Wild Rose Press, Inc.
www.thewildrosepress.com

CPSIA information can be obtained
at www.ICGtesting.com
Printed in the USA
LVHW050503091221
705721LV00010B/530